THE SABBATICAL DIRECTIVE

M.M. BUSBY

Patent Print Books
Panama City Beach, Florida

THE SABBATICAL DIRECTIVE

Published by PATENT PRINT BOOKS
www.patentprintbks.com
PATENT PRINT BOOKS and the fingerprint colophon are registered trademarks of PATENT PRINT BOOKS

Copyright ©2020 by M.M. Busby
Cover design ©2020 by PATENT PRINT BOOKS
Edited by Ann W. Carns

First Edition: March 2020
Printed in the United States of America

ISBN 978-0-9850731-6-9
Library of Congress Control Number: 2020904180
10   9   8   7   6   5   4   3   2   1

Dedicated to my parents,
who encouraged me to pursue
continuing education, and F.W. Busby,
who has always been my champion.

FOREWORD

"I've noticed a fascinating phenomenon in my thirty years of teaching: schools and schooling are increasingly irrelevant to the great enterprises of the planet. No one believes anymore that scientists are trained in science classes or politicians in civics classes or poets in English classes. The truth is that schools don't really teach anything except how to obey orders. This is a great mystery to me because thousands of humane, caring people work in schools as teachers and aides and administrators, but the abstract logic of the institution overwhelms their individual contributions. Although teachers do care and do work very, very hard, the institution is psychopathic—it has no conscience. It rings a bell and the young man in the middle of writing a poem must close his notebook and move to a different cell where he must memorize that humans and monkeys derive from a common ancestor."

~ John Taylor Gatto,
Dumbing Us Down:
The Hidden Curriculum of Compulsory Schooling.

"We destroy the disinterested (I do not mean uninterested) love of learning in children, which is so strong when they are small, by encouraging and compelling them to work for petty and contemptible rewards—gold stars, or papers marked 100 and tacked to the wall, or A's on report cards ... in short, for the ignoble satisfaction of feeling that they are better than

someone else ... We kill, not only their curiosity, but their feeling that it is a good and admirable thing to be curious, so that by the age of ten most of them will not ask questions, and will show a good deal of scorn for the few who do."

~ John Holt,
American Author,
How Children Fail

PREFACE

As a former educator, I have seen and worked alongside some of the best and the worst teachers. That there are what are considered "good teachers" and "bad teachers" is largely due to the perceptions of educators by administrators, colleagues, boards of education, students, parents, and state or federal departments of education. Programs come and go like the inexorably moving steamroller, and teachers are forced to comply with the numerous mandated and often ill-thought-out systems of instruction or risk being crushed by its wheel.

The burn out rate is extremely high, due to the stresses of dealing with a pervasive lack of respect from the general public, oppressive district paperwork, and expectations to conform to whatever are the hot button teaching methods at the time. The complacent educators appear to succumb to the pressure and "go with the flow," teaching what is handed down year after year with no end goal but to eke out their 20, 25, 30, 35 years until retirement. They don't mean to be poor teachers; they are just unable to fight the good fight.

The rebels hang on and try to affect educational change and reform. They are the so-called "best" teachers—the ones who question the very efficacy of programs such as common core math, merit pay for student performance, standardized testing, *No Child Left Behind* (which is mockingly called *No Teacher Left Standing*) and the ping-pong ball that bounces back and forth between proponents of *STEM* (Science, Technology, Engineering, Math) and Reading Literacy. They shun the old axioms and look for new and exciting ways to stay within the guidelines while operating outside the box and instilling a love for learning among their pupils. To avoid crashing and burning, teachers take short leaves of absence—returning to college to pursue advanced degrees and alternate certifications with continuing education, attending workshops that focus on a wide variety of new or interesting instructional topics or methodologies, or traveling abroad.

Throughout the years, education in America has been targeted by politicians and activists who seek to dumb down the intellect of the general population in order to control the masses. The first line of defense is comprised of the notable teachers who are hard-wired to color outside the lines. They are the thorn in the side of administrators, but they get results. However, even these determined men and women often feel like throwing their hands up and saying, *"The hell with it."*

To compensate these champions for their outstanding efforts, they are courted by benefactors who offer renewal in the form of elite retreats that can only be attended by the cream of the crop, the selection of which is determined by demonstration of superior educational talents, abilities, and skills. The motivation for being recognized as highly capable achievers in education is in the form of a prestigious award, but is it possible that some of these awards exact a heavy price? What if America's choicest educators were being seduced annually by *The Sabbatical Directive*? If so, only a few may survive.

~ M.M. Busby

THANK YOU

I want to thank those who had a part in the inspiration and completion of this book: my publisher, my editor, my fellow educators, my friends, and my family.

INTRODUCTION

<u>MITZIE GALLOWAY</u>: *"What if the world is holding its breath—waiting for you to take the place that only you can fill?"*

~ David Whyte,
Writer

<u>COLBY CARSON</u>: *"From the sadness, learn something; from the happiness, learn something. From the setback, learn something and even from the success learn something. Never stop learning from any situation in life, for that is where the wisdom lies."*

~ Gift Gugu Mona,
South African poet,
philosopher, philanthropist

<u>CASSIDY PHELPS</u>: *"I was bold in the pursuit of knowledge, never fearing to follow truth and reason to whatever results they led."*

~ Thomas Jefferson,
American President

<u>GLENN HARDING</u>: *"Education is and will be the most powerful tool for individual and social change, and we must do all that it takes to facilitate it."*

~ Shiv Nadar,
Indian Businessman

KEN SCHAFFER: *"Our job is obvious: We need to get out of the way, shine a light, and empower a new generation to teach itself and to go further and faster than any generation ever has."*

~ Seth Godin,
American Writer,
Former Dot Com Business Executive

STELLA COOKE: *"Curiosity is the wick in the candle of learning."*

~ William Arthur Ward,
American Writer

CARMINE WELLS: *"If you were born with the ability to change someone's perspective or emotions, never waste that gift. It is one of the most powerful gifts God can give—the ability to influence."*

~ Shannon L. Alder.
American Author

CHESTER OSCEOLA: *"Knowledge, like air, is vital to life. Like air, no one should be denied it."*

~ Alan Moore,
English Writer

PAULETTE JAMESON: *"If your actions don't live up to your words, you have nothing to say."*

~ DeShanne Stokes,
American author, sociologist,
progressive human rights activist

"The Risk is real ... The fate of our country hangs in the balance ... The minds of our nation's children are in jeopardy."

~ Cheryl K. Chumley,
<u>The Washington Times</u>

CHAPTER ONE
The Award

"If in your mind it was possible to take a year's sabbatical from work to reassess your life, what would you do and where would you go?"
~ David Whyte,
Writer

THE OVERSTUFFED LETTER LAY UNOPENED, resting atop her cellphone in the center desk drawer. It silently beckoned her, making her heart thump so loudly she was sure the entire combined group of ten-year-old students could hear it beating as she struggled to lead a discussion on why Peter, Edmond, Susan, and Lucy were put on a train in London and sent off to live with their uncle in the English countryside during the war. C. S. Lewis's *The Lion, The Witch, and The Wardrobe* was one of Mrs. Mitzie Galloway's favorite novels, and she took great pleasure in presenting it each year to the fourth-grade classes in the Jefferson County, Florida elementary school in which she taught.

The first book in *The Chronicles of Narnia* series was always a hit with the children, who delighted in hearing Mrs. Galloway read aloud in the distinctive voices of all the characters. She could speak in the Pevensie children's proper British accents and change seamlessly to the high-pitched Cockney of Mr. Tumnus or the nasally dismissive tone of the White Witch, and even provide sound effects for Mr. and Mrs. Beaver as they chucked and fretted in their underwater dam.

The reading always culminated just before Christmas break with a Narnia-themed party during which the students got the opportunity to display art work centered on the story, present vignettes of selected scenes in which they dressed as their favorite characters and performed memorized passages from the book in their own interpretations of the character voices, and got to make (and consume) different varieties of Turkish Delight. It was a unit of study that brought the students in that grade level together as a cohesive group, where they were not segregated into four distinct classes but were able to mix with their fellows and exchange varying ideas and points of view. It encouraged creativity, critical thinking, personal expression, problem solving, and venturing outside the box.

Mrs. Galloway's story time was a rite of

passage in the school: only the fourth graders were afforded the opportunity to experience Mitzie's epic performance, and they never failed to lord it over the younger students. The other teachers in "the pod"— the large open room divided into four sections by means of heavy accordion-pleated partitions—loved the storytelling just as much, but for another reason: it gave them a full hour in which to catch their breaths. They remained in their own classrooms (with the partitions pulled apart), gave pretense at monitoring the four combined classes, and during the 60-minute respite, they were able to surreptitiously text on their phones, grade papers, drink a coffee or cold soda, run to the restroom, grab a smoke, or even lay their heads on their desks and just relax.

This is not to say that the other three teachers were lazy. Far from it. Teaching was a tedious job, and they struggled to engage with their students in a world where video games, the internet, and smartphones took precedence and shortened children's attention spans. It was an overwhelming responsibility and an all-encompassing eight hours with barely enough time to eat, not to mention use the bathroom—which was why so many teachers had digestive issues and urinary tract infections.

Even the principals (and there had been three in the dozen years during which 34-year-old Mrs. Galloway had been reading the story) enjoyed the performance as much as they appreciated the time it allowed the other pod teachers to have the much-needed extra break. But the real reason the principals were fans of Mrs. Galloway's reading was the residual opportunity it afforded the fourth grade teachers to expand upon the themes and auxiliary content inherent in the book, such as Nazi Germany and the part played by the Allies in World War II and the dangers of substance abuse related to Edmond's betrayal of his siblings because of his addiction to Turkish Delight.

Mr. Knox, the current principal, was a champion of the story time because it allowed his teachers to touch on moral issues that were all but forbidden in the current political climate: the classic battle between good vs. evil and even the religious elements C. S. Lewis imparted in the story in which Aslan the Lion was an archetype of a resurrected Savior who sacrificed his life to save the lives of the children, including their brother Edmond, who was the betrayer like Judas Iscariot. Mr. Knox went so far as to attribute it to higher order thinking, and the fourth-grade classes in his elementary school typically led Jefferson County in their language and writing acquisition, garnering the highest scores on the annual standardized tests.

Story time had become so popular that many of the other grade levels followed suit with age-appropriate, mind-expanding novels for their own classes: *The Dark is Rising* by Susan Cooper in fifth grade (Celtic and English traditions, good vs. evil, fate vs. free will, perseverance, coming of age), *Charlotte's*

Web by E. B. White for the third grade (friendship and love, loyalty, sacrifice, mortality, self-esteem), and *Dear Max* by Sally Grindley for the children in second grade (letter writing, friendship, overcoming personal issues). And story time came with a bonus: through the storytelling practice, there emerged many talented readers among the teachers; however, none were as flamboyant as Mitzie Galloway. Perhaps it was because Mitzie had been a devotee of community theater growing up and had spent a few years in Hollywood rubbing shoulders with actors and actresses. It was an exciting time of her life, but much too fast-paced and filled with so many shallow people. She preferred the small-town setting in which she currently lived, raised her family, and taught school.

Today Mitzie was a little off her game, due to the insistent letter in her desk drawer, but she trudged on, nonetheless, and delivered a stunning portrayal of Lucy telling her brothers and sister she'd just been in a wardrobe and met a fawn in the land of Narnia. At the end of the hour, the boys and girls were dismissed to their own classrooms within the pod and thankfully sent off to Physical Education with Coach Elliott. During that time, Mitzie and the other three teachers had 50 glorious minutes of an uninterrupted planning period.

Downing the last of her Fanta Orange soda, Mitzie finally sat down at her desk and addressed the elephant in the room—the letter. She dreaded finding out she had been turned down for the award, and her hand shook as she pulled open the drawer and stared at the thick envelope. It was an ordinary looking white envelope—not too awfully large, the lettering not too ostentatious, nothing singularly remarkable about it at all except the return address: National Foundation for Academic Excellence in Education. Swallowing the gigantic lump in her throat, she carefully peeled open the envelope and took out the enclosed papers inside. She adjusted her glasses on her nose and began to read the letter:

"Dear Mrs. Mitzie Galloway,

We are pleased to announce that you have been specially selected as an award winner by the National Foundation for Academic Excellence in Education, based on your entry questionnaire, your teaching philosophy, your written essay, and the letters of recommendation from you're your principal, your district superintendent, and your fellow teachers at Monticello Elementary School.

You are one of the 67 candidates chosen from the state of Florida to attend an all-expenses-paid three-month educational sabbatical at the Lower Eastern NFAEE Center in Richmond, Virginia.

At the end of your sabbatical, you will travel to the NFAEE headquarters in Washington D.C. where you will be joined by your family and the winners from each of the 3,142 counties in the United States of America, during which you will be recognized in a private formal ceremony.

Please return your signed, dated, and notarized acceptance packet in the enclosed envelope, along with your preferred course of study and one alternate course of study for the sabbatical. We will make every effort to accommodate your preference.

Congratulations on your award! You should be proud to be one of the premier educators in America.

Sincerely,
Ronald A. Bowry, President
National Foundation for Academic Excellence in Education"

Mitzie's eyes misted, and she had to reread the letter several times to be sure she was not imagining the content. This was an extremely prestigious award, a once-in-a-lifetime opportunity, and she never dreamed she could win. She glanced at her watch. Twenty minutes remained in her planning period, but she debated on trying to call her husband Phillip. While she wanted him to be the first to know, he was a builder and on the job in an area with spotty cell phone reception. She could call her parents, or she could tell her principal or her co-workers, or she could just wait until she got home and tell her family all at one time. She could barely contain her excitement. Fortunately, once the children returned from P.E., it would be time to get them to the buses. Then she had only to wait until 3:15 to go home. She doubted she could last another hour without telling a single soul, and she was right. She told her team-teaching partner on the other side of the partition and gave her strict instructions to keep it a secret.

By 3:15, the whole town of Monticello knew.

*   *   *

COLBY CARSON reflected on his day at school as he drove home to his two-bedroom brick house in Perry, Georgia. It was September, but there were definite hints of the approach of autumn; he could see it in the barely changing colors of the leaves on the deciduous trees. Before long, the oppressive suffocating Georgia heat would let up, and he was looking forward to it.

The children had been restless all morning, instinctively feeling the tiny bit of change in the weather, so he took them outside. Never one to waste a teaching opportunity, Colby directed them to search for examples of various rocks and minerals, and he was rewarded with a plethora of examples as they diligently rose to their teacher's challenge.

Among the treasures his fifth graders collected were excellent examples of colorful conglomerated rocks fused together into large chunks, a jar full of some perfectly striated layers of sediment soil, and evidence of fossilized material in a brick of red clay.

The outdoor exercise gave rise to a rousing lesson, and before they could even scratch the surface of the science behind the processes required to create these examples, it was time to come back in for their lunch period.

When the students returned from eating, they were still buzzing about the rocks and minerals, so Colby postponed the math lesson until the following day and continued with the science discussion. He was always a proponent of "strike while the iron is hot," and because he taught in a self-contained classroom, he had the freedom to rearrange his lessons for maximum impact instead of being a regimented slave to schedules.

Colby's principal made a determined effort to look the other way when he deviated from his lesson plans because he so effectively captured his students' interest, and their soaring scores on the Georgia state assessment tests reflected his teaching style. Year after year, parents clamored for their children to be enrolled in his classroom, and many late-night calls were known to be placed to the principal ranging from impassioned pleading to veiled threats of going to the school board. To assuage them, the principal allowed Mr. Carson to conduct an afterschool science lab. The demand to be in Colby's lab necessitated a second day to accommodate the additional students, so he spent his Tuesday and Thursday afternoons facilitating the more challenging science lessons, albeit with no additional pay. Teaching autonomy was the trade-off that motivated Colby Carson.

Today being Friday, Colby was able to go home at his normal quitting time without having a mountain of papers to grade like most of the other teachers. That was by his own design. He never assigned his students additional homework; they had ample time during class to finish their work, and he was able to circulate around the room checking their understanding of the day's concepts, correcting them as necessary to ensure skill mastery. Whatever was not finished in class became homework. It was the theory of Occam's razor at its finest: the simplest solution is usually the best one.

As he pulled into his carport, Colby scooped up the stack of letters sitting on his car seat and took them into the house where he deposited them on the counter. His Russian blue cat Caboodle swirled in a figure eight around his ankles demanding attention. He kneeled and patted Caboodle for the customary allotment of time before the cat sauntered away toward the living room. He reached into the refrigerator and brought out a half-full jug of orange juice. After pouring a tall glass of juice with crushed ice, he replaced the container in the fridge, gathered the mail, and settled himself into his easy chair.

Bill, bill, bill, advertising flyer, another bill, another flyer, two political advertisements, and a bulging envelope. Tossing the other mail on the end table, he turned the hefty letter over and read the return address: National Foundation for Academic

Excellence in Education.

Eyebrows raised, he sliced open the top with a letter opener and read the contents:

"Dear Mr. Carson,

We are pleased to announce that you have been specially selected as an award winner by the National Foundation for Academic Excellence in Education, based on your entry questionnaire, your teaching philosophy, your written essay, and the letters of recommendation from your principal, your district superintendent, and your fellow teachers at Perry Elementary School.

You are one of the 159 candidates chosen from the state of Georgia to attend an all-expenses-paid three-month educational sabbatical at the Lower Eastern NFAEE Center in Richmond, Virginia."

Colby looked up, pursing his lips. *Hmm. National Foundation for Academic Excellence in Education? I don't remember this one*, he thought. He had applied to so many, searching for a place to get away from teaching for a while. It had been 22 years, and he desperately needed a break. He was really hoping to be selected for one of the out-of-country awards, but none of those applications had come through.

Richmond, huh? That's cool. Lots of history

there. Three months should be a great leave of absence. He read the rest of the letter while Caboodle kneaded a place on his lap in preparation to settling down. Colby sipped his juice and imagined the time he would have in Virginia's capitol city.

*   *   *

CASSIDY PHELPS was so tired of fighting with the administration. The school had been allocated minimal funding for another new program that was a clear dead end, in her opinion. Cursive writing had been discontinued, and her beloved Accelerated Reading program was being cut as the district leaders were jumping on yet another bandwagon that only benefitted the textbook writers—a new reading series, correlated with new social studies books from the same publisher. And to make that program work, they were going to take funding away from the AR program, a project for which she had personally campaigned and raised money.

Cassidy devoted countless hours of her own free time researching appropriate books for the different grade levels that both interested and challenged the children. She placed colored stickers on the spine of each book, numbered with the reading level and a point value that reflected the child's possible score on the corresponding computerized reading comprehension test that accompanied the book. She shelved these books in the library and prominently arranged them by sticker color so the students could easily locate the ones that were recommended for their individual reading levels.

The AR program was wildly popular with the students in Grady County as they strived to read their books carefully to attain maximum points on the tests. The accumulated points could be used to "buy" items such as new books from several booksellers who regularly distributed to the schools. Cassidy herself had purchased a cache of new books which she kept in a separate section of the library. These books were not for general checkout; they were exclusively for "purchase" with AR points. Now, to her dismay, the district administrators were once again moving away from a highly successful program in favor of a new unproven one.

As the school's librarian, Cassidy was on the committee to evaluate the proposed textbook series, and she was overwhelmingly unimpressed. Besides being too complicated for the elementary level child, the series featured uninteresting stories, marginal illustrations, and language that was too trendy and would be outdated in just a few years. After a master's degree in library science and 17 years on the job, Cassidy knew from experience that the students would be bored, and the teachers would struggle to include all the components. In addition, the series demanded the purchase of four other consumable workbooks *per student* which had to be replaced annually. It was just another way to get more money for the publishers.

Cassidy could recommend precisely the right

story for a particular student that would ensure the child came back for more of the same. She knew how to foster a love of written language. She believed children learned to read by reading, not by dissecting every little piece of a story, and that was what made her such a successful librarian. *Sometimes an author made a dog brown because he or she liked brown dogs! Why read anything more into it?*

To make matters worse, the social studies companion texts in the new series were completely unacceptable. Notable Civil War landmarks had been omitted from the early chapters, and well-known history had been edited and homogenized, reflecting the current politically correct environment of the United States. As a proud woman of African American heritage, Cassidy felt children should be exposed to history exactly as it occurred, even if it proved to be embarrassing.

George Washington owned slaves in Mount Vernon for 56 years. He acquired the first ten slaves from his father at the age of eleven. But Washington freed all his slaves in 1799. In fact, he was the only slaveholding Founding Father to do so. That was an important fact the children should know, but it was not in the books.

George Washington Carver (another famous George Washington) was *the* most prominent black scientist of the early 20th century, but he had been credited in the social studies book with the invention of peanut butter. *Carver didn't invent peanut butter;*

he invented hundreds of uses for peanuts which helped poor southern farmers vary their crops and improve their diets! She said to herself.

Cassidy was always careful to let the children know the facts. *We live in twenty-first century Cairo, Georgia,* she reasoned, *yet our kids know little about their own state. We must learn our unadulterated history and understand our culture if we are to advance our civilization!* Cassidy was a modern-day pioneer, but she was tired of the journey, even though her young students put into practice her unrelenting commitment to the whole truth.

"Mail for you, Ms. Phelps," the custodian said as he stuck his head inside her office and held out a bulging letter.

"Oh, thank you, Sam," she responded. "It's always good to see your smiling face." She took the letter and walked slowly back to her desk. Her next class was at lunch and would be returning in just a few minutes. Time enough to read the thick letter:

"Dear Ms. Cassidy Phelps,

We are pleased to announce that you have been specially selected as an award winner by the National Foundation for Academic Excellence in Education, based on your entry questionnaire, your teaching philosophy, your written essay, and the letters of recommendation from your principal, your district superintendent, and your fellow teachers at Cairo

Elementary School.

You are one of the 159 candidates chosen from the state of Georgia to attend an all-expenses-paid three-month educational sabbatical at the Lower Eastern NFAEE Center in Richmond, Virginia."

Cassidy read on in surprise:

Congratulations on your award! You should be proud to be one of the premier educators in America.

Sincerely,
Ronald A. Bowry, President
National Foundation for Academic Excellence in Education"

Cassidy Phelps laughed aloud and clasped the letter to her chest. She read it again to make sure she wasn't dreaming, and then she closed her eyes and bowed her head.

"Thank you, Mr. Ronald A. Bowry, for the honor. And Thank you, Lord, for this opportunity to renew my spirit for the coming years of teaching Your children. Amen."

* * *

At roughly the same time as Mitzie Galloway, Colby Carson, and Cassidy Phelps were receiving their award notifications, teachers throughout the eastern time zone of the United States opened their mail and read similar messages:

"Dear Mr. Glenn Harding,

We are pleased to announce that you have been specially selected as an award winner by the National Foundation for Academic Excellence in Education, based on your entry questionnaire, your teaching philosophy, your written essay, and the letters of recommendation from your principal, your district superintendent, and your fellow teachers at Annandale Elementary School.

You are one of the 95 candidates chosen from the state of Virginia to attend an all-expenses-paid three-month educational sabbatical at the Lower Eastern NFAEE Center in Richmond, Virginia."

———

"Dear Mr. Kenneth Schaffer,

We are pleased to announce that you have been specially selected as an award winner by the National Foundation for Academic Excellence in Education, based on your entry questionnaire, your teaching philosophy, your written essay, and the letters of recommendation from your principal, your district superintendent, and your fellow teachers at Graysville Elementary School.

You are one of the 159 candidates chosen from the

state of Georgia to attend an all-expenses-paid three-month educational sabbatical at the Lower Eastern NFAEE Center in Richmond, Virginia."

"Dear Ms. Stella Cooke,

You are one of the 100 candidates chosen from the state of North Carolina to attend an all-expenses-paid three-month educational sabbatical at the Lower Eastern NFAEE Center in Richmond, Virginia."

"Dear Miss Carmine Wells,

You are one of the 67 candidates chosen from the state of Florida to attend an all-expenses-paid three-month educational sabbatical at the Lower Eastern NFAEE Center in Richmond, Virginia."

"Dear Miss Paulette Jameson,

You are one of the 55 candidates chosen from the state of West Virginia to attend an all-expenses-paid three-month educational sabbatical at the Lower Eastern NFAEE Center in Richmond, Virginia."

"Dear Mr. Chester Osceola,

You are one of the 67 candidates chosen from the state of Florida to attend an all-expenses-paid three-month educational sabbatical at the Lower Eastern NFAEE

Center in Richmond, Virginia."

Across the United States in the three remaining time zones, other teachers opened their mail to read:

"You are one of the 3 candidates chosen from the state of Delaware to attend an all-expenses-paid three-month educational sabbatical at the Upper Eastern NFAEE Center in Annapolis, Maryland."

———

"You are one of the 92 candidates chosen from the state of Indiana to attend an all-expenses-paid three-month educational sabbatical at the Upper Eastern NFAEE Center in Annapolis, Maryland."

———

"You are one of the 64 candidates chosen from the state of Louisiana to attend an all-expenses-paid three-month educational sabbatical at the Lower Central NFAEE Center in Frankfort, Kentucky."

———

"You are one of the 254 candidates chosen from the state of Texas to attend an all-expenses-paid three-month educational sabbatical at the Lower Central NFAEE Center in Frankfort, Kentucky."

———

"You are one of the 53 candidates chosen from the state of North Dakota to attend an all-expenses-paid three-month educational sabbatical at the Upper Central NFAEE Center in St. Paul, Minnesota."

———

"You are one of the 114 candidates chosen from the state of Missouri to attend an all-expenses-paid three-month educational sabbatical at the Upper Central NFAEE Center in St. Paul, Minnesota."

———

"You are one of the 15 candidates chosen from the state of Arizona to attend an all-expenses-paid three-month educational sabbatical at the Mountain NFAEE Center in Santa Fe, New Mexico."

———

"You are one of the 64 candidates chosen from the state of Colorado to attend an all-expenses-paid three-month educational sabbatical at the Mountain NFAEE Center in Santa Fe, New Mexico."

———

"You are one of the 5 candidates chosen from the state of Hawaii to attend an all-expenses-paid three-month educational sabbatical at the Pacific NFAEE Center in Salem, Oregon."

———

"You are one of the 58 candidates chosen from the state of California to attend an all-expenses-paid three-month educational sabbatical at the Pacific NFAEE Center in Salem, Oregon."

———

On that day, with the help of the United States Postal Service, across four time zones, the 2020 bi-annual Sabbatical Directive began.

CHAPTER TWO
The Courses

"There is nothing more notable in Socrates than that he found time, when he was an old man, to learn music and dancing, and thought it time well spent."
~Michel de Montalgne,
The Complete Essays

MITZIE GALLOWAY WOKE EARLY on that cool Saturday in November, but she laid in bed for an extra hour thinking about her upcoming trip. She had eagerly completed her acceptance package and now awaited word from the NFAEE as to what course of study she had been assigned. She was given 21 choices for in-depth workshops: three courses in performing arts (music, theater, dance), three visual arts courses (drawing, painting, sculpting), two courses of culinary arts (healthy cooking, baking), five choices of literary arts courses (creative writing, editing, publishing, journalism, poetry), five American histories (indigenous Natives, European immigrants, African immigrants, Asian immigrants, early American pioneers), and courses in cartography, archaeology, and forensic anthropology. Determining the first and second choices for Mitzie's courses of study became a family activity.

"Take cooking," her youngest daughter said.

"No, Sarah. Mom already knows how to cook," her teenager Kristin disagreed. "Oh, I know! How about taking cartography?"

"Really? Who wants to learn stuff about carts?" Sarah complained with all the seriousness of a clueless middle-schooler.

"Cartography is really about creating maps, sweetie," Mitzie explained with a guarded smile.

"Yeah, early American pioneers is about carts," her first-grade son Gabriel said. Seeing his family's puzzled looks, he shrugged. "You know. The pioneers went west with their hand carts."

The laughter from his sisters made his face turn red, but Mitzie averted a crying jag by agreeing with him. "That's exactly right, Gabe. You are quite the clever one. I don't know. Maybe as my second choice. What do you think, Phil?"

Phillip Galloway put down his newspaper and leaned over to glance at the choices. "Well, right away I'd strike off the performing arts. You're already well versed in those. That'd just be a waste of your three months. Ditto on culinary, ditto on literary. I don't see you doing cartography, Mitzie. That leaves you indigenous Natives, archaeology, and forensic anthropology. What's your first instinct?"

Mitzie closed her eyes for a moment. "Ummm. Native Americans or archaeology. That's what comes to mind first." She looked up to see the family nodding, favorably considering her choices. "What do y'all think I should do?" she asked.

"Would you be happy with either one of those, Mitz?" he asked.

"I would," she confirmed.

"Then, I'd say to put them down in that order, babe. Sounds like a plan to me."

Having made the decision, Mitzie quickly wrote down her first choice: Indigenous Natives. Then, she filled in her second choice: archaeology. She bundled the papers back into their neat stacks, folded them, and carefully replaced them in the return envelope.

"Can I lick it?" Gabe asked.

"Not tonight. I want to read through the whole thing again in the morning to make sure I've completed everything. Then, you can be the licker," she said.

Gabe jumped around with the unbounded enthusiasm only a seven-year-old child can muster. "I'm gonna be the licker. I'm gonna be the licker," he sang.

"As if I cared," Sarah huffed, sticking her nose in the air.

"You care," Kristin mumbled with a lopsided grin directed at her sister.

That was two weeks ago. There was one week left until Thanksgiving, then three weeks of school before Christmas break, and then, she would be leaving for Richmond, Virginia on the first of January. The time had raced by while she went about her day-to-day business of teaching school and being a wife and mother.

Today, being the weekend, her activities were more of the latter. She sent Phillip off to his jobsite with a packed lunch, prepared breakfast for herself and the kids, cleaned house, laid out fruit and sandwich fixings for make-it-yourself lunches, rummaged in her closet for the hundredth time selecting different outfits to take, made sure they were clean and pressed, played Jenga with Gabe, and tried to relax and read a book, but all she was doing was marking time until the mail came.

"Mail man," Sarah called as she ran out the door and sprinted down the driveway.

"Mommy, I wanted to go," Gabe cried.

"Go catch up to her," Mitzie suggested. The boy was out the door almost before she finished talking. The two children came in the house arguing, both struggling to hold on to the letters that had been in the box.

"Mom make him stop," Sarah whined, pulling away. The action made the mail fly out in all directions and land in a heap on the floor.

"Hey! Both of you just stop it," Mitzie commanded. "Thanks for getting the mail, kids, but I'll take over from here. Please leave it on the floor and go play."

As the kids ran up the stairs, Mitzie bent down to retrieve the scattered letters. Her breath caught in her throat when she spotted the envelope from the NFAEE. She left the other mail on the floor while she carefully unsealed it.

"Dear Mrs. Mitzie Galloway,

We are pleased to confirm that you have been accepted into the HISTORY—INDIGENOUS NATIVES course. This is one of the more popular workshops and includes field trips to visit nearby Native tribes, instruction in dress and culture, ceremonials, cooking, music and dance, and language classes. You will need comfortable footwear and clothing suitable for outings in wooded areas, a warm coat, and a cap or hat. Please pack accordingly. All other items pertaining to the course will be provided you upon your arrival.

We are also excited to announce that you are one of the few candidates who have been selected to receive a stipend of $2,500 for each month that you participate in the course. We hope this will offset the costs associated with your leave of absence. To avoid hurt feelings, we ask that you keep this information *confidential and do not divulge the receipt of this stipend to your colleagues at Monticello Elementary School or with the other participants. We are confident you will adhere to this request; failure to do so will result in your termination and loss of your stipend.*

We look forward to meeting you at the airport on January 1, 2020 for the start of a most Happy New Year!

Sincerely,
Ronald A. Bowry, President
National Foundation for Academic Excellence in Education"

Mitzie was thrilled and immediately let the children know she had gotten her first choice. She quickly stuffed the letter back into the envelope; Phillip would be the only other person to read it and know of the unexpected stipend.

* * *

Colby Carson sat stroking Caboodle as he read his letter again. He was pleased that he had been granted his first course choice—Forensic Anthropology. The second part of the letter was a huge surprise:

"We are also excited to announce that you are one of the few candidates who have been selected to receive a stipend of $2,500 for each month that you participate

in the course. We hope this will offset the costs associated with your leave of absence. To avoid hurt feelings, we ask that you keep this information confidential and do not divulge the receipt of this stipend to your colleagues at Perry Elementary School or with the other participants. We are confident you will adhere to this request; failure to do so will result in your termination and loss of your stipend."

While he was happy to be getting $7,500 during his time at the Center, Colby felt vaguely disquieted with the tone of the wording. *Failure to do so will result in your termination and loss of your stipend. That sounds like a threat,* he thought. As if in agreement, Caboodle flexed her claws and dug them into his leg.

*   *   *

Cassidy Phelps had the same feeling. "I'm not so certain I want that money," she told her friend Edna Mae in confidence over the phone. "I surely didn't ask for it, and I don't much like the way the letter sounds."

"Now Cassidy, you just keep your mouth shut and take that money. They're offering it to you because you deserve it. Lord knows you need it, honey," Edna May replied.

"I suppose you're right. The good Lord's giving me blessings galore. Tell you what, though. I'm going to have them send my checks to your address, Edna Mae. I know I won't need all that extra money up there while I'm digging around in the dirt. I am going to be an archaeologist for three months. Now isn't that something for a 40-year-old black woman to do?" she joked.

Edna Mae laughed heartily at the thought of her friend Cassidy with a trowel in her hand excavating the ground. "Just don't you be unearthing no mummies, you hear me?"

"Maybe I'll find a dinosaur bone, then I'll know for sure whether God created them right along with all the other animals. Good night, Edna Mae."

Now wouldn't that just be something to find a thing like that. Cassidy pondered, just before she recalled the ominous sounding language at the end of that second paragraph in her letter. *Failure to do so will result in your termination and loss of your stipend.* She closed her eyes and sighed.

"Dear God, You wrap me 'round with a hedge of protection, please. And if things aren't just right, give me strength and make me a warrior in Your army so I can protect others. Amen."

Later that night, Cassidy Phelps dreamed of dinosaurs, and mummies, and warriors with swords.

* * *

Across the country, over 3,000 teachers read:

"Dear Mr. Chester Osceola,

We are pleased to confirm that you have been accepted into the <u>CARTOGRAPHY</u> course.

... you are one of the few candidates who have been selected to receive a stipend of $2,500 for each month that you participate in the course. We hope this will offset the costs associated with your leave of absence. To avoid hurt feelings, we ask that you keep this information confidential and do not divulge the receipt of this stipend to your colleagues at Holopaw Elementary and Middle School or with the other participants. We are confident you will adhere to this request; failure to do so will result in your termination and loss of your stipend."

———

"Dear Miss Paulette Jameson,

... to confirm that you have been accepted into the LITERARY ARTS—JOURNALISM course.

... receive a stipend of $2,500 for each month that you participate in the course ... To avoid hurt feelings, we ask that you keep this information confidential and do not divulge the receipt of this stipend to your colleagues at St. Albans Elementary and Middle School or with the other participants. We are confident you will adhere to this request; failure to do so will result in your termination and loss of your stipend."

———

"Dear Miss Carmine Wells,

... you have been accepted into the LITERARY ARTS—

POETRY course.

... To avoid hurt feelings, we ask that you keep this information confidential and do not divulge the receipt of this stipend to your colleagues at St. Augustine Elementary School or with the other participants. We are confident you will adhere to this request; failure to do so will result in your termination and loss of your stipend."

———

"Dear Ms. Stella Cooke,

_... have been accepted into the _HISTORY—EARLY AMERICAN PIONEERS_ course._

... we ask that you keep this information confidential and do not divulge the receipt of this stipend to your colleagues at Boone Elementary School or with the other participants. We are confident you will adhere to this request; failure to do so will result in your termination and loss of your stipend."

———

"Dear Mr. Kenneth Schaffer,

_... been accepted into the _CULINARY ARTS— HEALTHY COOKING_ course._

... keep this information confidential and do not divulge the receipt of this stipend ... We are confident you will adhere to this request; failure to do so will *result in your termination and loss of your stipend."*

———

"Dear Mr. Glenn Harding,

... *accepted into the* HISTORY—INDIGENOUS NATIVES *course.*

... *We are confident you will adhere to this request; failure to do so will result in your termination and loss of your stipend."*

———

"... accepted into the PERFORMING ARTS—MUSIC *course.*

... *confident you will adhere to this request; failure to do so will result in your termination and loss of your stipend."*

———

"... into the HISTORY—AFRICAN IMMIGRANTS *course.*

... *you will adhere to this request; failure to do so will result in your termination and loss of your stipend."*

———

"...into the PERFORMING ARTS—THEATER *course.*

... *adhere to this request; failure to do so will result in your termination and loss of your stipend."*

———

"... into the VISUAL ARTS—DRAWING *course.*

… failure to do so will result in your termination and loss of your stipend."

———

"… CULINARY ARTS—BAKING … will result in your termination and loss of your stipend."

———

"… HISTORY—ASIAN IMMIGRANTS … result in your termination and loss of your stipend."

———

"… VISUAL ARTS—PAINTING … in your termination and loss of your stipend."

———

"… HISTORY—EUROPEAN IMMIGRANTS … failure … will result in your termination …"

———

"… PERFORMING ARTS—DANCE … will result in your termination …"

———

"… your termination …"

CHAPTER THREE
The Arrival

"Those people who develop the ability to continuously acquire new and better forms of knowledge that they can apply to their work and to their lives will be the movers and shakers in our society for the indefinite future."

~ Brian Tracy,
Canadian American Writer,
Motivational Public Speaker

"WELCOME, WINNERS OF THE NFAEE AWARD— THE NATION'S EDUCATIONAL MOVERS AND SHAKERS!" the sign proclaimed.

Mitzie couldn't help but see it as she entered the airport terminal in Richmond. After all, it was three feet tall and festooned with balloons and ribbons, and beneath it stood several smiling men and women, smartly dressed in matching navy-blue suits with gold buttons, holding smaller signs with names written on them. Mitzie spotted one which read, "Mitzie Galloway, Monticello, Florida." She veered off in that direction toward a lovely young Asian woman with shiny black hair cut in a chin-length pageboy. The woman's red lips parted in a dazzling smile when she noticed Mitzie walking in her direction.

"Mitzie Galloway from Monticello, Florida? I thought I recognized you from your picture. My name is Koji Yoshitaka. I will be your guide during your time at the Lower Eastern NFAEE Center. Welcome to Richmond. If you'll stand here by me, please, we're waiting on a few more people to join our group, and then we'll retrieve your luggage. I hope your flight was satisfactory," she said in a high, heavily-accented voice.

"Oh, it was quite nice, thank you," Mitzie replied, pushing in beside her guide. Mitzie noticed she didn't respond.

Koji spotted a tall good-looking man with close cut light brown hair, bright blue eyes, and deep dimples. She waved to him.

"You are Colby Carson from Perry, Georgia? I recognized you from your picture. My name is Koji Yoshitaka. I will be your guide during your time at the Lower Eastern NFAEE Center. Welcome to Richmond. If you'll stand here by Mrs. Galloway, please, we are waiting on a few more people to join our group, and then we'll retrieve your luggage. I hope your flight was satisfactory."

The man blushed slightly and nodded to Mitzie. "Thank you. It was fine," he mumbled as Koji ignored him and waved at an attractive, slender black woman.

"Cassidy Phelps from Cairo, Georgia? (She pronounced it like the Egyptian city) You look just like your picture. My name is Koji Yoshitaka. I will be your guide during your time at the Lower Eastern NFAEE Center. Welcome to Richmond. If you'll stand here by Mr. Carson and Mrs. Galloway, please, we're waiting on a few more people in our group, and then we'll retrieve your luggage. I hope your flight was satisfactory."

Cassidy took her place beside Mitzie and was about to respond to Koji and correct her on the pronunciation of the city, but the guide was already addressing another passenger. Mitzie shrugged, a look of puzzled amusement on her face. She leaned in closer to Cassidy.

"She's given the same speech to each of us. I'm Mitzie Galloway, from Florida. It's very nice to meet you."

"Hello Mitzie. I am Cassidy Phelps, and I'm from Cairo (she pronounced it KAY-ro). It's spelled like the city in Egypt, but it's pronounced like the syrup. It's good to meet you, too." She turned toward Colby. "And you are…"

He grasped her outstretched hand firmly, without hesitation. "Colby Carson. I'm from Perry, Georgia. I guess we're the Deep South delegation," he joked, and both women laughed.

A total of 25 people joined Koji's group before she directed them to the baggage claim area and then into a white passenger van with the words "National Foundation for Academic Excellence in Education" emblazoned on the side in gold and navy. Mitzie looked around and saw at least seven or eight more vans lining the curb, loading people much like herself into them. It appeared they were going to be a huge group, and she suddenly felt nervous. She had never attended a workshop with so many participants, and she realized she really knew very little about this sabbatical, despite her many internet searches. She wondered where they would be housed, how the courses would be conducted, and just how large the groups would be in each.

"Mrs. Galloway ..." Cassidy said.

"Mitzie. Please call me Mitzie," she said.

Cassidy smiled kindly. "Mitzie, it looks like there's going to be a whole lot of people here, and I'm not too good with crowds. Would you mind if I stuck with you for a while?"

"Oh, Cassidy, thank you for asking! I'm feeling pretty overwhelmed myself. I have severe claustrophobia. I've had it for a while. Please, please let's stay together," Mitzie gushed, patting the seat beside her.

Cassidy gratefully slid in next to Mitzie, and then impulsively grasped her hands and squeezed them before settling her purse on her lap. Colby took the seat behind them and leaned up between the two women.

"Hey, you two. I heard you talking up here, and I want to be part of this team. The 'Three Musketeers,' if you will," he said.

Mitzie and Cassidy laughed and turned around, placing their hands atop his. "One for all and all for one," they said in unison. The gesture put all three of them at ease and set the tone for the rest of the three-month sabbatical.

Half an hour later, the vans pulled one behind the other into a long circular driveway. The building at the end of the marbled walkway was ultra-modern—a colossal eleven-story edifice with gleaming windows and shiny bronze accents reminiscent of an expensive luxury hotel. The teachers collectively exclaimed and sighed and whistled as they exited the vans.

Koji made her way to the front of the group and rang a little high-pitched silver bell.

"Hello. Remember me? I am Koji, and I am the guide for the red group. If we get separated, please listen for my bell," she said, ringing the bell for emphasis. "Your luggage will be brought up to your rooms. Please follow me." And with that, she led them through the massive revolving doors and into an immense lobby with enormous fresh flower arrangements, glossy green potted plants, and brocade armchairs and settees in navy patterns.

Mitzie had never seen anything so opulent,

and she had to remind herself more than once to close her mouth. Koji rang her bell and moved on through the lobby to a bank of three elevators where she directed the participants to enter. Behind her, Mitzie could hear the identical spiel being played out by the other guides.

"Hello. I am Doovid, and I am the guide for the blue group. If we get separated, listen for my bell," he said, ringing a lower-pitched bell. "Your luggage will be brought up to your rooms. Please follow me."

"I am Helga. Jah. I am the guide for the yellow group. If we get separated, please listen for my bell," she said, ringing a tri-toned bell. "Your luggage will be brought up to your rooms. Please follow me."

The elevator doors closed, and Mitzie felt Cassidy nudge her. "Are you salivating yet?" she asked with mock seriousness.

"Am I hungry?" Mitzie questioned.

"No, girl. Are you salivating? Ding, ding, ding. Pavlov's dog?"

"Oh my gosh. I completely see what you mean. Creepy," Mitzie replied.

"Woof," Carson chuffed.

The elevator opened on the tenth floor. Koji stepped out and rang her bell. "Hello, red group. This is your floor. You will each have a private room on the right side of the hall. Please, do not change rooms with anyone else. That is not allowed. Come this way and get your room key from Koji."

The members of the red group moved forward

one by one and obtained a navy key card with a room number engraved on the face in gold. Mitzie was disappointed that her new friend Cassidy was not beside her. Mitzie's room was 1006, and Cassidy's was 1011. Colby was down the hall and around the corner to the left in room 1021.

"Please be sure your card works in your doors now," Koji said. "You will have one hour to relax before dinner is served on the main floor. I will meet you at the door to the ballroom. Remember, listen for Koji's bell." She rang the bell vigorously. "Again, welcome to the Lower Eastern NFAEE Center! Bye-bye."

Koji disappeared into the elevator while the teachers entered their rooms. Mitzie checked to be sure her key worked, and then she walked down to room 1011.

"Knock, knock, knock. Pavlov's dog here," she said.

Cassidy threw open the door and greeted Mitzie with a hug. "Listen for Koji's bell!" she mocked, "Come on in, Mitzie."

Mitzie entered and took a seat in a leather barrel chair. The room was lavishly furnished, and she felt out of place. Cassidy followed Mitzie's eyes as they darted around the room.

"Yeah, I know. Thinking the same thing. I don't belong here!" Cassidy admitted.

"No, no. You absolutely do belong here, and so do I, but I almost feel guilty, you know?"

"Yes, I do. Well, what are you going to do for the next hour or so?"

"I'm going to take a long, hot bath … without somebody knocking on the door with a boo-boo or wanting to ask me a question," Mitzie said. "I teach fourth grade, but you'd think they were little whiney babies sometimes."

"Oh, I hear you! I'm the librarian at my school, but honestly, I think the older kids are as wimpy as the Kindergarteners," Cassidy said.

"It looks to me like our rooms line the outside wall of this place, so I'm assuming across the hall must be our classrooms, or workrooms, or whatever they call them," Mitzie observed.

"That was my thinking as well. Koji kept calling us the red group. I noticed that our carpeting is a red pattern. I'm dying to find out if the carpeting in front of the other groups' rooms is a different color. Would you like to go explore after dinner?" Cassidy asked.

"You read my mind! I have so many questions, and based on her behavior at the airport, I have a feeling Koji is not going to give us answers," Mitzie said.

"Oh yes. I have to agree. She was just this side of rude, bless her heart," Cassidy mugged.

The two ladies broke into conspiratorial laughter at the comment. In the south, when one ended a phrase with "bless her heart," it was code meaning that person being discussed was stupid.

"Oh wow. I really needed to laugh. Thank you, Cassidy. I feel much better now. I'm going to let you rest, but before I go, can I get your cellphone number in case we get separated?" Mitzie asked, taking her phone from the side pocket of her jacket.

"Sure, unless you'd rather I ring a bell."

The two women laughed again, looking around guiltily as though the walls had ears. "I'll give Mr. Carson a call on the room phone. He's in 1021. We can meet up for dinner together."

"Great idea. I'll see you in about 45 minutes or so," Cassidy said as Mitzie exited the room. When the door closed, Cassidy turned toward the bed and ran her hand across the thick duvet, shaking her head in disbelief. Then, she knelt on the floor and laid her head on the coverlet. "Oh Lord. This is quite a place, and I thank You. But Lord, the Spirit's tickling my gut, and something don't feel quite right. Gird me with your strength and protection and protect my new friends Mitzie and Colby. Amen."

*   *   *

While Mitzie and Cassidy were resting in their rooms, Colby did some reconnaissance and mental calculations. As soon as they exited the elevators, he immediately noticed the red floral-patterned Berber carpeting and idly wondered if it had anything to do with their red group designation. He paced and counted his steps down the hall and estimated the room dimensions. There were 12 doors on the right side of the hall, and Colby figured each room to be approximately 15 feet wide. A 13th door at the end of the hall was clearly larger than the other rooms. He didn't see anyone enter it, nor did he see any handicapped persons in the group, but there was no doubt in his mind that room 2012 was designed for a disabled workshop participant.

The hallway took a sharp turn to the left, and he counted 12 more rooms on the right side, also 15 feet wide. Colby's room was numbered 1021—10th floor, 21st room. There were three doors beyond his, and then there were three elevators side-by-side, and a door at a right angle to the others which led to the stairwell. So far, that made 25 rooms on the 10th floor, numbers 1000 to 1025.

He kept walking and turned the corner. The carpeting in front of the elevators was grey—a stark contrast to the patterned red—and the carpeting from that point on was identical to that on his hallway, except its predominant hue was orange instead of red. *Ah! I was right about the carpet. I bet these are the orange group's rooms.*

The orange carpeted hallway held rooms configured in the same way: 12 rooms, handicap accessible room, 12 more rooms, three elevators, door to stairwell. He finished the loop and ended up back in the red corridor. Looking to the left, he counted two double doors three-quarters of the way down the first hallway, and two double doors three-quarters of the way down the next. The orange hall was identical to the red—two double doors down one corridor, and two double doors down the other corridor. From the locations and sizes of the doors, he speculated the center of the building on this floor contained one huge room divided into four sections. All total, the central room could probably hold 100 persons at desks or tables comfortably. He couldn't verify his theory as all the doors were locked, and the keycard in his hand certainly didn't open them.

Colby walked on to his room and inserted the key, pleased to find the room was as deep as it was wide. The carpeting was plush (and thankfully a soft neutral beige instead of red flowers) and the bathroom flooring was terra cotta tile squares. The Queen bed on the right wall was springy and soft, and from the feel of it, he knew it was one of those expensive hybrid mattresses of coiled springs and memory foam. It was covered with a thick raw silk duvet and two pillows of differing firmness. Flanking the bed were two nightstands with lamps.

On the left side, a traditional style mahogany dresser and a matching desk and chair completed the furnishings. Mounted on the wall over the desk with a telescoping arm was a 32-inch flat screen television that could be pulled down and used as a computer monitor by means of a USB cable.

Colby carefully set his utilitarian-looking backpack on the desk, amused at the stark contrast to the expensive furniture. Having brought no computer or laptop, the flat screen would be used for viewing whatever cable programing package the NFAEE

Center offered.

A floor-to-ceiling window filled the wall space between the foot of the bed and the desk and afforded him a view of the city of Richmond. There was no balcony, and the window did not open except for a six-inch high screened jalousie section across the middle that could be cranked open for ventilation should one desire fresh air; however, the room was light and airy enough it did not feel confining.

The closet had bi-fold louvered doors which allowed the pleasant smell of cedar paneling to waft through. Colby was surprised to find that both of his bags had been unpacked, and his clothes were neatly arranged on hangers within the closet. A check inside the dresser revealed that his small clothes (socks, undershirts, and briefs) had been folded and placed in the deep drawers.

Although this was a luxury not granted him on stays at other workshops, the intrusiveness of it made Colby uneasy. He was basically a private person, and it displeased him that someone had access to his personal property without his permission. To make it even more uncomfortable, he knew that his suitcase had been locked, and he had the only key.

Colby was distracted by a flashing red light on the room phone on the bedside table. He picked up the handset and pressed the red button.

"Hi Colby. This is Mitzie Galloway in room 1006. How about meeting Cassidy Phelps and me in front of my room about five till so the Musketeers can go to dinner together? OK. Bye."

Colby Carson smiled as he thoughtfully replaced the receiver, and then he hurried into the bathroom to take a shower before meeting his newfound friends. He was anxious to get their impressions of their lodgings for the next three months. He particularly wanted to know if their toiletries had also been neatly laid out on the bathroom counter.

CHAPTER FOUR
The Dinner

"Engage people with what they expect; it is what they are able to discern and confirms their projections. It settles them into predictable patterns of response, occupying their minds while you wait for the extraordinary moment—that which they cannot anticipate."

~Sun Tzu,
The Art of War

"HELLO. IT IS KOJI," the guide said ringing her silver bell. "Hear my bell and follow me to your tables." She turned and entered the Center's Grand Ballroom.

Mitzie, Cassidy, and Colby followed with the rest of their group. As they stepped into the massive banquet hall, Mitzie's gut feeling was utter panic. She did not see the leaded glass chandeliers hanging from the ornate tray ceiling; she did not make out the champagne beige flocked wallpaper with the gold metallic flecks; she did not notice the gleaming Italian marble floor tiles. Mitzie only saw an endless ocean of people milling about elbow to elbow in a closed space, and her claustrophobia became as tangible as an anchor trapping her beneath the surface of the suffocating depths of the sea.

She had a flashback of a trip she took with Phillip to a Florida State University bowl game in New Orleans on New Year's Eve. They wanted to ring in the new year with the Big Easy's version of a ball drop. A six-foot tall papier-mâché statue of a diapered Baby Bacchus stood atop the roof of the Jax Brewery in Jackson Square, and at midnight, the baby's diaper was supposed to fall, exposing his naked butt. Phillip thought it would be hilarious, and Mitzie, having had more than a couple strawberry daiquiris, had to agree, so they walked along with the throng of people on Jackson Square.

Due to the awareness-numbing effects of the alcohol, Mitzie failed to realize the crowd around her was getting closer, pressing in against one another until they were no longer walking but standing. The people shoved and elbowed as they jockeyed for the best position with which to see the baby drop his poopy drawers.

Suddenly, her hand slipped out of Phillip's grasp, and Mitzie found herself surrounded by strangers. She struggled to find her husband; but, being a petite woman only 5'3" tall, she was dwarfed by the figures around her, and their heads and shoulders obscured her view of anything but their undulating bodies and laughing faces. She had an irrational thought: *With my halo of auburn hair, Phil won't be able to see me in the darkness. I should've gone blond like he suggested.* She panicked and began calling his name as loudly as she could, but even she couldn't hear her own voice over the shouts of the others. To make matters worse, her left arm was pressed up against her side, and her right arm was cocked at such an angle that her hand was flat against the back of her head. She couldn't wave; she couldn't move at all.

Soon, the crowd began to sway, and the motion rocked Mitzie along with it, back and forth, and each time they rocked, she was pushed lower to the ground until her knees were forced to bend. She began to scream over and over, coughing and choking as tears ran down her cheeks and mucous poured from her nose and into her throat. She could not wipe her face because her hands were firmly held in place by the people flanking her on all sides.

She slid lower and lower, knowing that soon she would be on the ground and would inevitably be trampled to death. When her knees hit the pavement, she pulled them to her chest and rolled to her side. There was more space among the crowd's legs, and she was able to free her arms and wrap them around her head as she tucked herself into a fetal ball. Her vision grew dark, the shouting became muffled, and

Mitzie Galloway said goodbye to her children and passed out.

The next thing she knew, she opened her eyes and saw Phillip. His face was ghostly white as he stared at her, and she wondered vaguely if she lay in a coffin at her own funeral. Though Phillip was talking, Mitzie could not hear him. Little by little, her senses were restored—first her sight, then her hearing, and then her sense of touch. She realized she was lying on cold wet grass surrounded by an ancient iron fence. Trees stood guard above her, and there was crisp air to breathe. Phillip lifted her into a sitting position, holding tightly to her hands. He knew better than to constrict her with an embrace.

"Mitz? Babe? You're OK. Breathe slowly. You're all right," he murmured.

"I thought I died," she whispered.

"Me, too, for a moment. I found you curled up on the ground. Got you out of the crowd. Think I'll have to pay for that little fence, though. I kicked it down, but this was the only clear spot I could see. I'm so sorry, Babe. So stupid of me." His face reflected the pain he felt.

Mitzie looked at the people beyond the fence and saw the crowd celebrating, still flowing back and forth like the tide. She smiled at her husband, and then she vomited into his lap.

"Oooh. Sorry. Couldn't help it," she said with an embarrassed grimace.

"Ummm. Guess I deserved it, bringing you

into such a huge crowd of people," he said. "I'm really, really sorry, Mitz."

She pulled her eyebrows down and fixed her husband with a steely stare. "You let go of my hand!" she accused.

"I didn't mean to let go. We got pulled apart. What can I do to make it right, Mitzie? I told you I was sorry," he retorted.

She thought for a fraction of a second before answering. "You can help me up, for one thing, and then I want to see that damn baby's butt. And then, you take me back to the hotel, Phillip Galloway!"

Mitzie was surprised at how raw and vivid the recollection was of that night. She even had the same insistent ringing in her ears that she heard just before she passed out.

"Mrs. Galloway! Mrs. Galloway! Listen! Koji is ringing the bell. Please follow me to the table with the rest of the group," Koji demanded, her voice a tad shrill, much like her silver bell.

Mitzie looked up to see Cassidy and Colby standing in front of Koji, looking back at her with concern. Colby stepped around the harried guide and put his hand out, reaching for Mitzie.

"No, no. We must get to the table. You go, please," Koji said to him.

Colby ignored her and grasped his friend's hand. Cassidy appeared on Mitzie's other side and put her arm around her waist. "She has claustrophobia, Koji. You lead on. We will follow," she explained. Her tone of voice left no doubt that Cassidy Phelps had taken charge of this situation. Koji turned around abruptly.

Colby and Cassidy led Mitzie to a chair at one of the round tables. There were three for the so-called red group, and they were set with white linen tablecloths and decorative red china charger plates between an array of gold and silver utensils. Around the room, other people were being seated by the bell-wielding guides by groups at similar tables with corresponding colored charger plates.

After sipping some ice water from an Austrian leaded crystal glass, Mitzie started to count tables—a trick her therapist devised to help her alleviate the debilitating claustrophobia and panic attacks. His method entailed focusing the problem-solving part of her brain on a linear task so she could force the emotional part of her brain to keep the anxiety at bay.

Being gifted with great spatial awareness and visualization abilities, Mitzie was able to mentally divide the ballroom in half and focus on one hemisphere at a time. There were 52 round tables, all with distinctly colored charger plates. The groupings appeared to be in clusters of three. She identified eight sets of three, with two opposing rows of six tables dividing the two hemispheres of the room. Two of the tables in each cluster sat eight persons, and one sat nine, so there was seating for 25 guests per grouping, including several she noticed in wheelchairs.

As far as the charger plates were concerned,

she counted ten different shades: red, orange, navy blue, turquoise, lavender, purple, green, yellow, white, and black. Her mind immediately reordered them into the colors of the rainbow and applied the acronym she taught her school children: ROY G. BIV—red, orange, yellow, green, blue, indigo, violet. She added PIE, which stood for purple, ivory, and ebony.

The arrangement of the six black and white tables reminded her of the Chinese Yin-Yang symbol—three whites across from three blacks, and three blacks across from three whites. Elsewhere, the groupings were like a reverse letter L opposite an inverted letter L. All total, there were 20 groups with 25 people. Mitzie gasped when she realized that the room held over 500 people, including guides and waitstaff.

"Mitzie, what's wrong?" Cassidy asked.

"Cassidy, did you know there are more than 500 people in this dining room, not including the servers and guides?" Mitzie responded, smoothing her hair self-consciously, its blond highlights a permanent addition in response to that horrific incident many years ago.

"Yes. Yes, I do. Colby and I counted them when we entered. Sip some water, honey. Nod and smile. It'll be all right," Cassidy purred.

So Mitzie did exactly that, noticing that the other two Musketeers were doing the same. Colby caught her eye and winked, a fixed smile on his face.

A ringing unlike any of the bells they had heard thus far directed their attention to a raised platform in the center of the far end of the room.

A distinguished-looking man in a navy-blue Armani suit stood behind a podium at the front center of the platform, tapping a spoon on the side of a crystal water glass. The high-pitched tone was picked up by the microphone and reverberated throughout the room. The guests immediately quieted, as much from the sound as for their reaction to the man.

He was well over six feet tall, with coal black eyes, a square jaw, and thick razor-cut and purposely tousled black hair that was shot through with silver at the temples. At a rectangular table behind him sat two women, one in white, and one in dove grey.

"I would like to welcome all of you esteemed educators to the Lower Eastern Center of the National Foundation for Academic Excellence in Education and wish you a Happy New Year on this first day of 2020. I am Ronald A. Bowry, and I am your host," the man said.

The room immediately rang with applause, along with some whistles and shouts. Bowry raised his hand and the guests quieted again.

"We are delighted that you have accepted the NFAEE Award and are here with us for the next three months. We will do everything we can to make your stay enjoyable, exciting, and memorable. You are among the finest teachers in America, and we celebrate you. Before we start our dinner, it is my honor to recognize the award winners from each of the counties in the lower Eastern time zone. When I call your state, would you please stand and receive applause from your fellow teachers.

"From Florida, we welcome 63 winners from the 67 counties." Mitzie stood and graciously smiled and then sat down with the rest of the Florida awardees.

"From Georgia, we welcome 100 winners from the 159 counties." Colby and Cassidy both rose. When their state awardees sat, Bowry recognized the rest of the award winners in turn.

"From the state of North Carolina, we welcome 92 winners from 100 counties. From South Carolina, we welcome 46 participants from all 46 counties. Yes, give them a hand; they all accepted. From Virginia, we welcome 75 winners from the 95 counties. And from West Virginia, we welcome 54 winners from the 55 counties. I thank all of you winners for accepting your award. I will speak to you again ... *after* dinner. Please enjoy!"

As soon as Ronald Bowry returned to his table, servers appeared through the enormous front doors of the room and began placing china plates covered with sterling silver cloche food domes onto the plate chargers at each table. Water glasses were refilled, and baskets of homemade bread and Irish butter were delivered. As the dinner guests began removing the silver food domes, the vigilant waitstaff appeared and whisked them away.

Looking around the room, Cassidy decided that it was proper to go ahead and see what she was served. She was overjoyed to discover that the menu was not the same workshop fare she had endured for so many years: dry roast beef or over-cooked chicken, soggy green beans, sloppy mashed potatoes, and a roll hard as a lump of coal. Instead, her dish revealed a perfectly baked medium rare beef wellington, lemon butter roasted asparagus, creamy mushroom risotto, and a baby lettuce salad with raspberries, cranberries, and feta cheese. She bowed her head and silently blessed her food, and then she attacked her dinner plate and ate with unfettered gusto.

Colby's plat du jour was a thick, glistening filet of wild-caught Alaskan sock-eye salmon with drawn butter and lemon, sautéed haricots verts with brown butter almonds, roasted purple fingerling potatoes, and a fresh tropical fruit salad with pomegranate. He wasted no time in devouring the meal, barely making eye contact with his tablemates.

Mitzie lifted her cover and was delighted to find they had taken her food preferences into account. Her menu consisted of a fat juicy chicken breast that had been stuffed with thin slices of pancetta wrapped around Gruyère and provolone cheese. The chicken cordon bleu had been covered with panko breading and baked to a golden crispness. When she cut into the chicken, the gooey melted cheeses flowed. To complement the dish, there were roasted rainbow carrots, parmesan lemon orzo with baby peas, and an apple endive salad with sugared walnuts and blue cheese. The aromas were almost overpowering, but she forced herself to savor every single bite.

When all the sabbatical participants had finished scraping the last morsels of food from their dinner plates, the desserts arrived. The guests had their choice of a double chocolate molten lava cake, a fresh strawberry topped cheesecake, or they could select a tall crystal parfait glass that was filled with fresh blueberries, strawberries, blackberries, and raspberries, and layered with crème fresh and mascarpone cheese. Cassidy chose the lava cake, Colby selected cheesecake, and Mitzie opted for the parfait. There was very little talking throughout the room during the entire meal.

Now that the dinner had been served, and the tables had been cleared, the guides began circulating and handing out tote bags filled with swag and course essentials. Colby was pleasantly surprised to note that the customary workshop tote bag was leather instead of cotton/polyester. The NFAEE had spared no expense. His brow furrowed as he did some mental calculations. *I wonder where all the money came from. Somebody in the NFAEE has deep pockets.*

Inside his worship satchel, Colby found an information badge detailing his name, room number, course choice, and the floor where his class would be held. The badge was hard plastic, not laminated paper or a flimsy vinyl pocket, with a braided navy cord attached to gold metal fasteners. The face of the rectangular ID on the lanyard was white with black lettering, and the back of it was a bright cherry red.

He glanced at the dinner guests at the tables around the room and was not surprised to see badges with backs of other colors. He instinctively applied visually descriptive adjectives to the colors—a skill he encouraged his fifth-graders to develop so their writing scores would be improved: burnt orange, butter yellow, jade green, cobalt blue, soft lilac, dark plum, azure blue, coal black, and snow white. He expected to hear, *"I am Koji. You will wear your red badge please."* She didn't speak, but she did ring that damn bell while pointing to her own lanyard. Colby grimaced and reluctantly slung it over his head.

The buzzing in the room came to a halt as Ronald Bowry approached the podium once again. He gave them a flawless white smile.

"Ladies and gentlemen. I hope you enjoyed your dinner ..." His words were cut off as the room erupted in applause. "I don't know about you, but I am stuffed!" Throughout the banquet room came peels of polite laughter as others acknowledged their full stomachs.

"There is now a bit of business we must go over," he said. "In all seriousness, you are not here to merely eat, although you will be doing plenty of that. You are here to experience renewal and arm your minds for battle against the institution of education that has sadly been failing you as teachers. At the end of your stay, most of you will be going back into the same battlefields from which you came. We want you to be ready to be exemplary movers and shakers in the field of education. We want you to lead. We want you to mold our young ones' minds so they can go on to be movers and shakers in their own generations. Think it cannot be done? I am here to tell you that it *can* be done, and *you* will be the ones to do it."

Bowry stopped as the applause became a roar. He smiled and looked out over the packed dining room.

"You have each been given a course of study that will hopefully expand your minds to include possibilities you have never before dreamed. We have decided upon these topics after great debate, after reading your essays, and after conducting field research to see what interests our best and brightest teachers have.

"I am pleased to introduce you to Dr. Elizabeth Ford, the brains behind this organization. By that, I mean she is the one who disaggregates all the data and designs the courses especially for the group of participants we have with us tonight. Dr. Ford, please come up and share your thoughts."

To rousing applause, a striking woman took the podium after a handshake and side-face-air-kiss from Ronald Bowry. She stood tall and erect, with an effortless grace that only came from years of practice. Her white high-necked sleeveless dress fit like a spray-on tan and displayed a perfect size six figure.

"Isn't that Jamie Lee Curtis?" Mitzie asked.

"You know, she's the one from the Halloween horror movies?"

Cassidy shook her head. "No, I think that's Charlize Theron. She does those sexy abstract perfume commercials."

"You're both wrong," Colby said. "That's the chick from *Basic Instinct*. Sharon Stone."

Elizabeth Ford smiled at the audience, aware that she evoked a response in them. She knew she was an exquisite woman, with her platinum blonde hair cut in a short pixie style that left her tiny ears and long neck exposed. Wispy bangs feathered across a high forehead that was without any wrinkles. She had almond shaped blue eyes, high arched eyebrows, and perfect white teeth in a diamond-shaped face.

She looked as though makeup never touched her skin; however, her coloring was satin-smooth, and her high cheekbones had a rosy blush. Cassidy held her napkin up to her lips and mouthed a word to nobody in particular: *airbrushed.* Colby nodded and raised his eyebrows in response. Mitzie also nodded, having come to the same conclusion.

Elizabeth knew everyone in the room was looking at her with awe, with wonder, with admiration, and with recognition. Her appearance was by design. She bore a remarkable resemblance to all the sexy actresses that had been speculated by the participants. She was certain that all men (straight *or* gay) wanted her; all women wanted to be her. She reveled in the crowd's adoration.

"Ladies and gentlemen, teachers all. Thank you for being here. We are honored by your presence. My job is to give you information about your courses of study and complete the materials we have prepared to ensure you get the most out of this sabbatical. In your satchels you will find a portfolio with a course outline, a detailed map of the NFAEE Center, dining schedules and locations, and important guidelines you must follow while you are with us.

"I realize this is the last thing you'd like to do tonight, but please bear with me so we can get the details out of the way, and then you can go to your rooms and relax after this big meal in preparation for your first day of NFAEE Center learning tomorrow!

"Now, will you please raise your hand when I call your course? And as I do so, please check your ID badges to make sure you have the correct course indicated on the front.

"Those of you in Performing Arts, please show your hands for Music. Thank you. You will meet for your course on the 10th floor.

"Hands, please, for Dance. Thank you. You will be on the 8th floor.

"Hands, please, for Theater. Thank you. You will all be meeting on the 6th floor.

"Those of you in Visual Arts, please show your hands for Drawing. Thank you. You will meet together on the 10th floor.

"Raise your hands, please, for Painting. Thank you. You will meet on the 8th floor.

"Hands, please, for Sculpting. Thank you. Your course will meet on the 6th floor.

"Those of you in History, please show your hands for Indigenous Natives. Thank you. You will meet for your course on the 6th floor, as well.

"Give me a show of hands, please, for European Immigrants. Thank you. You will meet on the 4th floor.

"Hands, please, for African Immigrants. Thank you. You will be on the 2nd floor.

"Hands, please, for Asian Immigrants. Thank you. You will also meet on the 2nd floor.

"Please raise your hands for Early American Pioneers. Thank you. You will have your course on the 6th floor.

"Those of you in Literary Arts, please show your hands for Creative Writing. Thank you. You course will be held on the 4th floor.

"Hands, please, for Poetry. Thank you. You will meet on the 4th floor.

"A show of hands, please, for Journalism. Thank you. You will also be on the 4th floor.

"Hands, please, for Editing. Thank you. You will meet together on the 2nd floor.

"Please raise your hands for Publishing. Thank you. You will meet on the 2nd floor, as well.

"Those of you in Culinary Arts, please raise your hands for Healthy Cooking. Thank you. You will meet in the kitchen area we have set up on the 10th floor.

"Hands, please, for Baking. Thank you. You will also be working on the 10th floor.

"Those of you in Archaeology, please show your hands. Thank you. You will be meeting on the 8th floor.

"Those in the Forensic Anthropology course, please show your hands. Thank you. You will be the 8th floor, too.

"Those of you in Cartography, please raise your hands. Thank you. You will be meeting on the 4th floor.

"Did I miss anyone? Anyone with an incorrect badge? Wonderful! Your classes will begin tomorrow morning at 8:00 a.m. on the floors I read off. If you get confused, the floor number is printed on your badge.

"Guess what, ladies and gentlemen? There is no bus duty, no cafeteria duty, no students to supervise. Isn't that great?" She giggled and rotated her shoulders to rousing hoots and applause throughout the room. "I truly hope you enjoy what we have in store for you. I'll let you in on a little secret. Some participants enjoy their course of study so much they go on to make careers of them. You may find you want to change what you teach, and that is OK. We have advisors on staff to help you if you decide to transition to another field of education. But no matter what you do, we want you to enjoy yourselves and be renewed. Teaching is hard work. You deserve to be pampered.

"Now, to go over the guidelines, I will turn the

time over to my colleague Ashley Lawrence. Mr. Bowry and I have a plane to catch to another center in Santa Fe, New Mexico, so we will bid you good evening. Thank you. Ashley?"

Elizabeth beckoned to Ashley who looked fresh out of college. A lovely young woman with hazel eyes and light brown hair in long waves to her shoulders moved to the podium. Ronald Bowry and Elizabeth Ford descended the platform and made their way to the doors amid waves and applause from the audience, and then Ashley spoke into the microphone with a soft, deferential voice, giving them a sweet, shy smile.

"Hello. I'm Ashley, and I'll be talking to you about our guidelines. With so many people here in the NFAEE Center, we would be tumbling all over each other without some type of order, so we've come up with a set of reasonable guidelines. You'll find these guidelines in your portfolios, if you'd please take them out now and read along with me.

"1. Your living space is assigned specifically to you. It is a single occupancy room, but we do not mind if you have visitors or even an occasional sleepover with a friend. You may not, however, move permanently into another person's room. As cell calls and tablets are not permitted in the course areas, you have been provided a lockbox you may use to safeguard your devices.

"2. Your dining area is chosen to allow the least amount of movement possible. With such a large group of people going to classes all over the building, it is imperative that you only eat in your assigned dining area. Floors 10 and 11 dine on floor 11. Floors eight and nine dine on floor nine. Floors six and seven dine on floor seven. Floors four and five dine on floor five. Floors two and three dine on floor three.

"3. Courses begin promptly each morning at 8:00 a.m. Breakfast is from 6:30 to 7:45, lunch is from 11:30 to 12:45, and dinner is from 6:30 to 7:45. The dining areas will only be open during those hours. If you find you want a snack, you may call down to the kitchen, and food will be delivered to your room. Those of you who like to drink cold sodas, juices, water, coffee, or tea throughout the day will find drink and snack dispensers in the dining areas and within the classrooms. You are welcome to take drinks and food items back to your rooms. There are no refrigerators, but you may obtain a six-drink cooler or a thermos by calling the kitchen.

"4. You are free to roam the grounds around the NFAEE in the event you have extra time or in the early morning or evenings; however, you may not take personal excursions off-site unless you are participating in a scheduled group outing. The perimeter path is handicap-accessible and there are several adjacent seating areas for your convenience.

"5. Certain areas are unavailable for personal use. The Grand Ballroom will remain locked and is accessible only when the entire group meets together or when a course instructor schedules an event. The stairwells on each floor are off limits as they are used for kitchen and maintenance workers and in the event of a fire. If you have a medical problem that prohibits you using the elevators, please inform the front desk and a guide will be sent to escort you up or down the stairway. If you must smoke or vape, you may not do so in the room or on the stairway. Please smoke only in the designated smoking areas outside on the grounds. Vaping is allowed in the hall corridors only.

"6. Your guides have been specially trained and assigned to your individual floor's color group. Please listen for your guide's unique bell tone and follow his or her instructions. Please, be polite and respectful of your guide. He or she is here for your own safety and to facilitate your overall experience at the NFAEE Center.

"7. The courses have been designed based on your feedback and your areas of interest. Each course has materials, lessons, outings, and activities planned for a specific number of participants. You may not change courses, audit courses, or accompany friends in other courses. If you are unhappy with your choice, please inform your guide. You will be allowed to meet with the administrators to discuss moving you to another course of study under the terms of your award and subject to seating availability. The decision of the administrators is final.

"8. If you are caught engaging in any physically, emotionally, or verbally abusive behavior, you will be removed from your course of study for the day. You will be required to confer with the administrators to discuss the terms of your award relative to the harm caused by you as a participant. If you are found to be a danger to yourself or others, or if your presence is determined to be detrimental to the program, your time at the NFAEE Center will be terminated and you must leave. The decision of the administrators is final.

"9. If you are caught engaging in any type of illegal or illicit behavior, such as drug use, alcohol consumption, or theft of property, you will be removed from your course of study for the day. You will be required to confer with the administrators to discuss the terms of your award relative to the harm caused by you as a participant. If you are found to be a danger to yourself or others, or if your presence is determined to be detrimental to the program, your time at the NFAEE Center will be terminated and you must leave. The decision of the administrators is final.

"10. If you fail to follow the guidelines set forth by the NFAEE for the duration of the awards program, you will be required to confer with the administrators to discuss the terms of the award relative to the behavior of you as a participant. If you are found to be in violation of the terms of the award guidelines, your time at the NFAEE Center will be terminated and you must leave. The decision of the administrators is final.

"There is a final page attached to the guidelines for you to sign and date, showing your agreement to abide by them. As the hour is growing late, you may take your tote bags and materials back to your rooms now, and we will arrange to collect the agreements in the morning at your dining locations."

She looked up from the stack of papers and graced the group with a girlish grin before she opened her eyes wide in mock surprise.

"Oh, wait! Before we go, I almost forgot to mention something! On your way out the door, please be sure to grab a swag bag with some late-night treats for you. I picked them out myself. Goodnight all!"

Ashley waved and left the podium to a final round of somewhat less enthusiastic applause, and the guides appeared with their bells to escort the 500 participants to their appropriate floors.

Colby, Cassidy, and Mitzie were not the only ones deep in thought. As they scanned the faces in the room, there were more than a few frowns and puzzled looks. They collected their swag bags and trudged along behind Koji and her annoying silver bell. As they walked along, they loudly and conspicuously sang the praises of the delicious dinner with some of the other participants in their group, but they deliberately refrained from recapping the rest of the evening's events; that was something they decided to do in Mitzie's room ... in private.

CHAPTER FIVE
The Recap

"Fear is not a good teacher. The lessons of fear are quickly forgotten."

~Mary Catherine Bateson,
American Scientist

"I AM NOT AFRAID," Mitzie insisted, looking around the room at her new friends. "I am *concerned*!" She shifted in the easy chair, crossing and uncrossing her legs.

"Well, *I'm* a little afraid," Colby admitted. "It's only been one day, and I have a feeling I am not going to feel renewed and energized at the end of three months. That's a long time to be unhappy with my circumstances. Ringing bells, can't leave the Center, can't have cellphones in the class, restrictive guidelines, threats ..."

"Now Colby, I wouldn't exactly say threats

..." Cassidy began.

"What else would you call it? It's right here in these guidelines: '... *you will be removed from your course of study ... confer with the administrators to discuss the terms of your award relative to the harm caused by you as a participant. If you are found to be a danger to yourself or others, or if your presence is determined to be detrimental to the program, your time at the NFAEE Center will be terminated and you must leave. The decision of the administrators is final.'* And guideline number 10: '... *If you are found to be in violation of the terms of the award guidelines, your time at the NFAEE Center will be terminated and you must leave. The decision of the administrators is final.'* Is it not implicit in this document that they can bounce us out at any time if we appear to be *'in violation'* of one of their rules? Wouldn't you call that a not-so-thinly veiled threat?" he insisted, shaking the paper in his fist.

"Don't you think it's more like some legal mumbo jumbo to protect themselves?" Cassidy asked.

"Protect themselves from what? A group of teachers, for God's sake? I hardly think we're going to be harboring any political activists or terrorists. Frankly, I'm pretty damned insulted," he huffed.

"Colby, you're taking this all rather personally, aren't you? It's basically a list of rules—just like the ones we set for the kids in our classrooms—only a lot stronger because we're adults in a private facility," Mitzie reasoned. "You know good and well that in a group this size, somebody's going to get out of line. In all honesty, it makes me wonder what's happened in the past years that's made it *necessary* to have these kinds of rules."

"Mitzie, if you put rules like this in your own classroom, I doubt you'd have any students! The parents would rip you to shreds," Colby said.

"Yes, but we have *children* at school, Colby. Adults—*especially* teachers—are going to push the boundaries far more vigorously than kids. Tell me you have a smoothly run faculty meeting with no teachers acting out, and I'll call you a damn liar!" Cassidy stated. She crossed her arms and bobbed her head in a defiant nod that broke the tension and caused Colby to laugh and throw his hands up.

"Ahhh, you girls are gonna kill me. OK. I see your point. All the same, let's be observant. Seriously, I've had a hinky feeling about this ever since I got the second letter," he said.

There was no mistaking the shock on Mitzie's and Cassidy's faces at the mention of the second NFAEE letter.

"Um, you mean the one that told us what course we had been approved for?" Mitzie asked.

"Yeah, that's the one," Colby said, noting with interest their reactions.

"What made you wary about that, Colby. Didn't you get your choice?" Cassidy offered.

"Well, sure I did. It was the last part. You know ... the *'you will be terminated'* part."

Mitzie and Cassidy suddenly became blank canvasses. Their emotions were inscrutable, and Colby immediately backed off from the topic. Instead, he got quiet and started to meander around the room.

"Like I said, Colby. They've got to set rules. It shouldn't be a problem for us. We certainly don't intend on causing any trouble," Cassidy said.

"Yeah, you're right. Guess I'm getting the letter mixed up with the guidelines. I'm kind of a word nerd, so the syntax is bound to be different than what we Southerners speak." He realized his near faux pas and tried to explain it away.

"Sure, that's what it is, *and* we're all kind of tired," Mitzie said.

"True. True. What did you think of our host and hostesses?" Cassidy asked.

"Ronald Bowry strikes me as a Cosmopolitan sort of guy," Colby said.

"Did you think he was handsome?" Mitzie asked with a slight smile.

"Yes!" Cassidy responded with a leer. "He has that smoldering bad boy vibe."

"Aw hell no," Colby interjected. "We are not going there. I didn't think he was handsome at all. But Dr. Ford? Smoking hot." He shook his hand like he was putting out a match.

"Ew. My kids would call her a 'fakie-fake-faker' to her face," Mitzie claimed.

"Your kids are not grown men," Colby observed.

"I'm with Mitzie. She was as phony as a pig with lipstick," Cassidy said.

"What? I've never heard that before," Colby admitted, though Mitzie was laid back on the bed in a fit of giggles.

"You haven't? My granny always told me 'you can put lipstick on a pig, but it's still a pig.' That's our movie-star-wannabe Dr. Ford," Cassidy responded with another bobble of her head.

"What about Ashley Lawrence? You've gotta admit, she's a sweetheart," Colby said.

The ladies alternated responses rapidly.

"Too sweet."

"Too saccharine."

"Too cutesy."

"Too coquettish."

"Too too," they said in unison.

Colby was taken aback and stared at them in confusion. "Who *are* you women? What did Ashley Lawrence ever do to you?"

"Nothing," Cassidy said in all seriousness.

"Yeah. We liked her," Mitzie added. "It's a girl thing, Colby, that the older kids do at school. Boys don't play the word game."

"A *mean* girl thing?" he asked.

Cassidy shrugged. "Not really. Just a girl thing. But Mitzie's right. We liked Ashley. She just had the misfortune of being the one to read the guidelines."

"And we're just blowing off steam after the

day," Mitzie said with a barely concealed yawn which made the others follow suit.

Colby blinked his eyes and stretched "You're right. It's been a long day. I think maybe I need to head on to my own room. How about you Ms. Phelps? Can I drop you off on my way?" he asked.

"I'd be delighted, Mr. Carson. Mitzie, will you be all right now if we leave?" she asked.

"Oh, sure. I'm worn out. I didn't realize it'd be such a big place with so many people. I'm going to call Phillip and say goodnight to him and the kids. Want to meet at my room in the morning to ride up to the eleventh floor for breakfast?" she said.

"Sounds good to me," Colby said, opening the door. He lifted his arm and tapped his smartwatch. "OK, ladies. Ready to synchronize." He looked back and saw Cassidy on tiptoes looking over his shoulder and Mitzie at his elbow admiring his watch. "Oh, yeah. I guess I'm a bit of a geek."

"Cool. I've been wanting one of those, but, you know, pricey," Mitzie said shrugging.

"Well, I actually … um … never mind. What time do you want to meet? Breakfast is at 6:30," he said, his hand poised over his watch face.

"I don't want to be the first, and I do want to be early, but not that early. How about 7:00?" Cassidy said, "but just let me synchronize my Timex. Very high-tech, you know."

The comment, for some reason, struck Mitzie as hilarious. She fell against the closet and burst out in an explosive guffaw that surprised her friends. The effect was infectious, and the three of them laughed so hard that the person in the adjacent room knocked on the wall, which made them laugh even more. Wiping their leaky eyes, they covered their mouths with their hands, a pillow, and even a leather tote bag as they struggled to be quiet. Finally, exhausted, they agreed on 7:00, and Colby left the room with Cassidy on his arm. Mitzie could still hear them giggling as she watched Colby escort Cassidy to her room and disappear inside. *Hmm,* Mitzie thought as she closed the door, *I wonder if something is developing there?*

Something was indeed developing, but it was more conspiratorial than romantic. As soon as they entered Cassidy's room, Colby put his finger to his pursed lips and began walking around, seemingly examining her room and its furnishings.

"Nice room you have here," he said.

"But, isn't yours just like it?" Cassidy asked, frowning in confusion.

"Oh, um, yeah. Sure, it is. Well, pretty much. I've got different bedspread colors. Mine's a little more masculine, I guess. Scarlet and chocolate plaid instead of cherry and gold paisley. My pictures are different, too," he said, examining the art on the wall, looking behind the frames. "My window view's not quite as nice as yours." He peeked behind the drapes. His gaze drifted to the television over the desk. He raised his eyebrows and nodded to Cassidy, his back to the wall mounted flat screen, finger still to his lips.

Then he stepped into the bathroom, all the while keeping his eyes on her face.

"Oh crap. Hey Cassidy, can you come here a minute. I've lost my contact lens and I need some help finding it," he called, kneeling down on the terra cotta tile floor.

Cassidy looked up in surprise, and then she came into the bathroom. Colby reached over and closed the door slightly.

"I think it may be back here near the door. Help me look," he said, pulling her down beside him behind the closed door. "Don't say anything," he whispered, "but I think we are being observed."

Startled, she rose up, only to be pulled down again close to the floor. He motioned for her to stay there and moved about the room, feeling under the sink, looking into the overhead vent, peering into the mirror while rapidly blinking his eyes, and then he stepped into the tub and examined the showerhead. Finding nothing, he pulled the shower curtain closed, knelt back down next to Cassidy, and whispered into her ear. "When we go back, I want you to throw your jacket over the television. I know it sounds paranoid but humor me. Be careful what you say," he urged.

Standing up, he pulled the door open. "Found it! It was floating around in my eye. Thanks for helping me look, though."

Moving back into the bedroom, Cassidy removed her jacket and casually draped it over the television. Then, she sat down at the desk. Colby nodded. "You're a bit of a messy housekeeper for a librarian, Cassi," he said with a forced chuckle.

"Oh, yes. You know what they say about us librarians. We're so buttoned up and organized at school that we just let it all hang out when we go home," she managed with a wan smile.

Colby gave a short "hah" as he walked to the bed and sat down facing the window. He carefully looked at the phone on her nightstand, and then he turned to her, side-eying the phone.

Cassidy stood and removed it from the table. "Well, I don't have anyone at home to call like Mitzie, so I'm going to put my phone to bed. Yes, I know it sounds funny, but at home, I usually put my phone under a pillow, so I don't hear it ring at night. I'm an extremely light sleeper, and I want to get plenty of rest before tomorrow."

"Oh, I completely understand. I never do the front desk wake-up call when I'm in a hotel. I hate when the ringing pulls me out of a good dream. I always set the bedside clock. That's a really good idea, Cassi, putting it to bed like that. I may do the same," he said as he watched her place the phone on the floor underneath two pillows and the extra blanket. She got up, and Cassidy saw him standing against the wall on the other side of the bed, surreptitiously pointing upward at the blinking light of the smoke detector.

She forced a big yawn, and then she moved toward the door and opened it. Colby followed and casually scanned the corridor.

"I will see you in the morning, Miss Phelps, at 7:00 at Mrs. Galloway's room, then," he said loudly. "I hope you rest well, Cassi." He covertly slipped his watch off and put it into her palm as he shook her hand. "Take it into the bathroom and wait for my text. Don't use your cell phone," he whispered before walking down the hall, whistling softly.

Cassidy watched him turn the corner before she pulled the door closed and locked it. Trembling, she removed her bed clothes from the drawer and carried them and Colby's watch into the bathroom.

In the time it took her to get ready for bed, Colby entered his own room, covered his television, put his own room phone to bed, and entered the bathroom. He pushed up the handle on the faucet and listened to the sound of the water running into the sink, and then he removed a second iWatch from his pants pocket. He powered it up and tapped on the face as he began texting.

"CASS. SORRY 4 SPY STUFF. SURE WE R WATCHED.
U B CAREFUL."

Cassidy responded, texting from his iWatch.

"I M SCARED. Y?"

"DON'T KNOW. BAD FEELING. DID U GET $$ LETTER?

"YES!!! U 2?"

"MITZIE?"

"MAYBE. SHE LOOKED STARTLED"

"READ LT AGAIN WHEN U CAN. READ IN BATHROOM. ONLY SAFE PLACE IN UR ROOM"

"WHAT MADE U THINK?"

"THE WORDING. TERMINATED… STRONG WORD. MADE ME WARY. I PROBLY WATCH 2 MUCH TV"

"WHAT 2 DO?"

"WATCH N LISTEN. DON'T TELL MITZIE YET. U + ME ONLY. OK?"

"SCARED!!"

"ME 2. MUST B CAREFUL. WATCH N LISTEN."

"BUT Y? Y WATCH US?"

"HAS TO BE THE $$"

"DIDN'T WANT THE DAMN $$"

"BIG BANKROLL HERE. LOTS OF $$ IN THIS PLACE. SOMETHING NOT RIGHT. 2 MANY RULES. BAD ATMOSPHERE. B SAFE. B ALERT. WILL B OK. C U IN AM. K?"

He added a thumbs up smiley face emoji to his text for reassurance.

Cassidy smiled wanly as she replied.

"K. THX COLBY. NITE"

Cassidy wiped away a tear. She stayed in the bathroom a few more minutes, and then she tried to inconspicuously walk to the bed, painfully aware of the smoke detector, the phone, and the television. Turning out the lights quickly, she snuggled under the thick, warm duvet and, despite her fears, fell fast asleep.

CHAPTER SIX
<u>Day 1 - Breakfast</u>

"Knowledge is a weapon. I intend to be formidably armed."

~ Terry Goodkind,
American Writer

MITZIE OPENED THE DOOR at 7:00 on the dot to see her friends smiling from the corridor.

"We're nothing if not punctual," Cassidy said.

"Not to mention clean and impeccably attired," Colby mugged, indicating his freshly pressed khaki pants and wrinkle-free blue and white checkered button-down collar shirt.

"Gads, all you need is a bow-tie, glasses, and a pocket protector," Mitzie said.

"Are you referring to my geekiness?" he asked with a mollified look on his clean-shaven face.

"Yes, she is," Cassidy replied with a grin.

"You look a little like Howdy-Doody ... emphasis on the doody."

Colby feigned a shocked expression. "I wanted to look my best, and I intend to get a red apple at breakfast to give to my teacher," he said, "but first, I have a little something for you, Mitzie. I noticed last night that neither of you ladies wore watches. I happen to have extras of these little cheap look-alike smartwatches that I got for my nieces and nephew from one of the stores at the airport. Voilà." He reached forward, took her arm, and fastened the white round-faced watch around her tiny wrist.

"Colby! I can't accept this. It's too expens ..."

"... Mitzie, can I just use your restroom before we go. In all the excitement over the day, I forgot before we left my room," Cassidy asked hurriedly to distract Mitzie from finishing her sentence.

Flustered, Mitzie ushered her in, and Cassidy dashed into the bathroom.

"Colby, really, I don't think ..." Mitzie started.

"No, no, no. It's just a plastic knock-off LED watch that all the kids like. Looks expensive, but it's not. Mine's an imposter, too. A gift from one of my students to make me look cool. $13.99 plus tax. Here, I've already synced it. Please, accept it with my compliments for being my new friend and so we can meet for lunch on time," he insisted.

Cassidy emerged from the room and winked at Colby. "Oh, do you like your watch, Mitzie? He gave me one, too, to use instead of my imaginary

Timex. Several of my fifth-grade students had these pretending they were smartwatches. They look remarkably realistic. No frills, but they keep good time." She brandished her own watch, which had a black band and square black face.

"Thank you, Colby. I appreciate the gift," Mitzie said with a grin.

"Well, ready all?" Colby asked, extending his elbows for both ladies to grasp. They walked down the corridor as a trio and made their way to the elevators where several others were gathering. Remembering her panic attack the night before, the three of them hung back as the first elevator filled and boarded the less crowded second one.

When they got to the eleventh floor, they moved toward the first double doors on the left of the hallway. Already, the corridor was abuzz with excitement as people talked about their courses, last night's dinner, and got to know one another.

"Listen," Colby said.

"Getting noisy, isn't it?" Cassidy said.

"No. That's not what I was meaning. Listen again. No bells!" he said.

"Well hooray! I really hate those stupid bells. *'I am Koji. You will eat your breakfast now.'* Thank you, Lord. By the way, have you noticed they're all foreign—Japanese, German, Romanian, Swedish, Hispanic? Every guide I've heard speak is ESOL," Cassidy pointed out.

"I know, right? Why would they have guides

for American teachers who all speak English as a second language? Weird," Mitzie said.

"Shhh. Don't you be disrespecting our specially chosen guides. Argh, that reminds me. Did you sign your guidelines agreement?" he said.

"Yes, but reluctantly" she said, pulling the paper from her tote bag and rolling her eyes.

"Here, let me take it over to the drop box at the door. Mitzie, got yours?" he said.

Mitzie pulled out her paper and handed it to him, and then she entered the double doors and took stock of the 11th floor dining room.

The dining area was huge, though not as immense as the ballroom. As Colby had deduced, it was a square in the middle of the four corridors, and there were folding partitions pulled back and secured to the centers of each wall to allow the full measure of the room to be used. Round tables were arranged all around a central square of tables which served as the buffet setup.

One row of rectangular tables held stainless steel chafing dishes with burning Sterno cannisters beneath them to keep the contents of the dishes warm. A perpendicular row of tables featured breads and pastries of all sorts and toasters in which to warm them. Silver bowls held jellies and fruit preserves. There were three cream cheeses—traditional, herbed, and fruit flavored—and trays of smoked salmon, pancetta, and sliced cheeses—cheddar, gouda, swiss, and provolone. Fresh fruit in baskets completed the food choices.

The next perpendicular group of tables held five different cold or hot cereals in crank handle dispensers, along with milk—whole, 2%, and almond. There were several flavors of Greek yogurt, as well as yogurt and fruit parfaits, honey, maple syrup, agave, and Irish butter. On the next tables beside them were double Bunn coffee pots, electric kettles of water for a wide variety of black, green, and herbal teas, and chilled juices in ice—orange, grapefruit, and apple. This table also contained trays, cups, glasses, china plates and bowls, and baskets of silverware.

The final tables completing the square were manned with cooks in tall paper chef's hats. They stood behind induction cooktops and prepared special-order items—omelets, hashed brown white or sweet potatoes, and pancakes and waffles—plain or with bananas, chocolate chips, or berries.

Colby loaded a tray with plate, bowl, cup, and silverware and headed down the buffet line. He was pleasantly surprised to find the fare fresh and appetizing. He piled his plate with fluffy soft scrambled eggs, grits, and crisp applewood bacon. He crumbled two flaky biscuits into his bowl, covered them with peppered white sausage gravy, and liberally sprinkled shredded cheddar cheese over everything. Catching Cassidy's eye, he headed for an empty table and smiled broadly.

Cassidy opted for an omelet with crispy home fries. She watched as the chef whipped up three large eggs and expertly cooked a perfect omelet stuffed to overflowing with mushrooms, ham, and cheese. She set her tray down beside Colby and headed back for a cup of strong coffee.

Mitzie, in the meantime, made herself a bowl of oatmeal with butter, cinnamon, and maple syrup. She also grabbed another yogurt and fruit parfait and a cup of red rooibos herbal tea with honey. She sat down next to Colby and shook her head.

"This is like being on a cruise, only the boat's not rocking. I'm going to be so fat at the end of this sabbatical," she said with a self-conscious giggle.

"Enjoy it while you can. In three months, it'll be back to peanut butter and jelly," he said through a mouthful of scrambled eggs mixed with grits.

"I've never seen so much food in my life," Cassidy exclaimed. "Do you think we'll get this every day or are they just courting us now and by the end of the month we're going to be back to peanut butter and jelly on white bread?"

Colby shot her a covert look. "Oh, who knows? Eat up, Cassi. Lookie here, they have grits! Did you know, in the North and the West, they don't even know what grits are? Can you imagine? You ask for grits; they give you cream of wheat. Ever eat cream of wheat? It sucks, especially if you put butter and cheese on it, because it's sweet. Only Southerners know what good food is, huh?" he said, giving her a playful wink.

Cassidy responded by agreeing with him as

she savored the melted cheese that oozed from her omelet. "Yes, sir. I'm hoping they'll serve us some turnip greens and hog jowls for lunch. Maybe even some chitlins."

Colby dropped his fork, and Mitzie nearly spit out her tea. "Do you cook those foods at home, Cassidy?" she asked, hoping not to offend her newfound friend.

"Are you out of your mind? Those are nasty tasting and even nastier smelling. I do like me some greens, but I hate to cook them. Smells up the whole kitchen. If I want that kind of soul food, I go to my Auntie's (she pronounced it Ohn-TEE's). No ma'am. I like what I'm eating now ... and I especially like it when somebody else is doing the cooking and especially the cleaning."

"Yeah, you should see her room," Colby smirked, laying his dirty fork on the table and continuing eating with his spoon.

"Hmmph. Told you about that last night. We're on a kind of vacation. We can afford to let down our housekeeping standards a bit, don't you think, Mitzie?" Cassidy asked.

"Well, to tell the truth, I'm going to enjoy myself and not worry about keeping everything so tidy like I have to do at home. No kids or husband to pick up after, right? You know what? Tomorrow, I'm not even going to make my bed," she said with a smile.

"Good for you," Colby said. "Are you excited about your class? What do you hope to learn?"

"My husband is Creek Indian, and there are a lot of people around my area that are Creek, so I'm really interested in learning more about the early indigenous Native Americans. I hope the instructor is Native American. That would make it even more authentic, you know?" Mitzie said.

"I am going to *dig* digging," Cassidy joked, "and by that, I mean I really hope we get to do a lot of excavating on a type of historical site. Maybe I'll find a dinosaur bone or something. Do you know, I knew another lady from around my area in Georgia that came here just a few years ago. Olivia Roberts. She was in the archaeology course, too. Olivia was handicapped—had that condition where the hand is like a lobster claw ..."

"... Ectrodactyly," Colby said.

"Yeah, what he said. She only had a thumb and two fingers, but she could hold a trowel and dig. Anyway, she unearthed some piece of a bone and she determined it to be part of a foot bone from a human being—a Native American. Of course, they had to shut the site down because anytime you find any Indian skeletal remains, the tribes come in and declare it a burial ground."

"Wow! That's fascinating. What did the lady do afterwards?" Mitzie asked.

"Well, from what I heard, she got offered a position in a university up north in their archaeology department. She never went home after her sabbatical because they started her job at the college right away.

Her whole family—husband and two little boys—moved from Georgia lock, stock, and barrel. Now I hear they live up in a big house in New York state, or something. Can you imagine? They must be living high on the hog because I was told they never came back to visit Georgia again. Don't even answer phone calls or texts from friends," Cassidy said.

"That's wild! Money changes people, I guess. I don't know what I'd do if I were offered a job, like that woman was saying last night. I'd have to turn it down, I think. We're very settled in Florida. What about you, Colby?" Mitzie said.

"I would sail along where the wind blows. Who knows?" he replied dramatically, "over hill or dale or on the back of a whale."

Cassidy elbowed him in the ribs. "Go on with your fool self."

He smiled broadly. "I don't know. It would have to be something really good, with great pay, of course. But I'm doing forensic anthropology. I don't have the schooling or credentials to make it big in that kind of department. I just took the course because it sounded interesting ... and I'm a geek for figuring out puzzles and mysteries, too. Hey, I know what: Cassi can dig up a bone, I'll do a forensic analysis on it, and if it turns out to be Native American, Mitzie can publish a paper on it. Win-win-win! Regardless, I intend to learn something I never knew before. I believe that's the whole point of sabbaticals, don't you think? Expand your horizons. Branch out. Take the road less traveled and all that."

"I agree with you. This is our opportunity to gain knowledge we didn't have before and may never have the opportunity to get again. Will I be an archaeologist in my lifetime? Not very likely. But can I use that information to enrich the lives of my pupils? Absolutely," Cassidy said.

"And I can take what I learn about indigenous Natives to not only know more about my husband's and my children's ethnic background, but I can use it to guide my fourth-graders. I question many of the things I read in our social studies texts. I don't think they're entirely accurate." Mitzie said frowning.

"Oh, Mitzie. You have hit one of my hot buttons. I just did an examination of a reading series with social studies companion texts that my county insists on adopting, and I know for certain that the historical information is inaccurate. It's one of the reasons I applied for this award. I'm so sick of our country rewriting history to suit someone's idea of political correctness. The facts are the facts. Let's don't mess with them and tidy them up," Cassidy announced.

"Peace be still, Cassi. I agree with you, and I wholeheartedly admire your passion, but this may not be the right forum. Go on to your class, acquire what knowledge you can, and be observant of everything you see and hear. That's what we all need to do," Colby said with calm aplomb.

"I know, I know, Colby. But those who forget

or ignore history are doomed to repeat it," she said, her eyes burning fiercely.

"Those are true words. So, let us not forget or ignore. How about we go into this sabbatical with our eyes wide open and gain insight into these different fields of study? What do you say?" he countered, placing his hand gently on her forearm and squeezing.

Cassidy graced Colby with a warm smile. *Oh yes, something is developing here*, Mitzie said to herself. She looked at the two of them fondly, thankful that she had met them yesterday at the airport. Her stomach was full, and her fearfulness of the unknown subsided. She remembered something she took from the buffet table.

"Colby, I got you this for your first day," she said, holding out a shiny red apple.

He released his grip on Cassidy's arm and took the apple with a grin.

"Why, thank you, Mitzie. This may come in handy on my first day of school," he said.

"No, Colby. Thank you, for being my friend and for giving me this cute watch," she replied, "and looking at it, I see we have exactly nine minutes to take a potty break and get to our classes."

Mitzie pushed her chair back and picked up her tray. Immediately, a server took it from her hand and retrieved the trays of her tablemates. She poked out her lower lip and giggled, shrugged, and lifted her tote bag to her shoulder as her friends also got up from the table and joined her in walking to the door.

As she boarded the elevator, she wondered how the first class would turn out. She wished she could have been on the same floor as Colby and Cassidy, but they would meet at the lunchroom in four hours, and she was excited to hear what they had to say about their first day of the sabbatical courses.

CHAPTER SEVEN
Day 1 - Indigenous Natives

"I cannot emphasize enough the importance of a good teacher."

~Temple Grandin,
American Educator

THE VERY FIRST THING MITZIE NOTICED, to her disappointment, was that the instructor was Caucasian. She was hoping to be taught by an authentic Native American. Nonetheless, she took a seat and appraised her surroundings. She was in a central room exactly like the dining area, except it had been partitioned off into four segments. She sighed. *Great. I'm in a pod again.*

The room was much larger than her classroom at school, however, and designed to easily hold 25 participants with plenty of space. That was a plus. Rather than desks, they were seated two or three to a table with comfortable rolling desk chairs. Mitzie's tablemates included Nancy Jenkins, a skinny blond fifth-grade teacher in her twenties from Alpharetta, Georgia who wore way too much perfume, and Glenn Harding, a congenial man with serious-looking reading glasses in his mid-fifties who hailed from Annandale, Virginia.

The three of them exchanged a little pleasant conversation while they waited for the rest of the participants to appear. At ten minutes past the hour, it was apparent that five of their classmates would not be arriving, so the guide at the front asked them to spread out and sit two to a table. Mitzie was glad that Nancy chose to move to another seat; the perfume was already beginning to give her a headache. She found Glenn to be quite charming and was glad to have him as her tablemate.

Glenn leaned close to Mitzie's ear, making his fine blond hair flutter atop his head. "Restrictive guidelines," he whispered.

"Beg pardon?" Mitzie said.

"We've lost five people. I'll bet it was the restrictive guidelines. Maybe they were smokers," he said with an exaggerated shrug.

"I don't know. Do you really think that would cause people to leave?" she asked.

"Maybe. Can't really say. I'm not a smoker, but I'd be a little upset if I had to exit the building every time I wanted to light up."

"I suppose so. Well, glad I'm not either, then."

"Why'd you sign up for this course?" he asked.

"I have Creek Indians in the family."

"Ah, me too. Not Creek, though. My wife is full blooded Cherokee. I understand those tribes were at war with one another. Maybe we should sit at separate tables." He chuckled and winked at her.

"Well, technically, *we* are not from *either tribe*, so I think we may be safe sitting together," she said.

"*Touché*. I have a smart partner. I like this class already," Glenn confided before turning his attention to the instructor who was approaching the wooden lectern.

"Good morning, teachers. Welcome to the Lower Eastern NFAEE Center. My name is Mikhail Melnyk, and I am the instructor for the Indigenous American Natives course. By a show of hands, how many of you have seen the Hollywood film of *Dances with Wolves*?"

More than half the class exuberantly raised their hands, including Mitzie and Glenn.

"How many of you have read *Last of the Mohicans*' by James Fennimore Cooper or have seen the movie version?"

Again, a large number raised their hands along with Mitzie and Glenn.

"How about the book or movie *Windwalker*? *Bury My Heart at Wounded Knee*? *A Man Called Horse*? *Geronimo*? *Windtalkers*? *Little Tree*? Well, it appears Mrs. Galloway has seen them all," he said with a nasty smirk.

There was general laughter in the classroom, and Mitzie felt her cheeks burn.

"I'm a mother and a fourth-grade teacher, Mr. Melnyk. We like watching movies about historical things." She was embarrassed at being singled out.

"I am sure you do. I am teasing you Mrs. Galloway," he said with no trace of a smile. "We have all grown up on Hollywood's version of the American Indian. But I am here to teach you about the *real* early indigenous Native American Indians. They were neither romantic nor inspirational. They were savage, pagan, lawless people who worshipped animals and the elements of nature. They lacked education and brutally eked out a living that involved thievery and murder. We cannot romanticize them; if we truly want to learn about them, we must accept the cold hard facts. That is what our course is all about."

Melnyk leaned forward on the lectern and fixed them with a hard glare. "You as American educators should know and teach your classroom students that traditions like Edward Winslow's account of the first Thanksgiving in 1622 are myths, that the Indians possessed slaves, and that they were perverse and often subscribed to depraved pluralistic sexual practices."

Mitzie raised her hand.

"Mrs. Galloway, from Monticello, Florida is it?" he said, consulting a list on his podium.

"Sir, my husband is a Creek Indian, and even though what you say may very well be true, I don't find his tribe to be anything like what you describe," she said, her lower lip beginning to tremble.

"Oh no, of course you do not," he said with a dismissive gesture. "The modern-day Indians are nothing like their ancestors. They have been educated and have adapted to societal norms. Many of them have intermarried with other ethnic groups, so there are very few full-blooded individuals around. Your husband's people are, in all likelihood, a rather diluted bloodline living primarily as Caucasians. That is not a criticism, of course. It is a fact. I think you and he should be proud of his lineage and that of your children, but remember, we are here to learn about the *early* indigenous native people. All right?"

Mitzie took her course syllabus and fanned her face briskly, not daring to look at the instructor. Glenn Harding leaned closer. "He's a jackass," he offered. "Don't pay any attention to his high-handed crap, dear. Not only isn't he a Native American, he isn't even a *regular* American!"

She gave a wan smile and nodded her head, wishing desperately that she had selected a different course. She had to agree. Sadly, Melnyk was going to be a horrible teacher.

Mikhail Melnyk continued. "In this course of study, we will look at the history of the early indigenous natives. We will study their cultures, their dress, their food, their philosophies, and learn some of their languages. We will have at least four outings—weather permitting—to visit local tribes and gain some first-hand experiences of these indigenous people after they have been modernized.

"My assistant will be distributing some texts that we will use: *A Comprehensive Atlas of North American Indians* by James Langtree, *Indians in the New World* by Henry Collins, *A History of Indigenous People in the United States of America* by Jeffrey Turner, and *How! The Indian Book* by Percival Clark. You may keep these texts and mark them freely. They will be your bibles, so to speak, for this course. Are there any questions so far? Yes … Miss Jessica Cristo from Reston, Virginia."

"Mr. Melnyk, are you of Native American descent?" Jessica Cristo asked.

"Absolutely not! I am Eastern European by birth. My family originated in Ukraine. But I assure you, I am quite well versed in this subject. I have a master's degree from Charles University in Prague," he boasted.

"Kinda seems like we'd be better off having your husband or even my wife as the instructors for this class," Glenn whispered, finally coaxing a smile from Mitzie.

"You there, sir. Mr. Glenn Harding from Annandale, Virginia. Have you something you wished to share?" Melnyk said.

Glenn stood up, removed his glasses, and congenially addressed the class. "Hi, everyone. I'm Glenn Harding. My wife's a Cherokee, and she's not diluted," he joked before sitting back down.

The class laughed in earnest, and Mitzie was again happy that he was her seatmate.

Mr. Melnyk was not amused. "Are there any other people who call themselves Indians or have Indian family members? Six of you. How very nice," he scoffed. "At some point, I may let you each share what you know of the modern-day tribes you or your families represent. Until such time, however, we will commence learning the truth about the early peoples. Please turn in your *Comprehensive Atlas of North American Indians* to page two and let us begin our course learning."

Mitzie opened her book and laid it flat on the table, holding it down with her left arm as she scanned the text with her right hand. Glenn casually reached his hand over and unobtrusively pulled her sleeve down to cover her exposed watch. Mitzie flinched and looked at him in alarm.

"Best keep that covered, dear. Not allowed, according to the guidelines," he whispered.

"Oh, no. It's not..." she began.

"What page did he say, Mrs. Galloway?" Glenn asked, his voice louder than necessary. He shook his head slightly as he looked her in the eye.

"Page two, I believe Mr. Harding."

"Mr. Harding," Melnyk said, "would you begin reading at paragraph one on page two for us?"

"I'd be delighted," Glenn said, clearing his throat. "There were four glaciations in the million years of the Pleistocene era. During the Wisconsin glaciation from about 90,000 B.C. to 8,000 B.C., the oceans were lowered due to the predominance of glacier ice, and land that is now submerged was exposed. Big game in the Ice Age migrated across that land bridge, along with people who wielded spears that hunted the animals for food. These Paleo-Siberian people who crossed the Bering Strait land bridge were the first Indians ...."

CHAPTER EIGHT
Day 1 - Archaeology

"What we ought to know we never be taught in the classroom."

~ Lailah Gifty Akita,
Ghanaian Writer

CASSIDY ENTERED THE ROOM with high hopes. After parting from Colby with an admonition to watch and listen, she was determined to be observant, but deep down in her soul, she hoped he was wrong. As she looked around, she imagined every eye was on her, the microphone on the lectern contained a recording device, and the overhead smoke detector housed a camera ... and she would have been correct as far as the microphone and camera were concerned. Cassidy shuddered and subconsciously pulled her shirt sleeve down farther on her wrist to completely cover her newly acquired smartwatch. She hoped she was wrong, but she instinctively knew she was right.

Touching the watch made her think of Colby, with his startling blue eyes and easy manner. He intrigued her in more than a platonic way. The realization was a little surprising. She had never found white men attractive. It was not a racial bias; she simply had never had occasion to date any men outside her own race.

Cassidy's parents died when she was a teenager, and she went to live with her Auntie in the house next door. Throughout school, books were her constant companions. Through them, she lived vicariously in worlds which she knew were financially beyond her reach.

When she graduated high school, Cassidy won a full scholarship and went straight to college, living and working off campus to pay her bills. Library Science was always her first and only choice for a major, and she continued through graduate school, obtaining her master's degree, graduating with honors, and keeping a 3.95 grade point average.

Returning to Cairo, Cassidy moved into her small two-bedroom childhood home. Her Auntie had rented it out for many years to help support the two of them, and it was in poor condition. Cassidy lovingly restored it with the help of her friend Edna Mae and some of the boys from around town.

She was hired in the fall at the local elementary school and immediately knew she was meant to be a librarian, for she flourished in her job. She embodied collegiality and cooperation, and the other teachers loved her so much she was elected teacher of the year four times.

Throughout the years, there were many dates and boyfriends and even one fiancé, but none of the men ever seemed to be the complete package Cassidy sought. Edna Mae attributed it to the "knight in shining armor syndrome." No man ever lived up to the picture of the men in the many books she had read ... until she met Colby Carson. So far, he punched all the right buttons except for physical compatibility, and she wondered if that might possibly happen while they were at the sabbatical. A tap on her shoulder startled her.

"Would you like to sit together?" a young African American woman of about 30 asked.

"Sure," she replied. "I'm Cassidy Phelps from Cairo, Georgia. Nice to meet you."

"I'm Angelíque Tanaka, from Charleston, South Carolina. What do you teach?" the young woman said.

"I'm the librarian at my elementary school."

"Oh, then you teach *everybody*."

"That's about right. Why did you choose this course, Angelíque?" Cassidy asked, looking at the woman's expensive manicured nails and high-heeled black leather Louboutin pumps.

"Well, to be honest, this was my second choice. I really wanted to do Asian Immigrants. My husband is from Japan. I don't know why I even put this as a second choice. I know absolutely nothing about archaeology, and yes, I saw you checking out my nails, and no, I can't imagine me digging in the dirt. Oh well, it's a vacation, right? And I can't complain about the extra pay, so here I am," Angelíque said.

Cassidy's eyes widened when Angelíque mentioned extra pay. Not knowing the woman, she felt it was not prudent to ask if she meant the $7,500 stipend, but she tucked the comment into her mental file cabinet and kept up the small talk.

"How do you like living in Charleston?" Cassidy asked pleasantly.

"Oh, very much. I've lived there all my life, except when I visited Japan one time. I was a singer, see, when I was in my 20s. That was before I became a schoolteacher. I took a gig in Tokyo, and that's where I met Hiro. That's my hubby. Hiro came to my show every night and proposed after only a month, and I accepted. He didn't want me to do singing gigs anymore, and since I'd always be an outsider in Japan, we moved to Charleston and got married, and I got my teaching degree. I teach third grade. Hiro is a high school teacher. I'm 32. He's older. Teaching is a really honorable occupation in Japan, you know. How about you, Cassidy?"

"Born and raised in Cairo. It's a smallish town, but it's quaint. I've just turned 40 years old and I've never been married—by choice, not by circumstance. Haven't found the right man that challenged me intellectually. Found plenty that I thought were physically attractive, but I've always been looking for that total package," Cassidy said.

"You mean there's nobody that meets all your criteria for a husband?" Angelíque asked with a shocked expression, followed by an impish grin.

"Not all of them, no, although some have come close. I have lots of nieces and nephews, so I don't lack for child companionship. I enjoy being Auntie Cass, just like I enjoy being the school librarian. I can send the kids away when I've had enough of them," Cassidy said with a wry smile.

Angelíque laughed aloud. "I like you Cassidy Phelps. Even if this ole digging course doesn't really excite me all that much, at least I've found a friendly sister who makes me laugh."

A heavyset middle-aged woman wearing an unattractive pink boiled wool frock entered the room and approached the lectern. She had a bouffant hairstyle and large teeth.

"Oh no! It's Professor Umbridge from *Harry Potter*," Angelíque whispered, suppressing a squeal.

Cassidy clapped her hand over her mouth to stifle her laugh. As soon as the instructor spoke, she and Angelíque exchanged wide-eyed looks.

"Good morning. ladies and gentlemen. Do come in and get settled at one of the tables. We seem to be missing a couple of participants, so I think we can fit two to a table. Do find an empty seat and let us get to know one another. I am Constance Wright, and

I am your course instructor," she said in a sing-song voice with a distinct English accent. "I have supervised several digs in the northern Virginia area, and you shall be pleased to know we shall be getting in the field during your time in this sabbatical. Before we do, however, we must learn the correct methods for archaeological work, including what tools to use, how to correctly grid a location, how to preserve artifacts, and so on and so forth.

"My assistant shall be giving out textbooks for your use. Please feel free to make notations in the books. They are yours to keep. The first text is *A Practical Handbook of All Things Archaeology* by Donald Kingsley. You will use that quite often. Next, you are getting a copy of *Archaeology: The Theory, Methods, and Practicum of Historical Unearthing and Preservation,* written by Hans Gudendorff. Very good information in that book. And finally, two light-humored books: *Archaeology for Dummies*, and *I Can Dig It!* By Sandra Cummings." She tittered after she named the last books, pressing her lips together in a wrinkled pucker.

"Excuse me, Ms. Wright. Will there be a test?" a dark-haired man in the front asked, to the giggles of the class participants.

"*Mister* Ronald Smith from Brunswick, Georgia. There will not be a written examination, but you must become well-versed in the information you learn from the books and lectures before you are out in the field," she replied with aplomb.

There were more than a few groans at the mention of the word *lecture*s, but Ms. Constance Wright did not acknowledge them.

"Moving on, have any of you ever *been* on a dig?" She pronounced the word *bean,* like the green vegetable. "No hands? All right then, we have loads of work to do before we can have our first outing, so shall we get started? Please turn in your Gudendorff book to the first chapter and we shall begin reading," she said, putting on a pair of brightly bedazzled reading glasses that hung on a chain about her ample neck.

Cassidy turned to the first page and listened as Ms. Wright read the text word for word. By the end of the second page, she was thoroughly bored. She fiddled with her sleeve and considered texting Colby under the table, but she was afraid someone would see her, so she sat and squirmed and restlessly tapped her foot until at last the instructor announced a break *"for precisely one-quarter of an hour,"* during which they would be able to get a cold drink and walk outside into the empty corridor.

She hurriedly grabbed what she called a "loaded Coke" (i.e., full sugar, full caffeine) and rushed into the corridor, searching for Colby, but his class had not yet taken a break. Angelíque caught up with her outside the door to the room.

"OMG! Is this class not the *most* boring thing you've ever *been* in?" She mimicked Ms. Wright's pronunciation. "I might just die. I think I'd almost prefer going to a faculty meeting. At least we could cut up," she complained.

"I know what you mean. It's awfully dry, so far. I hope she's not planning to read every word of every book to us. I might go to sleep," Cassidy said.

"That's why I got myself a Mountain Dew. More caffeine than that Coke. You might want to consider switching. If it gets too bad, I've got some pepper-upper pills in my purse. Let me know if you want one."

Cassidy looked at the woman in shock, and Angelíque laughed at her expression.

"Oh Cassidy! Your face. You thought I meant speed? They're just *NoDoz* tablets."

"Oh, Lord help me, Angelíque. You gave me a start. Thanks, but I'm afraid I'd be so wired I might say something insulting to her. Better not," Cassidy said in a hushed voice.

"OK. Let me know if you change your mind. Where's your lunch floor?"

"Eleven. Yours?"

"Seven. Thought we could at least eat together. Oh, well. We'll just have to be classroom buddies. Aw crap, there's the old bat. Time to go in already. Two more hours until lunch," she said as she teetered along on her expensive designer shoes.

Cassidy drained her soda and threw the can in the "tin" section of the recycle bin near the door. Angelíque was already in her seat with her book open. Cassidy sat down, flexed her gluteal muscles, and prepared for more of the droning sound of Dame

Constance Wright's oral recitation, rueful that the practical experience for which she had signed up would not be found in the pages of the interminable course materials.

CHAPTER NINE
Day 1 - Forensic Anthropology

"I'm a good teacher and am great at observation and picking out what's wrong and fixing it."
~ Abby Lee Miller,
American Dancer

COLBY APPROACHED HIS CLASS with his eyes wide open. Despite Cassidy's reluctance to completely embrace his suspicions of being monitored, he had a kind of sixth sense about such things. To say that he was intuitive was entirely correct, but he was not clairvoyant in the sense that he could read minds or even have prophetic dreams. Nevertheless, he had what he preferred to call "inklings." Sometimes he just knew what he knew, and this time, he really felt like he knew what he knew. What's more, he had known it for a while.

He entered the doors and chose a seat by

himself at a table near the back, so he had a clear view of everything that occurred in the room, including the exit door. Colby held a concealed carry permit, and he wished he could have the comforting feel of his handgun in his pocket, but he had to leave it at home. He didn't like being unarmed, although he did have a wicked switchblade on his keyring that was all but undetectable. Likewise, he carried a special tool in his wallet that looked exactly like a credit card, but which could be dismantled to make just about any survival tool you could possibly think of. Not that Colby was a prepper; he was, instead, always prepared.

He scanned the room and pinpointed the different "types" among the other awardees. Without even speaking to them, he could get a bead on their personalities. It was an exercise he liked to do when he was in an unfamiliar place. It was an aspect of his constant vigilance and preparedness.

Today's classroom presented a smorgasbord of potential types. Beginning at the front, he observed a bookish looking man setting out three pens, a notebook, and a micro digital recorder on the table. He meticulously lined up the individual items parallel and perpendicular to one another. *Hmm. That one has obsessive compulsive disorder. He will be the first one to break if threatened,* Colby decided.

Beside OCD guy sat an overweight man of 50 or so, with unkempt hair splayed out on his collar, wearing a t-shirt and denim jeans. He had a hot beverage—probably coffee—in his hand that he cooled by blowing across the top before each sip. Each time he blew, it ruffled the syllabus on OCD's notebook. *A middle school science teacher,* Colby deduced. *Burnt out. Doesn't give a crap. Big, but cowardly. OCD will move away from him soon.* Sure enough, the first man abruptly gathered his supplies and rearranged them at another table. Colby smiled and continued identifying the people in the room and determining what they might do in a panic or emergency situation.

The ability to read others had kept Colby Carson out of more than one jam, but it was not a skill he advertised. He preferred to sit back and be a silent observer. He immediately thought about his new friends, Mitzie Galloway and Cassidy Phelps.

Mitzie was a doll. She was early 30s, attractive, with dark eyes and gold highlighted auburn hair that crowned her head in soft waves. She was a little harried with the sabbatical situation, but otherwise on the ball. He was certain her home was orderly, and her children were bright and well-behaved. Her husband was a Creek Indian, she had told him. Because of that and the fact she so readily attached herself to Cassidy—an unknown African American woman— meant Mitzie accepted all races as equals. He liked that about her.

She seemed comfortable with his friendship as a single man, so Colby was sure she was secure in herself and loyal to her husband. In her past, something must have happened to trigger the intense claustrophobia they witnessed at dinner. He saw a little of her fear when she entered the dining area at breakfast, but she pushed on and overcame the feeling. It showed him that she was brave, with an underlying strength and determination which could be counted on in an emergency. Colby felt great affection for her, as did Cassidy.

Now Cassidy? He reflected. *She is quite a woman.* She was not the type to whom he was usually attracted, but something about her caught his attention. Maybe it was her humor or her regal bearing. She was nearly as tall as he was, and when she talked with him, she looked him directly in the eyes. He found her to be smart, confident, and incredibly sexy, and he unexpectedly found himself thinking about being with her.

Colby sighed. He had not even been out with a woman in four years, not since his wife Letitia had died. Tish was petite, mid-length blond hair, and white. Cassidy was exactly the opposite—tall, closely cropped skullcap, and black. She had revealed she recently turned 40, making her younger than 45-year-old Colby. Cassi admitted she had never been married. With her tall, willowy frame, good figure, and her engaging eyes and natural smile, Colby was surprised. He was fairly certain her bachelorette status was not from a lack of suitors. In his eyes, Cassidy Phelps was a goddess.

What appeared in front of the class was decidedly less than a goddess. She was a short, boyish figured, wizened Asian woman with black hair twisted into a severe bun at the nape of her neck. The skin of her pale face seemed to be pulled tightly against her skull, causing her almond shaped eyes to become mere slits. For a moment, Colby thought she might ring a bell and say, *"I am Koji's mother. You will please sit up and listen."*

She did not ring a bell, but she did rap her knuckles on the wooden lectern to get their attention. She stepped up on a small platform which had been placed in front of the stand and looked out at them. The classroom quieted and waited for her to speak. When she did, it was with a surprisingly strong voice in a lower register than he figured.

"Good day. Welcome to NFAEE. This course is forensic anthropology. I am your instructor, Chen Mei. You may call me Professor Chen," she said, smiling broadly. She gave a little wave, and many in the class waved back. Colby almost laughed aloud at the incongruence of the severity of the woman's appearance and the pleasantness of her manner.

"I have been a forensic anthropologist after getting advanced degree at Peking University of Beijing. I have worked many years in the USA. I love USA. You too?" she asked.

The course participants smiled and nodded, charmed by the small, affable woman. Colby liked her, despite himself, and he smiled and nodded with the rest of the class.

"My assistant, Yi Ken, will give you textbooks.

You can write in them. Yes, yes. They will help you learn," she said as a slender Chinese guide began handing out a thick tome entitled *The Forensic Anthropology Handbook* and a much larger one entitled *Forensic Anthropology: The Comprehensive Pedagogy*. They thudded heavily as they landed on the tables, and Colby heard audible groans coming from his course mates as they looked at the books.

"I will teach you many things. You will like forensic anthropology. It is a good thing to know. You may ask, what do forensic anthropologists do? It is very exciting. We study human remains. Oooo," she said, making a sound like a ghost and waggling her hands, causing the class members to snicker. "Oh! You like crime TV shows? Yes? You know TV show 'Bones?' Yes? We will all be Dr. Bones!" she announced, spreading her arms out dramatically.

"You will learn to look at skeletons and see many things, like how the person dies, how tall, what sex. We will document much skeletal trauma and the postmortem interval. In forensic anthropology, we use many tools. You will get to use gas chromatograph, mass spectrometer, anthropometers, boley gauges, forensic radiology technology, spreading calipers, and heat-sensitive infrared cameras. Yes, yes!"

Colby, though he quite liked her manner, was beginning to realize that the content would be well over his head. He wondered if he had been overly ambitious in choosing this course. Professor Chen was obviously quite intelligent, and he worried that her presentation of the material would be more than most of the people in this class could handle.

"There will be bones in the ground outside that you will be locating. The archaeology class next door will unearth them, and then we will determine if they are human or animal. Very exciting. Some remains we work on will be decomposing. Smell very bad," she said, wrinkling her nose and waving her hand in front of her face, while still smiling. Colby observed OCD guy holding a handkerchief to his nose just thinking about it. *Oh yeah, that guy won't last.*

"I am pleased to be your humble instructor for this sabbatical. You are the very best teachers. We will learn much together," she said.

Colby could hear people talking in the corridor behind him, and he wondered if Cassidy's class was taking a break. He was anxious to see her, but it didn't look as though Professor Chen was stopping. He stared intently at her while fidgeting in his seat, drumming on the tabletop, and willing her to stop, but she continued talking. When, at last, she paused and announced a 15-minute break, it was too late. Cassidy's class had already gone back into their room. Colby checked his watch. One hour and 45 minutes to go before lunch. He could hardly wait. He downed a soda and went back into his classroom to listen to more of Professor Chen's excited discourse on *"forensic anthropology. Yes, yes!"*

CHAPTER TEN

Day 1 - Nationwide

"One time, the teacher was the storehouse of knowledge. That will no longer be so. So what would a teacher do? A very good teacher will play the role of augmenter. Also, the teacher will be located anywhere and helping students."

~Shiv Nadar,
Indian Businessman

ACROSS THE NATION, thousands of NFAEE award winners attended the first day of their chosen course of study, and almost unilaterally, thousands of teachers were disappointed. Not only were they given stacks of technical and outdated textbooks, they found that the "qualified, elite instructors" they were promised were anything but.

Gary Campbell from Laramie, Wyoming at the

Mountain NFAEE Center in Santa Fe, New Mexico entered his Visual Arts—Painting class expecting to learn techniques for using oils, acrylics, and watercolors on canvas. He left with a theoretical textbook for each type of medium. His instructor, an androgynous man of indeterminate ethnic origin, stated that he had a preference for painting nudes, so they should expect to focus on that.

Alma Downey, a veteran teacher from Butte, Montana in the same Center, attended her Performing Arts—Theater course and left with two textbooks: *On Acting* and *Theater for Beginners*. Her instructor was an Australian man with a lisp and bad breath.

Arlene Yazzi, a veteran Navaho teacher from Winnemucca, Nevada in the Pacific NFAEE Center in Salem, Oregon, entered her Performing Arts—Theater course and came away with the same books. Her middle-aged male instructor was clearly interested in the younger women in the course.

Annemarie Cummings, a fresh young teacher from Juneau, Alaska, anxiously went to her Culinary Arts—Healthy Cooking class at the same Center, ready to try out new healthy recipes and bring them back to the families in her community. She left with a Julia Childs cookbook, a Mario Batali cookbook, and a set of knives. Her instructor hailed from Puerto Rico and stated that they would focus on Hispanic cuisine.

Ken Schaffer of Graysville, Georgia at the Lower Eastern NFAEE Center in Richmond, Virginia entered his Culinary Arts—Healthy Cooking class and went back to his room with the same materials. His instructor was a sweet little old woman from Canada who was hard of hearing.

Clark Banning, teacher of the year from Beaver Creek, Ohio in the Upper Eastern NFAEE Center in Annapolis, Maryland eagerly anticipated his Performing Arts—Dance course. He was ready to learn the latest jazz, free-style, and pop and lock moves. Instead, he left the studio with two archaic textbooks: *Movement and Dance: The Fundamentals* and *Let's Dance*. According to his instructor, a 60-year-old Mexican man who was short and grossly overweight, theirs would be a more practical approach to dance through study and lecture. They would have four outings to local clubs, and they would learn the basic techniques of Latin Salsa, ballroom, Western line dancing, and beginning ballet.

At the same NFAEE Center, Inez Cohen from Ithaca, New York was early for her Performing Arts—Music course. She left early with a textbook from the 1970s about Music Theory and an anthology of classical vocal repertoire. Her instructor, an elderly rotund German man named Otto, sang for them in a breathy falsetto.

Andrew Thibodeau, a talented teacher from Slidell, Louisiana at the Lower Central NFAEE Center in Frankfort, Kentucky went to his Visual Arts—Sculpting class ready to create a statue he envisioned of a Creole woman. He left with several books about pottery methods and a bucket of slip to bring to class each day. His instructor was a woman who could most accurately be described as a 1960s hippie throwback.

Mariana Gonzales, a Galveston, Texas teacher who was also in the Lower Central NFAEE Center, arrived at her Literary Arts—Journalism course ready to write exciting pieces about world events. She left the course with a stack of outdated periodicals and newspapers. Her instructor, an Irish man from Belfast with a ruddy complexion and large ears, said they would learn much from interviewing each other and writing up their accounts.

Paulette Jameson of St. Albans, West Virginia left her Journalism course in the Lower Eastern NFAEE Center in Richmond, Virginia with the same materials. Her young female instructor was previously a proofreader for a fashion magazine.

Lou Anne Stevens, a beginning teacher from Cedar Falls, Iowa, was excited to attend her Archaeology course in the Upper Central NFAEE Center in St. Paul, Minnesota. Ready to hit the field and unearth artifacts, she left with the same books Cassidy received: *A Practical Handbook of All Things Archaeology, Archaeology: The Theory, Methods, and Practicum of Historical Unearthing and Preservation, Archaeology for Dummies,* and *I Can Dig It!* Her instructor was a 25-year-old graduate student from Hawaii.

Della Strongbow, a Lakota woman who taught in Watertown, South Dakota, entered her Cartography course at the same NFAEE Center wanting to learn how to map out the countryside. She walked away with a small world globe, a Rand McNally Road Atlas of the United States, and a huge textbook entitled *Practical Surveying*. Her instructor was a Nigerian gentleman who spoke heavily accented English and preferred large-scale colorful maps with lots of detail

Chester Osceola, a Seminole elder from Holopaw, Florida, left his Cartography course in the Lower Eastern NFAEE Center in Richmond, Virginia with the same textbook. His instructor, who told them he was legally blind, said he could read relief maps with his fingers, so they would be creating maps with modeling clay.

Stella Cooke of Boone, North Carolina, also at the Lower Eastern NFAEE Center, chose her History— Early American Pioneers course to learn of the men and women who crossed the country. She hoped to be able to experience the skills of cooking, sewing, and building from that time period so she could design and build an off-grid cabin and live sustainably. She was presented with two thick textbooks and the complete series of "Little House on the Prairie" on DVD. Her instructor was a large pale Austrian woman named Berta.

Carmine Wells of St. Augustine, Florida at the same Center entered her Literary Arts—Poetry class armed with a love and a talent for precise rhyme. Her instructor was a young Asian man who preferred the simplicity of haiku.

By the end of the second month of the Sabbatical Directive—a malicious plot to break talented teachers across the United States—these were some of the few remaining participants.

CHAPTER ELEVEN
<u>Day 1 - Lunch</u>

"Education is not the filling of a pail, but the lighting of a fire."

~ William Butler Yeats,
Irish Poet

"Education is the kindling of a flame, not the filling of a vessel."

~ Socrates,
Classical Greek Philosopher

COLBY WAITED BY THE DOOR for Cassidy to come out of her classroom. He was smiling and excited to talk with her; he was not prepared for her state of mind. She was a shell of the woman who had made his heart race since yesterday. Her perfect head was hanging, her twinkling eyes were dull and downcast, and the shoulders of her previously erect posture were slumped forward. It was as though her flame had been extinguished. He took a step back and blinked rapidly, unsure if his eyes were playing tricks on him.

"Cassi? Cassidy?" he said quietly.

She raised her head and met his gaze. He saw a light flicker as she recognized him, and then the tears spilled. Colby rushed over and took her elbow, leading her away from the crowd of people to a more secluded place along the corridor. She allowed herself to be moved along, never speaking, not taking her eyes from the floor, until he stopped and turned her to face him.

"Cassi, what happened?" he asked.

"Colby. Oh, Colby. I don't even know how to tell you. My course is so horrible. I am so unhappy with it," she said, wiping away the tears that traveled down her cheeks. "I was so excited. I imagined myself in a wide-brimmed khaki hat, digging in the earth, cradling a delicate artifact in my hands. I was so wrong, so wrong." She wept silently, her face in his shoulder as he patted her back awkwardly.

A few people walked by and cast curious glances at the pair.

"She's homesick. She'll be all right. Thanks for noticing," he stated, waving them on. "Come on, Cassi. Let's go to the room."

She stiffened up. "No, they'll see me, hear me. I want to go to lunch and see Mitzie. I'll be fine. Just so disappointed is all. Caught me totally off guard." She wiped her face and regained her composure.

Colby watched her transformation from a broken, wilted weed to a beautiful, strong, upright flower. She lifted her chin and met him eye to eye, and then she brought forth a smile.

"I will not be broken," she said, "and my flame will not be snuffed."

With those words of affirmation, Cassidy Phelps decided she would come out the winner in this obscene game that someone else was playing with their emotions and intellects.

"Come on, Colby. I am hungry!" she declared. She grabbed her surprised confidant by the hand and pulled him toward the elevators, and right then and there, the most unexpected thing happened: Colby Carson fell in love with Cassidy Phelps.

Cassidy and Colby entered the dining room hand in hand, a fact that did not go unnoticed by Mitzie Galloway. *I knew it!* she thought as a huge smile filled her face. *Thank God something good is happening out of all this.* She rose from her seat at the table and hurried over to them.

"Eat first, talk later," Cassidy said.

The three of them made their way through the buffet, which was set up as before, except with lunch fare. There were hot casseroles in chafing dishes, cold cuts on trays, sandwich fixings, desserts, fruits in baskets, crudité plates, and assorted beverages. They had just brought their trays to the table when Mitzie spotted Glenn Harding sitting alone. She rushed over and spoke to him, and Glenn came sauntering over to join them at the table.

"This is Glenn Harding, the saving grace of my horrendous Indigenous Natives course. Glenn, these are my new friends Cassidy Phelps and Colby Carson," she said by way of introductions.

Colby and Cassidy assessed the man Mitzie brought over. He was of average height and build, with fine blond hair and black framed reading glasses which he wore pushed up on top of his head. He was older, in his fifties, and his fair skin showed wrinkles beside his eyes and at the corners of his mouth which Cassidy called "grin lines" because his face had a look of a perpetual smile just about to break forth.

Colby called them "smartass lines." His inklings about Glenn were of a man who was comfortable in his skin who didn't take any crap, but he didn't peg him for a fighter. He seemed more of a "word warrior"—somebody who could cut his foes down to size with his acerbic wit and intelligent language skills.

They were both right. Glenn Harding had no fear of his fellow man or their opinions. He was firm, yet compassionate; serious, yet given to sarcasm and puns. He projected the appearance of someone who was harboring a secret which he would never disclose. He exuded confidence, and they were immediately taken with him.

Glenn beamed at them. "If you are Mitzie's friends, then I know I'm in good company. Thanks for letting me join you," he said.

"Where are you from, Glenn?" Colby asked.

"Annandale, Virginia ... outskirts of D.C. Ms. Mitzie tells me you're from Georgia, and you are from Georgia also," Glenn said.

"That's right. We consider ourselves the Deep South contingent," Cassidy said.

"So, Glenn, I take it your class was ... not the best?" Colby said.

"That's an understatement," Glenn replied. "Our instructor began picking on Mitzie right away. He's a jackass. Not even an American. He's Ukrainian. Can you believe they'd have someone like that teaching about Native Americans?"

"Seriously?" Colby said.

"Damn straight, and to make it worse, we got all these textbooks that we're expected to read, and *that's* how we're going to learn? Almost made Mitzie cry, too. That would've been the end of me. I'd have broken at least two of those rules. She reminds me of my daughter, and I'm a very protective daddy."

"I don't doubt that, Glenn. Cassi *did* cry," Colby said, reaching over to pat her hand.

"What? Oh Cassidy, I'm so sorry. What did they do to you?" Mitzie asked.

"Nothing that I cannot handle. I just lost sight of who I was for a moment. I am right as rain now, though. I am nothing if I can't rise above a fat prissy white woman from England with big ole buck teeth!" she announced with a wag of her head.

Her wide-eyed friends at the table were silent

for about two seconds, and then they erupted in laughter. Mitzie had to slap Glenn on the back after he aspirated his coffee. And Miss Cassidy Phelps kept right on eating her ham and cheese sandwich as though nothing was wrong with the world

Catching his breath, Glenn shook his head slowly from side to side. "Ms. Phelps, remind me to never get you mad!"

"OK, in all seriousness, can you tell us what happened now, Cassi?" Colby asked. "It's OK. The table's safe."

Cassidy looked around, noting that their table was situated in a corner against two back walls, somewhat removed from other diners.

"Well, this English woman is our instructor. She gave us the biggest books I have ever seen in my life, and then she proceeded to *read* from the first one, word for word. *The. Whole. Time.* We have to *earn* the right to have an outing *after* we finish reading the texts! That is *not* what I signed up for."

Mitzie's eyes grew two sizes. "Oh my gosh. That's just about the same thing that happened to us. Our teacher is from the Ukraine, like Glenn said. And yes, he did pick on me. It wasn't my imagination. He is so condescending. He made Glenn read from the first textbook for so long he grew hoarse. It was mean, but Glenn's a toughie. The instructor said that Native Americans were dirty savages in the beginning, and that the modern-day ones were ... what exactly did he say Glenn?" she said.

"He said they had diluted bloodlines and lived as Caucasians," Glenn said with a sardonic smile.

"Oh yeah, that's right, and Glenn made a comment to me, and the instructor asked him if he had anything to say. So, Glenn stands up and says, 'My wife is Cherokee, and she's not diluted.' Everybody laughed, and I thought the instructor would explode. We were toast from then on out. Glenn and I are the naughty kids in the class," she related with a giggle.

"That's funny," Colby agreed, "but listen, you two. I want you to be a lot more careful. Try not to rock the boat."

"Why's that, Colby? What do you know that we don't?" Glenn said, lowering his voice and leaning forward, elbows on the table.

Colby and Cassidy exchanged looks, then Colby leaned in closer and spoke softly. "We are being observed and monitored," he said, taking a drink from his glass of soda.

Mitzie frowned, but Glenn nodded soberly. "Uh huh. I understand," he said, his eyes darting around the room. "What about in here?"

"Pretty sure," Colby confirmed, "so don't say anything so loudly that someone other than us can hear. I've checked under the table and it's clean."

"Is that what you did when you dropped your napkin earlier?" Glenn asked with a half-smile.

Colby nodded, taking another sip of his soda.

"What about our rooms?" Glenn asked, biting

the end of a banana and chewing slowly.

"CCTV in the flatscreen. Telephone listening device. Video and audio in the smoke detector. The bathroom is clean."

"In the corridors?" Glenn wiped his mouth with a napkin and took another bite of banana.

"I'm sure, but I don't know every spot. There are wide-angle surveillance cameras at the corners. In and above the elevators, of course. Inside and outside the course classrooms and the dining areas. Look above each doorway. See that little blinking red light? That's it. It's a fisheye lens. Now everybody needs to laugh like I just told the best joke ever," Colby said.

The four of them snickered and guffawed. Cassi punched Colby in the shoulder. Mitzie covered her mouth with her hands, more to hide her trembling lips than to cover a laugh.

Glenn pretended to offer her a pear. "Your watch is a smartwatch, dear," he said with a gentle smile. "That's why I had you pull your sleeve over it in class."

Mitzie looked at Cassidy, who nodded as she reached over and took Glenn's pear.

"It is? But, Colby said … what if somebody … I mean, I didn't know … Oh my," Mitzie said, appearing to crumble.

"Just pretend it's a children's watch and nobody will be the wiser. We can text each other from our bathrooms. Never, never in the classes or in your rooms. Glenn, do you have one? I have one more, but it's pink," Colby said.

"I'll give him mine, Colby. I like pink," Cassidy said. "Later, though. Not here."

"I have an idea," Mitzie said, gathering some courage from deep within. "Why don't we all eat dinner together tonight, and then we can take a stroll around the NFAEE grounds?"

"You are a genius, Mitzie. That OK with you Glenn? I'll trade watches with you when we're in the dark," Cassi said.

"Sounds like a plan. Thanks for including me. I'll try to maintain a lower profile now that I know we're being watched. Mitzie, my dear, take a quick look at your watch and see what time it is. We can't be late getting back to Kaiser Melnyk," Glenn said.

Mitzie made a show of raising her arm and looking at her watch. "We've gotta go, Glenn. Colby, Cass, we'll meet you back here for dinner tonight. Everybody be cool," she said brightly as she and Glenn left the table.

Cassidy and Colby also left the table. Colby offered his elbow, and Cassidy linked arms with him. It was as though nothing else existed, at least until they separated into their classrooms. Colby settled himself back in his observation post at the back of the room, and Cassidy took her seat at the table. Angelíque Tanaka was conspicuously absent.

CHAPTER TWELVE
Thursday Night

*"No thief, however skillful, can rob one of knowledge,
and that is why knowledge is the best and safest
treasure to acquire."*

~L. Frank Baum,
American Writer

STROLLING IN 50° WEATHER may have seemed silly to
many, but for those who had been all but imprisoned
inside the classrooms all day long without even a view
of the outdoors, it was both invigorating and
necessary. Though dark, the grounds were lovely, and
the four friends walked along casually—Colby and
Cassidy with their arms linked, Glenn and Mitzie side
by side.

Their dinner meals had been every bit as
sumptuous as the night before, albeit without the
ambiance of the grand ballroom, but Mitzie was more

than willing to forego the opulence of the ballroom for the more intimate, and less crowded, space of the dining area. The tables were farther apart, the lighting brighter, and there were far fewer people because of the ability to come and go as one pleased. They enjoyed their food and made small talk while they ate, ever aware of their surroundings and anyone who could be within earshot.

After making stops at their rooms to don heavy coats and get their cellphones (at Colby's insistence), they met on the main floor and prepared to go on a night walk. Cassidy wisely inquired at the front desk if there was a rule for exploring the grounds and was told there was a well-lighted footpath that meandered around the Center and that seating areas were spaced here and there along the route. Most of them had small, already lit firepits to add a bit of warmth. She thanked the clerk and relayed the information to her friends as they exited through the central revolving doors into the night.

"Maintain an easy pace, laughing and talking. We have to assume every light fixture has a listening and maybe a viewing device, so we'll walk slowly and only talk of covert things while in the darker areas," Colby directed sotto voce.

"I hate to say it, but this is terribly exciting," Cassidy admitted. "I feel like a real spy."

"Yeah, but I'd feel a lot better if I were properly armed," Colby said.

"Colby, do you think we're in any real

danger?" Glenn asked, shuffling his feet to mask the sound of his voice.

Colby smiled and laughed. "I don't know, Glenn. I really don't know, but it never hurts to be prepared for any eventuality."

Mitzie raised her arm, seeming to point at the starlit skyline.

"This is scary, guys. Do you know that we only had 20 out of 25 people in our class today? Glenn thinks a bunch of them left because of the restrictive guidelines. What do y'all think about that?"

"I agree with Glenn, for the most part, but I noticed a couple more folks from my class were gone after lunch," Colby said. "That could be attrition because of the boring nature of the course more than because of the guidelines."

Cassidy stood still under the path light and stared upwards. "My, but aren't the stars lovely tonight? You know, I felt better after lunch, and my class seemed to move along more smoothly. I got a highlighter out of my tote and started marking passages that I found to be particularly enlightening. I'm determined to learn about my course subject," she said before leaving the halo of light. "On another, more serious note, my tablemate Angelíque was gone. She was a delightful girl, all full of millennial richness and spunk. I don't think she left because the class was boring. In fact, she flat out said she was staying for the extra money."

Glenn stumbled over an invisible rock and

knelt to check his shoelace. "Did she really say for the extra money? That brings me to a question, did any of you get a second letter that mentioned a stipend?"

"We all did, Glenn, and so did Angelíque. I am wondering just how many others received that same letter," Cassidy said, extending her arm to help him stand up.

Just then, they entered the boundary of another path light.

"And Professor Chen is a delight. She's fond of saying 'yes, yes' after every sentence. She envisions us as 'Bones' from the TV series. I think the course will be well worth my time. She liked the apple," Colby said, prompting Mitzie to call him a brown-nosed butt-kisser.

"What else, Cass?" Mitzie asked as they moved into darkness. "You sounded like there was more to it."

"Yes, actually there is. When we went on break, Angelíque offered me some *NoDoz* to help keep me awake. She called them her 'pepper-uppers.' When we returned from lunch, the instructor made a point of reminding us of the guidelines and said specifically that '*drug use would not be tolerated.*' I think they heard her offer me the tablets and maybe even the comment about the money. I don't know for sure, but she was sure enough gone after lunch!"

"Were you close to the door of the room, Cassi?" Colby asked.

"Oh, my Lord. Yes. We were right beside it,"

Cassidy said.

"I see what you mean about managing our behavior, Colby. Mitzie and I were model students after lunch," Glenn said as they edged closer to the light, "...and did you know that there was a land bridge over the ice millions of years ago that the early Natives crossed to reach the Americas? Fascinating stuff, I tell you."

"I'm reminded of a quote from L. Frank Baum who wrote *The Wizard of Oz*. It goes something like this: 'No thief, however skillful, can rob you of knowledge.' I believe, if we follow the lead of our course instructors, we *will* learn much. We *were* promised highly accomplished teachers, after all," Cassidy said while within the light.

"Good point. I feel better already. Tomorrow, I'll look at things with a different eye," Mitzie said.

"Which reminds me, Glenn, come over here. I've got a joke for you. You ladies just walk on ahead. We'll be right there," Colby said with a wink.

Glenn leaned in closer as Colby spoke softly in his ear. Afterward, they laughed heartily, and Colby put his finger to his mouth in a shushing gesture while indicating Cassidy and Mitzie. Glenn laughed again and shook Colby's hand, palming the square black iWatch and putting it in his pocket. Then, they caught up to the ladies in the next circle of light, still snickering guiltily.

"Are you men telling dirty jokes again? Shame on you," Cassidy said, linking her arm with Colby, who shrugged and patted her hand. "Are you sure you can get another fake smartwatch for your niece? I do like this pink one. All my little girls at school like to wear them. They are so growny, pretending to have the expensive Apple kind. I'll be glad to pay for it, Colby. I can afford $13.99 for a piece of plastic vinyl that keeps good time."

"No, no. I wouldn't think of it. I have a friend who gives them away like candy. My nieces and nephew won't go without. I'll get more," he said.

As they passed from the light into the darkness, Glenn fastened his watch on his wrist and admired it. "Nice piece of technology, Colby. Thanks," he said.

"Always good to be prepared," Colby said.

"Speaking of prepared, I spotted Mitzie's watch right away in our class today. If we're being observed, somebody'll notice sooner or later if a sleeve slips up or something like that. Best be sure we're extra careful with these things," Glenn said.

"That's a good point, Glenn. Hear that ladies? If your shirt or sweater won't cover it, keep your watch in your pocket," Colby suggested.

When they next emerged from the darkened area, Mitzie gave a little shiver and pointed toward a seating area where a bright blaze beckoned from the center firepit.

"I'm getting chilled, guys. Do you mind if we sit over there by the fire for a while and thaw out? And I need to text my husband, too," Mitzie said.

The party made their way to the cushioned wooden benches that formed a U-shape around an elevated bronze and cast-iron fire pit. The pit was square in shape, with a six-inch wooden shelf around the screened in box that was exactly the right height and distance on which to prop one's feet.

"Ah, heavenly," Cassidy murmured, casting a glance around the area. By now, she was becoming aware of incongruities in her surroundings and could pick out the monitoring devices. The light from the fire would certainly hamper any visuals directly in the area of the benches, but a solar garden decoration set within the shrubbery near the path had an unusual tiny red light on the top that directly faced them and flashed steadily.

Colby and Glenn unobtrusively ran their hands beneath the arms and over the backs of the benches and made a show of brushing dirt or leaves from the cushions to check for listening gadgets before sitting down and propping their feet on the fire box ledge. The ladies mirrored their actions. Colby smiled and put his arm on the top of the bench behind Cassidy, tapping his fingers meaningfully. Glenn, sitting across from Mitzie, laid his arm on the back of his bench and tapped it, as well, nodding and smiling. They had discovered listening devices on the backsides of the benches.

"This is just perfect. Great idea, Mitzie. Are you going to text your husband now? I think I will text my wife as well," Glenn said, pulling out his cell phone and palming it in his left hand. The cellphone illuminated his face while obscuring the watch he had twisted around on his wrist. Mitzie followed suit with her own cell phone, as did Colby and Cassidy.

"Well, *'when in Rome,'* as they say," Colby announced. "I'll just check on my cat."

"Your cat has a cellphone?" Cassidy said with an impish grin.

"Oh yes. She's the famous Cheshire Cat from *Alice in Wonderland*. I've taught her to text, and she can even use the toilet, but she doesn't yet flush."

"You are so full of it, Colby Carson!" Cassidy said, playfully slapping his shoulder.

"OK. She can't really text, but she does use the toilet. That's no lie. I'll tell you all about how I trained her sometime."

"Can't wait to hear it, but right now I need to text Edna Mae and see how my Auntie is doing. She had a bad cold when I left." She began tapping her wristwatch beneath the cellphone in her hand.

"COLBY. R U GETTING ME?"

"I GOT U CASSI."

"MITZIE?"

"YES."

"GLENN?"

"(THUMBS UP EMOJI)"

"K. OVER TO U COLBY."

Colby smiled and looked around, then he began texting them, using a group text so everyone saw the same messages.

"EVERYBODY SEND TEXTS ON UR CELL PHONES NOW 2 UR FAMILIES."

Mitzie nodded and began texting Phillip; Cassidy messaged Edna Mae; Glenn texted his wife Iris; and Colby sent a note to his neighbor who was looking after Caboodle. At the same time, Colby tapped on his watch face.

"NITE WALK. EVERY NITE. K?"

They each replied.

"K"
"K"
"K"

Colby responded to their acknowledgements.

"THE PLAN: SECRET TXTS ONLY HERE R BATHRM. NOD IF U UNDERSTAND."

The rest of them nodded.

"M...LAUGH (LAUGHING EMOJI)"

Mitzie laughed while looking at her cell and responding to a text from Phillip.

"G…LOOK UP (EYES LOOKING UP EMOJI)"

Glenn gazed at the stars for a moment, then he sent Iris another message on the phone.

"C…SHAKE UR HEAD (HAND ON CHIN EMOJI)"

Cassidy shook her head while reading and responding to a message from Edna Mae.

"MOVE NOW N THEN. K? NOD HEAD"

There were nods and shifting of feet and bodies all around.

"NEVER N CLASS. NEVER N ROOM. NEVER N DINING. NEVER N HALL. NEVER US ON CELL."

Glenn cleared his throat. Mitzie nodded with a smile directed at her phone. Cassidy casually patted Colby's leg as she texted a question.

"Y NOT CELL?"
"PROBABLY HACKED OR CLONED. IS Y WE R TXTG FAMILIES ON CELLS. DIGITAL TRAIL."

Mitzie looked up at him in alarm, then back down at her watch as he continued.

"WATCH N LISTEN. B AWARE. B COMPLIANT, BUT
NOT 2 MUCH. COMPLAIN SOMETIMES. NOTICE
WHO LEAVES. ASK Y BUT B INNOCENT. LOOK 4
EYES N EARS AROUND U. SIT W/SOME OTHERS AT
MEALS. B UNPREDICTABLE. B NORMAL. STAY
UNDER RADAR. K?"

There were nods and emojis from all of them.
Glenn texted the next question.

"WHAT DO THEY WANT?"

"NOT SURE. SAVE $$ MAYB?"

"N DANGER?"

Colby looked at Glenn before he responded.

"COULD B. HOPE NOT. JUST B CAREFUL"

Mitzie texted the next question.

"SHOULD WE JUST LEAVE HERE?"

"No!" Cassidy said it a little too loudly. "No.
Oh, Edna Mae. Now don't do that." She grimaced,
but Colby smiled.

"GOOD SAVE, CP. MG…CALL HOME. SAY G'NITE TO
KIDS N PHIL. GH…SAY ILY TO IRIS. WE R DONE
4 TONITE"

He stuck his cell phone in his pocket and
gazed at the stars.

"Oh, that Edna Mae," Cassidy said, pocketing

her phone "She is the worst speller, but she is my very best friend."

"Goodbye, and I love you, Iris," Glenn said, blowing a kiss to his phone as he switched it off and repositioned his feet near the fire.

The three of them sat together making small talk, enjoying the calming warmth of the blaze while Mitzie spoke softly into her phone.

"Things are good, Phil. I'll get over being homesick soon. Yes. OK. Put her on. Hi Sarah. Please don't fight with your sister, OK? Goodnight. I love you, honey. Give Kristin the phone. Hi Krissie. You're the lady of the house, but don't be bossy. I love you, sweetie. Let me talk to Gabe. Hi baby. Yes, I miss you, too. Don't cry. Oh really? Daddy let you sleep with him? That's nice. OK. I love you, and when I get back, I'll give you a million kisses. I will. I promise. Night night. Give me back to Daddy. All right, Phil. We're getting ready to go back now. I'll text and call you tomorrow night. Love you. Bye."

She brushed away a tear and turned back to the others. The four of them rose and retraced their path back to the Center. Cassidy and Mitzie linked arms. Glenn walked along beside Colby. There was very little talking on their return as each was consumed in thoughts of what the next day would bring. They would be hypervigilant, but at least now, they were prepared to deal with whatever the NFAEE might throw at them. They had a plan, and that was reassuring, and also a little exciting. The Three

Musketeers had become four. They hoped to pick up more along the way.

CHAPTER THIRTEEN
<u>Saturday Night</u>

"Curiosity is one of the permanent and certain characteristics of a vigorous intellect."

~Samuel Johnson,
The Rambler

THREE FULL DAYS INTO THE SABBATICAL, the Four Musketeers had developed a means of enduring the boredom and were gleaning useful chunks of information from their sessions. By tuning out their personal objections to the lackluster, incompetent, or browbeating instructors, they turned their attentions to the materials presented in the texts. Much of the material was outdated—one of Mitzie's textbooks had a copyright date of 1927—and there were erroneous facts that had been disproven by 2020, but the core knowledge was solid, and they sucked it up like water to a desert nomad. By the end of the day on Saturday, they felt much more empowered than they had the prior Wednesday.

Mitzie and Glenn had progressed from early Natives who crossed Beringia to Paleo-Indians who flaked stones in distinctive styles for their weapons, including Sandia points, Clovis points, and Folsom points. In the evenings, they walked with their heads down, scanning the walking trail for similarly shaped rocks that fit the illustrations. They knew what atlatls, bolas, and adzes were and how they were used. They went beyond the printed words and had discussions on how to prepare food with heated stones in boiling water and what they might use to create hooks for fishing or hoes for cultivating.

Colby and Cassidy discovered their chosen fields of study had many overlaps, and that led to some interesting comparisons of the two. They set about sharing with each other the random facts gleaned from their texts and realized their interests were more similar than they originally thought.

In just three days, the four of them had gone from despondent and defeated to alert and energized. They knew where the monitoring points were, and they were careful to avoid them when they talked of NFAEE things. They were observant, and they realized that the courses Center-wide were getting smaller. Editing and Proofreading had been combined into one class because of attendance drop off, as had Healthy Cooking and Baking. In those classes, the teachers simply rotated: one taught the morning session, and one taught the afternoon session. The Archaeology group now sat one to a table. The word was Creative Writing, Poetry, and Journalism would soon be combined as well. As Glenn put it, "people were dropping like flies." But the four of them remained steadfast.

They had also managed to increase their cadre of acquaintances. The first new friend they cultivated was Ken Schaffer from Graysville, Georgia, who was in the combined Healthy Cooking/Baking Class that met on the 10th floor. They bumped into him before dinner on Thursday, and he and Glenn struck up a conversation about the virtues of using stone ground corn meal for hushpuppies.

Ken was an affable man of 56 with grey hair, a goatee, and eyes that were a cross between green and brown. Until recently, he had been an Eagle Scoutmaster; however, with the decision to include young women in the formerly all-male Boy Scouts of America program, Ken opted to quit. His decision to apply for the NFAEE award came about because his wife of 30 years had passed away the prior year, and he wanted to take the cooking course to recreate some of her recipes to remember her. His marital status gave him something in common with Colby, who was also a widower. Ken was in room 916, so his meals had to be taken on the 9th floor, but he eagerly sought the rest of them out before breakfast, lunch, and dinner on both Friday and Saturday.

Cassidy made a friend on the 8th floor when

she was taking the first break in her Archaeology class on Friday. While leaning against the door of room 812, she suddenly found herself falling backwards as the door was snatched open from inside. A freckled, red haired woman of 59 caught her under the arms, and the two of them ended up crashing to the floor on their butts. The woman was Ms. Stella Cooke of Boone, North Carolina.

Stella had been a kindergarten teacher her whole career and was taking the Early American Pioneers course because she planned to retire soon in a little off grid cabin in the mountains with her Great Pyrenees dog Thor. Twice divorced and not looking for another husband, she wanted to piggyback on her childhood Girl Scout skills to design and build the cabin herself and was hoping the course would offer her some practical information on sustainable living.

Unfortunately, Stella was given four textbooks and a set of DVDs thus far and none of them seemed to be what she wanted to learn. Cassidy invited her to come to Mitzie's room after dinner that evening for an hour of "gal-gabbing," and Stella happily took her up on it. When they left the room to meet Colby and Glenn on the main floor for their walk, Stella went back to her own room, but she sent a text to Cassidy's cell phone asking if she and Mitzie would like to come to her room Saturday evening. After talking it over with Colby and Glenn, they decided to make Saturday night's walk a non-texting event and invited Ken and Stella both to come with them.

Although they had a very pleasant evening walking the grounds and resting along the way at the seating areas to warm themselves at the firepits, they felt the other two were not well known enough to be trusted with the information about the monitoring. They had, however, been able to ascertain through careful questioning that Stella and Ken had also been given a stipend. That gave credence to Colby's idea that everything centered around money. What he couldn't figure out was why they had been given the stipends in the first place. Nowhere in the application package had there been any language to indicate a cash prize was part of the NFAEE award.

As they continued down the walkway, they happened to come upon three people who were sitting around a larger fire pit. There were two young women in their 20s and an older man who was unmistakably of Native American descent. The trio waved them over, and they all sat on the benches near the firepit warming their feet.

The young women were Carmine Wells of St. Augustine, Florida and Paulette Jameson of St. Albans, West Virginia. Both were perfect examples of freshly turned out teachers from state universities. They were pert, attractive, and trendy, with plenty of mascara and unblemished, unwrinkled faces, but that was where the physical similarities ended.

Carmine was a curly blond with light blue eyes and quite visibly came from money, judging from her jewelry, designer coat, and ostrich skin half boots. She reminded Cassidy a little of the absent Angelíque who had never returned to class. She wore no wedding ring, but she sported gemstones on her right thumb and left little finger. She had a high treble voice and a musical, tittering laugh.

Paulette was a dark brunette who wore her straight hair in a high ponytail. Her sensible coat was clearly off-the-rack, and she wore jeans and white tennis shoes with silver reflective tape in a chevron pattern. She also had no wedding ring, nor did she wear any other jewelry. Her voice was somewhat raspy with a definite West Virginia twang, and when she smiled, her dark brown eyes nearly disappeared.

Despite the women's obvious socioeconomic and physical differences, it was evident that Carmine and Paulette were a matched pair of dispossessed girls who had somehow found each other in this place and had become fast friends.

Outside of their visible dissimilarities, they shared a number of things in common, one being that they were both second-year teachers who had excelled in their schools from the outset. Their home lives were also comparable. Carmine's parents had met at college, married, and had Carmine shortly thereafter. Paulette's parents married just out of high school, and she was born before they celebrated their anniversary. Both sets of parents were still married, and there were no other siblings in the families.

They told the group they had met on the 4th floor where they had their classes. Carmine was in

Poetry, and Paulette was in Journalism, and they each shared a love of the written word. But even though they were both voracious readers, they were not looking forward to the reading material of their chosen courses of study. Both were unhappy with their classes, and they were on the verge of quitting, but something held them back. *I bet I know,* Colby thought. *The money would be a factor for Paulette, but Carmine is in it for the love of language.*

The 61-year-old man, Chester Osceola, was an enigma. He was a full-blooded Seminole Indian from Holopaw, Florida who had taught in his hometown elementary and middle school for almost 30 years. He wanted to learn the art of Cartography to be able to map out the boundaries of his family's ancestral lands around Holopaw. So far, all he had to show were a big book, a road atlas, and an instructor who wanted them to make maps out of modeling clay.

"Who the hell makes maps out of clay?" he asked with a forceful exhale.

"Why does your instructor only want that kind of relief map when there are so many others?" Ken asked with a puzzled look.

"Because the fool can't see," Chester said. "He is blind. Why would you teach a class that depends on doing something by sight when you do not have sight? I do not understand." He shook his head slowly and ran his thick fingers through his stubbled black and grey hair. "I do not understand," he said again.

"Why stay if you're unhappy?" Stella asked. When they didn't respond she offered her excuse. "I'm staying because I'm stubborn as all get out."

The group laughed, but Stella persisted. "Seriously, why *are* you staying?"

The girls looked at one another guiltily and then shrugged. Chester was more vocal.

"It was that letter ..." he began.

Immediately, the girls shushed him, patting him on the back, trying to distract him.

Colby was curious. He got up and stood before the fire with his back to the solar light camera he had already detected to hide his face and hands from the device. He rubbed his hands together like he was warming them and got Chester's attention.

"Chester, I can see that you are upset. I know the letter with the guidelines was a big shock to all of us. Look, Chester. That's right. I get it. It's because of this, isn't it?" Colby made a sweeping movement with his right arm as if indicating the NFAEE Center and the grounds. At the same time, he made a smaller gesture with his left hand in front of his chest, rubbing his thumb against the tip of his fingers. It was a universally understood sign for money. "You don't have to say anything. Just nod, OK, Chester?"

Chester looked into Colby's eyes and pulled the side of his wrinkled mouth up into a wry grin. He nodded slowly. "Yes, it is as you say."

"I understand. We all feel the same way, but there's no need to let it ruin our time here. We will just stop complaining and mark down our days one after the other. Is that OK?"

Chester nodded gravely, as did the girls. Thus, his theory confirmed, Colby and his alliance of six became a band of nine.

"Let's all take a walk on the path, shall we? There's much we can learn from each other. For instance, my friend Glenn Harding here is married to a Cherokee, and he would love to talk to you about Native Americans, Chester," Colby said.

Glenn took the cue and invited Chester to walk with him, and while they walked, Glenn told him about the light and dark areas on the path and what to avoid within the building.

"I'd love to chat with Carmine and Paulette about writing. You know, that's something I've done a little of, and I want to pick your brains," Mitzie said, leading the girls to the walkway.

Cassidy confided in her new friend Stella, and Colby discussed his theories with Ken as they strolled behind the others on the path. Thus, each of the original Musketeers took the new initiates under their wings and explained what was happening at the NFAEE Center.

At the end of the evening's stroll, the nine of them approached the revolving doors and filed through into the lobby, armed with more knowledge than they had before they ventured out into the night. The first thing they noticed when they entered the building was a poster at the front desk that read:

"NFAEE SUNDAY EXCURSION. Those interested in taking an excursion, please listen for the bell and join your guide in the corridor outside your room at 8:00 a.m. Breakfast and lunch will be served on the excursion. Dress appropriately."

CHAPTER FOURTEEN
<u>1st Sunday</u>

"I was like a chocolate in a box, looking well behaved and perfect in place, all the while harboring a secret center."

~Deb Caletti,
Honey, Baby, Sweetheart

"I AM KOJI. HEAR MY BELL," she said, ringing her little silver bell in the corridor. "If you wish to take the Sunday excursion, please come now."

Doors opened all along the hallway and out stepped excited men and women dressed for a day outing, Mitzie and Cassidy included. Mitzie noticed that there were as many closed doors as there were open ones. She wondered if the participants did not want to take the day trip or if they were simply no longer residing in the NFAEE Center.

"Please, you may take along your cell phones

for the excursions. Take many pictures; send to your family. Come, please hurry. Follow Koji," she said walking toward the bend in the corridor. Mitzie caught up to Cassidy and they both trailed behind Koji's rapidly retreating feet.

"Hello. It is Koji," she said rounding the corner. "Hear my bell ring and please come into the corridor for the excursion. Bring cell phone and cameras. Take many pictures; send to your family."

About half the doors opened, their occupants milling into the hall. Cassidy waved to Colby, who joined them as Koji made an about-face and retreated down the first corridor toward the elevators. The three of them took up the rear of the line for the elevator. On the connecting orange rug corridor, they saw other people moving around a stocky blond young man in the requisite navy-blue suit ringing his bell.

"It is I, Hans. Listen to my bell. Do come out and meet me for the excursion. Kindly bring your phone. Take pictures for your families," their guide said before he turned the corner. About half a dozen people followed behind him.

When they got to the lobby, they were put into the same passenger vans which picked them up at the airport. Since there were fewer people than had arrived less than a week ago, Mitzie was able to have a seat to herself. Colby and Cassidy sat together in the seat just behind her.

While they waited to depart, Koji boarded the van and stood before them waving an itinerary.

"Every Sunday we do not have classes, but we have excursions in Richmond." She clapped her hands. "I will tell you where we go. Today, we visit the Virginia Museum of Fine Arts. It is very beautiful place. You will like. It is close, so when we get there, we have a breakfast in a coffee house nearby. After, we go to the Museum. You may have freedom to see what you like. No need to stay with group. Is a big place, so it takes many hours to see. You have watches? Good. We meet at van to go for lunch at 12:00. Please do not be late or you will have no lunch. If you have no watch, please ask people or look at clocks on wall. Koji will be at van. Listen for my bell. OK? Let's Gooooo!" She said the last phrase like a cheerleader at a varsity football game.

Everyone laughed, not because it was clever, but because it was so silly, but Koji did not know they were laughing at her.

*   *   *

Back at the Lower Eastern NFAEE Center, another excursion was taking place. Within the grand ballroom, Ronald Bowry and Elizabeth Ford were standing before the course instructors, who were eating breakfast. Elizabeth paced the room slowly while speaking to them.

"All right. I know it's been a trying week, but let's all get on the same page. Please, feel free to finish your breakfasts and get seconds, if you wish. When I call your name and course, raise your hand.

"Music - Otto Bruner.

Drawing - Larry Braithwaite.

Healthy Cooking and Baking, which will now be known as Culinary Arts - Lucy Prince and Javier Rojas.

Dance - Chaz Keller.

Painting - Ansel Olivetti.

Archaeology - Constance Wright.

Forensic Anthropology – Professor Chen Mei.

Theater – Dina Rosembaum.

Sculpting – Liesle Stumph.

Indigenous Natives – Mikhail Melnyk.

Early American Pioneers – Berta Strauss.

Creative Writing, Poetry, and Journalism. We're just going to call your combined class Literary Arts from now on – Holly Sapp and Ken Fujita.

Cartography – Lou Harris.

African Immigrants – Beau LaFage.

Asian Immigrants – Jonquell Jones.

Editing/Publishing – Carl Lytle and Oscar Grund.

Splendid. I'd like to get your impressions of this first week now. Who would like to give us a progress report?" she said.

Ansel Olivetti, the painting instructor rose. "I began with 25 students, and I am down to 21," he said with a serious face. "I expect to lose several more when I begin bringing in the nude models. Morale is low as I have not yet let them set up easels and paint." He smiled and sat back down.

"Excellent, Ansel. Remember, Monday starts

happy week. Let the participants paint whatever they want. Next?" Elizabeth said.

Lou Harris, the cartography instructor who was legally blind, raised his hand.

"Yes, Lou. How is your class going?"

"I have 20 students left. They are reading aloud to me because, of course, I cannot see. They are frustrated, and I can hear one man near the back grumbling about the clay relief maps. He sounds like he is old, and I'm not sure which one he is, but I expect him to leave soon. Next week I plan to let them map the grounds, and the following week, they will have to construct those maps of clay," he said.

"You never fail to deliver, Lou. That's good work. Constance? What do you have to report about your class?" Elizabeth asked.

"Well, I am happy to say that my class is down to 16 students. I am reading the text verbatim in my most monotone voice, and most of the students are bored silly. Except for one or two, that is," she said.

"Tell me about them. Are they a problem?"

"No, no. I don't think so. One of them is a Negro woman. She befriended a younger Negro woman on the first day, but she was *Exited* for drug possession, so that seemed to put a damper on the older one," she said with a slight smile.

"As I understand it, the woman did not possess any illegal drugs, is that right?"

"Ah, no, but the door recorder picked her up speaking of extra money, so she had to be sent away,"

Constance said.

"Did the other woman acknowledge the drugs or the money?" Elizabeth asked.

"She reacted to the possible drugs with alarm, but she did not appear to notice when the woman mentioned the money. The older Negro woman is now sitting alone and marking up her text. She is not interacting with anyone. I believe the loss of her seatmate upset her. She was seen crying on a white man's shoulder after class."

"That's wonderful news, Constance. A mixed-race romance on the first day! Next week, let the class handle some tools and encourage them to look about the grounds, and then the following week, get back to the tedious readings. Who's next?"

Mikhail Melnyk stood up.

"Dr. Ford, I would like to report I had some interesting developments in my class. I zeroed in on one woman who seemed especially eager. Her husband is from some Indian tribe, and she was insulted at my characterization of Indians in general. Her seatmate appeared to come to her defense. I thought he might act out, so I tried to provoke him to violence by making him read aloud for an hour, but he did not take the bait. After lunch, he seemed to have calmed down. Now the two of them are quietly listening and taking notes. They don't look like they will leave, but I believe their spirits have been damaged," he said, inclining his head in a little bow.

"Very good, Mikhail. You say he rose to her

defense and now they are compliant. Do you think there could be a romance there?" Elizabeth asked.

"No, he is much older. It seemed to be more of a fatherly role he was playing," Melnyk said.

"Oh, that's a pity. We all know that sabbatical romances tend to muddy up one's focus both here and at home. If any of you see chemistry developing between your participants, be sure to encourage it—subtly, of course," Elizabeth declared. "How about your class, Professor Chen?"

Chen Mei stood up and addressed the room. "My class is good. Yes, yes. We are learning much. The people are happy. Yes. They like being 'Dr. Bones' very much," she said with a broad grin.

Elizabeth frowned and sighed. "Professor Chen, this was to be sad week, not happy week. I see in my notes that nobody has left your class since the guidelines were rolled out. Is that right?"

Professor Chen nodded. "Yes, that is correct. Everybody stays and reads their books. They are good class. One nice man gave the teacher an apple," she announced with a giggle.

Elizabeth sighed again, heavily. "All right. Keep at it. The course material itself should be enough to cause their disinterest sooner or later, Professor. Thank you," she said, shaking her head.

"Thank you very much," Chen Mei said as she sat down and took a big swallow of her green tea.

"Anyone else have anything earth shattering? OK. Remember, next week is *happy* week. Make your classes exciting. Then the following week *must be bad*. We want to keep them off balance. They will all be on a high after the excursion today, so promote that high. That is all. Enjoy the rest of your day," she said as she dismissed them from the breakfast meeting.

The instructors hurriedly drank the last of their coffees and swallowed the remaining bites of food, and then they filed out of the ballroom and closed the doors, leaving only Elizabeth Ford, Ronald Bowry, and Ashley Lawrence inside.

"Ready for me, Elizabeth?" Ashley asked.

"Always, Ashley. What do you have from the surveillance reports?" she said, sitting next to Ashley and draping her arm around the young woman's shoulder affectionately.

"On day one, 112 sabbatical participants were *Exited* after refusing to sign the guidelines. Another twenty-six people were *Exited* when they received their course textbooks. No incidents have occurred in the stairs. Nobody has tried to leave the grounds. We had 13 smokers in their rooms, and they were all *Expelled*. That one black lady was *Expelled* for drugs. The pills she had were caffeine pills, but she didn't get to explain. Twelve brought their devices into the class—tablets, phones, smartwatches. They were confiscated and told they would have to keep them in the room. Five of them tried to sneak their devices back in, and we *Expelled* them. Fifteen people divulged their stipends. We *Expelled* them, along with the people they told," she said as Elizabeth casually stroked the back of her shoulder.

"There have been 32 romances started and several hook-ups in the rooms. Nobody appears to have caught on to the surveillance, but quite a few people have been suspicious of the flatscreen televisions. They've been turned to the wall, covered with clothing, and that sort of thing. The same with the telephones. Lots of people are covering them with pillows and blankets," she reported.

"To what do you attribute the paranoia about the TVs and the phones?" Elizabeth asked, pushing a lock of Ashley's hair behind her ear.

"Mostly television shows, I'd say. Facebook. Warnings that the smart TVs and computers can be remotely accessed, and phones can be bugged. Everybody forgets about the smoke detectors, though, so it's really not a problem. We still have eyes and ears in their rooms. And so far, nobody has stood out as really catching on," Ashley explained, with a shrug.

"OK. That's reassuring." Elizabeth patted her back softly. "Continue, please, sweetheart."

"We've had friendship groups spring up on all the floors and within all the classes. Nothing that warrants a flag, though. Several groups have evening walks along the path and take advantage of the seating areas with the firepits. None of them show any evidence of knowing about the viewing devices in the overhead lights or the solar garden lights, nor do the microphones pick up any conversations of concern. There is one group that walks every night and sits on the benches to text their families and friends. We've hacked their cellphones and have checked out their conversations. Nothing out of the ordinary to report. We seem to be on track," Ashley said with a smile.

Thank you, Ashley. Well done. Enjoy your day," Elizabeth said with a charming smile. She kissed Ashley on the cheek and shooed her toward the ballroom door.

Ronald Bowry waited until Ashley left the room before he approached Elizabeth's chair from behind and started kneading her shoulders with his strong fingers. She laid her head back and rested it against his wrists with a sigh.

"Good numbers, Lizzie. We started out down 22 from the 522 awards given. That's 4% right off the bat who didn't return their acceptance paperwork—right in the 4% to 10% refusal forecast. As we figured, they will likely be disgruntled because they couldn't stay for the three-month time frame, especially after they 'mistakenly' received the letter about the stipends. Then add another 182 gone in the first five days, leaving us 318 guests right now. That's a 39% reduction. It may be the best we've ever done. Those who've stayed appear to be malleable, I'd say. Wouldn't you, lover?" he said with a cold laugh.

"As malleable as my shoulders, Ronny. What have you got planned for the rest of your day?" she purred in a throaty register.

"Mmmm. Well, after we get the reports from the other Centers, I think it will leave just enough time for a quiet dinner and recreation in my loft. How does that sound to you?"

"Lovely," she replied. "When's the next Center due to Skype their report with us?"

"An hour," he said.

"What shall we do until then?" Elizabeth asked, arching her eyebrow suggestively.

"Sadly, I have to go over some figures in my office. Let's just plan on dinner and bed," he said, bending down to kiss her neck at the jawline.

Elizabeth pushed her lips out in a pout and sighed as he pulled away and walked toward the door.

"Oh, well. I guess I'll go find Ashley," she said, touching the tip of her tongue to her teeth.

*   *   *

As the NFAEE van rolled down Arthur Ashe Boulevard on the way to the museum after the breakfast stop, Colby kept his eyes on the stores they passed along the way. He was looking for something in particular. Seeing several possibilities, he counted the blocks and mentally determined the time it would take to reach each place on foot. A plan in mind, he turned his attention back to Cassidy and Mitzie as the van pulled up along the curb in front of the huge columned building.

Disembarking to the sound of Koji's bell, the passengers seemed to visibly brighten around him as they felt a sense of freedom from schedules, bells, and terrible instructors. They mounted the stairs in small groups, chattering excitedly. Colby heard a voice calling his name and saw **Glenn** waiting at the top of the steps. Being in room 1116, **Glenn's** van was the first in line, followed by the vans for each floor in order. Down the street, Cassidy saw **Ken** from the 9th floor and **Stella** from the 8th floor rushing toward them. Mitzie spotted **Carmine**, who had arrived on the 7th floor van, waiting on the sidewalk, watching as the other vans unloaded, looking for **Paulette** and **Chester**, who were from the 3rd and 2nd floors respectively. Once all the vans were unloaded, and the passengers entered the museum, they merged into traffic and parked down the street.

Built in 1936, the Virginia Museum of Art was owned and operated by the Commonwealth of Virginia and was one of the largest art museums in North America. It housed works from all over the world, as well as a 500-seat proscenium theater for the inclusion of performance arts in addition to static arts. Among its permanent collections were galleries devoted to African, American, Asian, European, and ancient art, as well as examples of art nouveau, art deco, modern, and contemporary art.

As soon as they were inside and had greeted one another, they migrated to different attractions. Cassidy was particularly interested in viewing the Lillian Ronald Pratt Collection of Fabergé eggs—the largest public collection outside of Russia, and though Colby did not find the jeweled objects that fascinating, he did find Cassidy fascinating, so he willingly accompanied her. Likewise, the others joined up and meandered along together—Mitzie, Glenn, and Chester in one direction, Ken and Stella in another, and the inseparable friends Carmine and Paulette elsewhere.

While Cassidy gushed over the Fabergé pieces and took countless pictures (without flash, as that was not allowed), Colby excused himself to the restroom. Using the internet browser on his iWatch, he had determined the exact distance to the nearest Wawa convenience store and calculated his travel time, and then he returned to Cassidy's side. He could see their guides casually strolling among the crowd, and he noted their positions relative to their probable listening ability. Leaning in closer to Cassidy, he murmured in her ear while pointing at a green lacquer jewel-encrusted egg.

"When our lunchtime arrives, I will suddenly become ill and will have to stay in the restroom. I'll miss loading up on the van, but I want you to be sure you are overheard telling Mitzie how sick I am. Don't look for me, and don't let Koji send somebody into the bathroom to get me," he said.

Cassidy, who by this time was becoming an expert at masking her emotions, simply nodded and moved on to take a picture of another egg. Colby pretended to read the placard beside it.

"I'll be waiting on the steps when you return. I have an important errand to run, and I need the hour reserved for lunch in which to do it. Don't worry. I'll explain afterwards," he said, peering closer into the display case.

"This is all so fascinating. I can't believe we're getting this opportunity. Come on, Colby. Let's keep going," she said.

Two hours later, Colby began to drag his feet, holding his midsection, sitting every time he saw a bench or disappearing into a nearby restroom. His head hung lower, and he sighed heavily from time to time. Cassidy looked at him in concern, patted him on the back, and returned to check on him when he sat down. He nodded as she spoke and managed weak smiles, all the while glancing around the galleries at the people milling about.

At ten minutes to noon, the sound of bells of different pitches and tones could be heard throughout the museum, although they were just short bursts instead of the sustained ringing heard throughout the NFAEE Center. People immediately moved toward the entrance to the museum. Some made dramatic 180° turns as though they were viscerally responding to their bell-tone conditioning.

Colby grabbed his belly and hunched over. "Go Cassi," he said quietly, and then he hobbled toward the men's room in apparent stomach distress.

Cassidy displayed real concern and followed him halfway to the bathroom, but he turned and waved her away. She bit her lower lip, looked around, and then she hurried toward the entrance. When Cassidy climbed into the van alone, Mitzie abruptly sat up in her seat.

"Where's Colby?" she asked.

"Oh my. Colby is very sick," Cassidy said, her voice elevated. "He's been spending time in the restrooms since we got here. I think he ate something for breakfast that didn't agree with him."

"We have to wait for him," Mitzie said, getting Koji's attention before Cassidy could stop her. "Koji, Mr. Carson is not here yet. He's sick in the bathroom."

Koji turned to face Cassidy. "Where is Mr. Carson? It is nearly 12:00. He must come now. The van must leave soon," she said emphatically.

"Oh dear, Koji. I'm afraid he will have to miss lunch. He is much too ill," Cassidy said.

"What kind of ill that he misses lunch?" Koji asked in alarm.

Cassidy put her hand to her mouth and lowered her voice, whispering dramatically. "He is sick to his stomach, Koji. He has diarrhea," she said, emphasizing the syllables *di-ar-rhe-a*.

Koji frowned, wrinkled her nose, and pulled her mouth down as though smelling something unpleasant. She turned to the driver quickly. "We go now. We cannot wait. Drive, please," she said.

As soon as Colby saw the vans had left, he dashed out the door of the museum and raced down the sidewalk. Six blocks later he arrived at the Wawa convenience store. He dashed inside and quick-walked down the aisles until he found what he hoped was there. *Oh, yes! These will do nicely,* he decided, examining the packages hanging on the metal hooks.

Pink Princess, black Batman, black Avengers, white Snoopy. Perfect!

Colby promptly took his items to the counter, along with a sandwich from the refrigerated coolers and a cold soda. Once he paid for them, he rushed out the door and sprinted back to the museum, his purchases safely secured in a hidden zippered compartment in his backpack. He checked his watch. The entire trip had taken 45 minutes, just about what he figured.

Colby entered the first restroom he found and locked himself inside a stall, and then he took the items from his bag and removed them from their packaging. After a few adjustments, he stuffed them back into the hidden compartment. He ate his sandwich and drank his soda while sitting on the unused commode. When he was finished, he threw all the trash and packaging into the rubbish bin, covered them with paper towels, washed his hands, and left the men's restroom.

He headed to the a la cart snack and drink café on the entry level near the Atrium of the gardens and bought a fountain drink and some soda crackers. Then, he hurried back to the front steps to sit, thankful that the museum's *Best Café* was too small, and the *Amuse Restaurant* was too expensive for the NFAEE participants to have their lunch.

When the vans arrived just moments later, Colby waved weakly as Cassidy and Mitzie scurried over to him on the steps.

"Are you all right, Colby?" Mitzie asked. "Cass said you got sick."

"I'm fine. It was something I ate for breakfast probably. Got a ginger ale and crackers from the little café. I'm over the worst of it, I think," he said, giving her a feeble smile.

Koji walked up, but she kept a discreet distance. "Mr. Carson. You miss lunch. We could not wait for you. Why are you so sweaty, and where did you get drink?" she asked with a concerned look on her face.

"I'm sorry, Koji. I got sick. Got the cold sweats. It couldn't be helped. I'm much better now," he said. "Somebody told me there was a cafe on the main floor where I could get a cold soda and some crackers. I hope that was OK."

Koji made the same distasteful expression as before and backed away in tiny little steps. "You cannot miss van for going back to NFAEE Center. You must be here. You, friends of Mr. Carson. You make sure he is here on time. We cannot wait," she said. "Koji is sorry you are ill, but please be on time this afternoon. 5:00, Mr. Carson. You get well soon."

After the young woman turned and went inside, Colby finished the last of his drink and crackers and threw the trash away. By this time, Glenn, Ken, and Stella had gathered around him.

"Better now?" Glenn asked.

"Oh, yeah. Much better. Let's go look at some art," Colby said, taking Cassidy and Mitzie by the hands and leading them inside. "I think we're all going to be just fine."

CHAPTER FIFTEEN

Sunday Night

"Ignorance is not bliss—it is oblivion."

~ Philip Wylie,
American Writer

EVERYONE WAS HIGH on the freedom they experienced with the Sunday excursion. They laughed and joked as they entered the NFAEE Center and even seemed to overlook the ringing of the bells. Most of the participants carried bags from the museum gift shop, this being the first opportunity they had to do some shopping, which always appeared to make people feel better after a disappointing and stressful week of courses.

In honor of his cat Caboodle, Colby bought himself an AndyCat6 t-shirt which had been designed by a local Richmond artist. It featured six different colored treatments of the same cat face looking out, inspired by the Andy Warhol cat series. He planned to wear it the following day—*Howdy Doody be damned.*

He also secretly purchased a two-inch replica of an emerald green colored enamel Fabergé egg inlaid with Austrian Crystals on a stand which opened with a small hinge to reveal a bonus item inside—a ¾-inch identical egg made into a pendant on an 18" gold chain. Both pieces were safely tucked away in the combination lock box he kept in the hidden backpack pocket—the same place he had originally stashed the iWatches and which now held his new purchases. His intention was to present the necklace to Cassidy when or if their relationship grew to a point where it would be appropriate to give her a gift. He had other plans for the egg itself.

Cassidy discovered a large book for herself in the sale section entitled *Fabergé Revealed* by Géza von Habsburg. It had been $65 but was marked down to $20. The book contained over 400 pages with 600 illustrations of some of the very pieces she viewed at the museum. She was giddy over her find and joyously told her friends.

"After our walk tonight, I am going to look at all these lovely pictures and imagine having a Fabergé egg of my very own," she confided. "I will probably dream of chickens and omelets."

Mitzie also hit the sale section and came away with two bargain art books to share with her students: *Jasper Johns and Edward Munch: Inspiration and Transformation* and *Champion Animals: Sculptures by Herbert Haseltine.* The first was a 140-page book with as many pages of color illustrations revealing Munch's influence on Johns that inspired his painting. It was originally $45, but Mitzie got it for $3. The second book was a collection of illustrations of horses, cattle, sheep, and pigs who had won awards in Royal Agricultural Society of England shows in Britain in the 1920s. She scooped it up for $1.00.

"My school kids will love it because we live in an agricultural community," she said.

"Did you get anything for your own children?" Cassidy asked.

"Well, duh. I got them an Andy Warhol Memory Game. You have to match pairs of soup cans that Andy Warhol used on his soup can art. It'll be a family thing. I got Gabe an eight-inch Good Luck Dragon. It's a white and gold Chinese dragon that has six legs, the tail and paws of a lion, blue eyes, and a smiling face. It's a dragon that's not scary," she assured them.

Inside the lobby and along the corridors, people could be heard discussing what they saw during the day and what items they had purchased in the gift shop.

At dinner that night, some of the men wore colorful printed t-shirts, and there were many ladies sporting newly acquired jewelry. From their dining table, Mitzie and Cassidy pointed them out as they saw them, including their price tags.

"Oh, I almost got those Nefertiti earrings.

They were only $16. And that Degas Little Dancer pendant. It was adorable, but it was $25, and I needed to get things for the family," Mitzie said.

"Oh look! She got a Fabergé bear pearl necklace. It was cute, and only $35, but I like the eggs so much better. I thought about you, Mitzie, when I saw those turquoise solid seed bead hoops that woman is wearing because of your husband and kids and your Indian course," Cassidy said.

"Yeah, I saw them. They were $30. So were the yellow Pueblo earrings. Darling!" Mitzie exclaimed.

"Oh, my Lord, look there. She's wearing a Fabergé calla lily locket pendant! $200 if it's a dime!" Cassidy squealed into her napkin.

"I'd love to have had that diamond fleur de lis egg pendant, but it was $75. I need to save for something else I might see later on," a woman at the next table piped in.

"Well, I got these gold and freshwater pearl drop earrings for only $90. That's a bargain," a woman behind her said.

"Oh yes. That was a bargain, all right." Mitzie rolled her eyes dramatically.

"What do you think of that gold filigree bracelet? I know for a fact it was marked down to $85," the first woman said.

"Pretty, but too delicate. The kids at school would bend it up in no time," Cassidy said.

"The kids at school are not *allowed* to touch *my* jewelry," the second woman remarked, to which

Cass rolled her eyes.

"That silver art nouveau charm bracelet was precious. I considered getting it for Edna Mae until I saw it was $45. She'd lose the charms down the sink washing dishes, and then she'd just have a $45 chain." Cassidy snickered at the thought.

During this exchange, Colby and Glenn sat quietly, eating their meals and observing all the women's conversation in amazement.

"How do they *do* that?" Glenn asked.

"What? Remember all the prices? I don't know. My late wife was the same way. She could spot a pair of designer shoes in a dark movie theater full of people and tell me exactly what the retail cost was. It's beyond me," he answered.

Cassidy and Mitzie saw a woman in the buffet line wearing a multilayered choker of translucent orange beads and crystals.

"Ew. I wouldn't *have* that tangerine crystal pom pom collar. $225 and uuug-*lee*," Cassidy stated, her nose wrinkled.

"I'd take that hammered silver domed cuff, though," Mitzie said, brandishing her arm.

"Girl? Are you crazy? That thing costs $400, and the first scratch you get, it's lost its goodie, just like a new car," Cassidy said, and the two women slapped their legs and laughed hysterically.

"See what I mean?" Colby said.

Just then, a well-dressed woman passed by the table wearing a gold ring with a huge multicolored gemstone. The women gasped and stared in awe.

"Did you see that?" Mitzie whispered.

"I did, I did, but I don't believe it," Cassidy responded, her voice low and breathy, "a Persian turquoise ring."

Their mouths gaped. Cassidy turned to stare at the men.

"She's wearing a Persian turquoise ring!" she said, her eyes wide, her hand painfully clamped around Colby's wrist.

"OK. I see the ring, Cassi. It's beautiful ... and really big," he said.

"It's a Persian turquoise!" Mitzie reiterated.

"I understand that," Colby said. "Glenn, it's a Persian turquoise ring. Did you see?"

Glenn shrugged his shoulders. "OK," he said.

"That ring cost more than $700 you guys! Who the *hell* in this teacher convention can buy a ring for $700?" Cassidy asked.

A woman sitting behind Glenn held up her hand and waggled her fingers, displaying the same ring. "I can," she said with a smug expression.

Mitzie stared open mouthed at the woman and her expensive ring, and then she morphed into a person she didn't even know.

"Who *gives* a crap? Eat your *damn* dinner and mind your own *damn* business," she cried, throwing her napkin onto her plate and stomping out the dining room door.

Cassidy jumped up and ran after her, leaving

Colby and Glenn in shocked silence at the table. Glenn's cheeks flushed. He turned and gave the woman a stern look, but he refrained from speaking. He took a few more bites of his food, and then he gave his friend a serious look.

"This is class warfare," he said quietly.

Colby considered his statement for a moment and then he let his eyes roam around the dining room. There were people of all types in this one area. Their dress, their decorum, their manners were all over the charts. He recognized the dainty and picky eaters who looked down their noses at the waitstaff and complained about the food, the hungry ones who got multiple helpings of everything from the buffet, the privileged who took one bite of steak and left it on their plates only to have an identical piece of steak prepared for them, the folks who stuffed fruit and rolls into their pockets, the condescending ones, the polite ones, the demanding, the easy going. They were all here in full view, yet he had missed it. His usually sharp powers of observation had failed him, and he realized it was not all about the monthly stipends.

"Haves and have nots," he said, and Glenn nodded in agreement.

"I think I'm done here. How about we find the ladies and go for a walk?" Glenn suggested.

The two of them exited the dining room calmly, aware that the incident with the women had been seen and heard. They found them in Mitzie's room. Mitzie had been crying, and Cassidy was holding a wet washcloth covered with black mascara smudges. She let the men in after they knocked and gave a slight smile. The ladies had already laid out their coats and scarves.

"I think she will be fine after a nice, brisk walk. She's overly tired from the excitement of the day," she explained to the men and for the benefit of the hidden bugs.

Colby and Glenn had their coats over their arms, anticipating the evening walk, and now they put them on and helped the women with theirs. They exited the room in silence and rode the elevator to the lobby. Cassidy linked arms with Mitzie after they went through the revolving doors, and the four of them headed for the path. When they reached the darkness between the lights, Mitzie spoke up.

"I apologize, everyone. I know you told me to stay under the radar, Colby, but I think I just put a big target on my back. I'm so, so sorry," she said.

"No, my dear," Glenn said, "I think you did exactly what someone wanted you to do."

"How's that?" she asked.

"You broke. Someone wants us broken. Think about it. Melnyk tried it the first day of class with you, and then with me. He wanted a reaction, but we didn't give it to him. What happened in the dining room was carefully orchestrated. Colby said it well. It's the 'haves and have nots.' We haven't noticed because we're all compatible, and if I had to guess, we are all in roughly the same socioeconomic bracket," he said.

"You think so?" Mitzie asked.

"Maybe. I'm not sure. I just can't put my finger on it, but there's an underlying current in this place promoting discontent," he said.

"I thought it was the stipend. Always follow the money. Maybe it still is, but there's more to it. Teachers are notoriously underpaid all across the nation. If you live in a mega-county like Miami-Dade, Florida or Los Angeles, California or Maricopa, Arizona, you'll get better pay, but it won't be on a scale where a person can afford a $700 ring, much less two people. There has to be more. I'm missing something here," Colby said.

"No, no. I think the money has a lot to do with what's going on. I did some figuring, and let's just use 3,000 as a nice round number. If 3,000 people are paid a stipend of $7,500 each, then whoever's bankrolling this is shelling out *$22.5 million*!" Who *is* this benefactor?" Glenn asked, waiting to see if there were any takers before he continued.

"What millionaire can afford that? And twice a year for the past five years? That's a quarter of a *billion* dollars," Colby announced.

"It can't be Bowry," Mitzie said.

"Oh, no, my dear. It's most definitely not Bowry. He's an entitled rich prig, but he's not the deep pockets. And it sure isn't the *Basic Instincts* woman. I'm thinking more along the lines of an organized *group* of people as opposed to a single random philanthropist," Glenn said.

"So, let's get back to the money. That's the reason for the class warfare ... to winnow the field," Colby stated.

"Exactly. Reduce the numbers in attendance; reduce the payout," Glen agreed.

"The four of us are going to be in the $40,000 to $60,000 income bracket, don't you think? And we don't get the stipends until we finish out each month," Cassidy pointed out.

They entered the circle of the light.

"… and you said you didn't sleep well last night, and today was a very tiresome day, so it's no wonder you were on edge. I think you just need a good night's rest," Cassidy said.

"I know. I hate that I was ugly to that woman. I will apologize to her at breakfast," Mitzie said.

"That's an excellent idea, dear," Glenn said as they moved out of the light's beam.

"Colby, what district in Georgia do you come from?" Glenn asked.

"Peach County, Georgia. Why?" Colby said.

"What would you say is the population?"

"Ohhh, probably 27,000 or a little more."

"And Mitzie. Tell me what district you're from, dear?" Glenn asked.

"I'm from Monticello, Florida, in Jefferson County," she said.

"Population?"

"I'd say, maybe 28,000."

He looked at Cassidy.

"Grady County, Georgia. Population 24,750," she said. "I know because I review textbooks for Georgia counties within the 20,000 to 30,000 range of population."

"So, you all live in counties whose populations are in that range—more than 20,000 but less than 30,000. And you are all on the 10th floor, and in the red group. What are you willing to bet that the people on your floor on the orange corridor have total populations either *well below* 20,000 or *well above* 30,000?" he suggested.

"How do you figure, Glenn?" Colby asked.

"I come from Annandale—Fairfax County. Population just under 40,000. I'm neither on your floor nor in your color group. I'm on the 11th floor. I'm willing to bet that the other people on the 11th floor, on my white corridor, come from counties whose populations are more than 30,000 but less than 40,000, just like me. And the people that are on the 11th floor on the black corridor have populations greater than 100,000," he pointed out.

"How could you possibly know that, Glenn?" Colby asked him.

"I say that because both of those women from our dining room with the Persian turquoise rings are on the 11th floor, in the black group. It's another piece of the puzzle we've all missed—money, yes, but also money tied with county populations and entitlement mentalities," he said.

"But what does population density have to do

with money?" Mitzie asked.

"OK. Think of it this way. If you're from a very small county, your employment options are going to be considerably fewer than those from a larger county, and that affects your household income. In your Florida county, I'd hazard a guess that the schools employ the majority of the women, and most of the men are likely to be farmers or tradesmen. Would that be a fair assumption?"

"Yes, I'd say that was accurate."

"But if you were from Miami, then Phillip would probably be a lawyer or a doctor or a high-profile businessman, and your combined household income would be substantially higher," he said.

"So that's why those women could afford $700 rings?" Mitzie asked.

"That's *exactly* why," Glenn confirmed.

"I think I'm getting this," Cassidy said. "So, if you put people who can afford $700 Persian turquoise rings on the same floor with people who can't afford $30 yellow Pueblo earrings, they're invariably going to run into one another and breed contention, just like what happened in our dining room. Right?"

Colby sighed and gave her a glorious smile. "Beautiful ... *and* smart!"

Cassidy stared at him, speechless, and Mitzie burst out in laughter. She was still giggling when they entered the light, but she held her breath and quietly walked through it. They slowed in the next dark area and spoke together quietly.

"What about Chester?" Mitzie asked.

"What do you mean?" Glenn asked.

"He's from Osceola County. That's one of the largest in Florida, but he's not snooty … and his county's even named after his family."

"Exception to the rule. I'd wager his town of Holopaw is rather tiny. Small fish in a big pond."

"Makes sense," Cassidy remarked.

"Yep. But good question, Mitzie," Glenn said.

"Thanks, Dad," she replied with a smirk.

When they reached the glow of the next area, they stopped and stood still, looking up at the stars beyond the path light.

Cassidy lifted her arm and sighed, displaying the new hot pink plastic *Disney Princess* digital watch on her wrist. "I'm tired, folks. Let's turn this thing around and go on back to our rooms."

"I agree," Mitzie said, holding out her arm to show her brand new round white *Snoopy* hidden LED digital watch. "I've still got to call Phillip, and I'd prefer to do it on my back than on my feet. I really am that worn out."

"I understand completely, dear," Glenn said as he pulled his sleeve back and exposed the square face of his new black vinyl *Batman* digital watch. "By my watch, it's time for this old man to get in bed, so let's go."

"I agree. Let's all meet for breakfast in the morning at 7:00," Colby said, touching the lighted square face of his brand-new black vinyl *Avengers*

LED digital watch.

They retraced their steps on the path and entered the lobby through the revolving doors, caught the next elevator, and returned to their respective rooms, with their expensive iWatches tucked safely in their pockets.

CHAPTER SIXTEEN
<u>Week 2</u>

"The mediocre teacher tells. The good teacher explains. The superior teacher demonstrates. The great teacher inspires."

~William Arthur Ward,
American Writer

MITZIE DREADED BREAKFAST. She entered the dining room and immediately looked for the woman she had cursed the prior evening. She sincerely wanted to apologize. She also kept watch for Koji or some other person from the administration seeking her out to send her home. Not seeing either, she went through the buffet line and got toast and a banana. It was all she felt she could keep down. She spotted Glenn at a far table and made her way there. Colby and Cassidy left the line with full plates and sat down with them.

"Help me look, Cass. As soon as I see her, I

want to go over and try to make amends before they send me home," Mitzie said, nibbling nervously at her buttered toast.

"No need to bother, dear," Glenn said.

"Why not?" Mitzie asked.

"Well, as the angel told the women when they reached the tomb ..." He gestured for her to complete the thought.

"'*Woman, why do you weep?*'" Mitzie said.

"No, not that," Glenn said with a chuckle.

"'*Why do you seek the living among the dead?*'" Cassidy's eyes widened. "Please don't tell me that woman is dead!"

"No, no, no. Colby, help me out," he said.

"'*He is not here?*'" Colby offered, with a shrug of his shoulders.

"Ding, ding, ding. You are correct, sir. She is not here ... but she has *not* risen," Glenn said.

"I don't get it," Mitzie said.

"When we got back last night, she was lugging her baggage to the elevator. She got bounced," he said.

"But why?" Cassidy asked. "I thought they'd come after Mitzie for being abusive, although I really didn't think what she said or did constituted abuse, in my humble opinion."

"I was told by a white corridor person who is friends with a black corridor person on the other side of Miss Persian ring's room that they heard the Gestapo visit her last night, and she was hammered when she answered the door. In addition to her pricey ring, she had bought several bottles of wine from the *Best Café* and hidden them in her gift bags. When she antagonized you, Mitzie, she was already three sheets to the wind. They accused her of breaking the alcohol consumption rule and said she instigated the abusive 'altercation,' as they described it, and then they sent her on her way." He smiled broadly. "You, my dear Mitzie, have been completely vindicated."

Mitzie pushed her chair back and stood up.

"What are you doing, Mitzie?" Cassidy asked.

"Going back to the buffet to get a plate. All of a sudden, I'm starving," she said as she hurried to the chafing dishes.

Once they had all eaten their fill, and it seemed the observers were not going to swoop in and send Mitzie home, they boarded the elevators and went off to their courses, dreading the inescapable monotony and condescension that awaited them.

When Glenn and Mitzie entered their room, they were greeted by a smiling Mikhail Melnyk standing behind three tables full of artifacts. There were authentic examples of the three spear points they had heretofore only read about, a representation of an atlatl, various stone cultivation tools, and many other items gleaned from archaeological digs. Melnyk invited all 12 of them to come up and view the items, and even handle them.

They were as children, exclaiming over the artifacts and applying their book knowledge to tangible examples. Mitzie held a split-twig deer talisman from the Grand Canyon that dated back to about 2500 B.C. She turned the object over and over, examining it with awe. She looked up at Melnyk, and he nodded to her with the barest hint of a smile.

Glenn ran his fingers reverently over an ancient Olmec celt of green jade and carved with a catlike baby face.

"Do you like that, Mr. Harding?" Melnyk asked. "Compare it to this Mayan carved shell pendant. See the similarities? The Maya decorated their carvings with jade inlays. And here is an Aztec pendant of a serpent with white shell teeth and red shell nostrils. What comparisons can you draw from these three styles?"

The next thing Mitzie knew, Glenn and Melnyk were engaged in a riveting conversation. Glenn looked back and her and winked, and she happily continued poring over the beautifully created toys and tools on the table, some of them crafted in gold and silver and adorned with the remnants of colorful feathers from exotic birds. Whatever had come over Melnyk on Sunday, she didn't know, but she hoped it continued. This was the course she was hoping to experience.

In Cassidy's classroom, the participants were buzzing excitedly. The tables had been pushed against the wall, and the class members were gathered into the center of the room. Constance Wright stood in their midst, dressed in khaki trousers and a white cotton button down shirt, thick walking boots, and a floppy brown hat. She demonstrated the correct way to create a grid at an excavation site, and all the students had a hand in pulling the string to create one-meter squares throughout the room. When they finished, they each were given a pair of canvas gloves, a four-inch pointing trowel, a hand shovel, and three sizes of paint brushes, as well as small tools comprised of makeup-sized brushes, a toothbrush, and a dentist's probe. They sat cross legged in gridded off squares while Constance described how to hold their tools and encouraged them to try them out. As they did, she moved about the class making minor corrective adjustments to their grips and giving them meaningful tips.

"Excellent technique Ms. Phelps," she said as Cassidy demonstrated brushing imaginary dirt off her trowel. "You should do very well when we go outside in the digging area tomorrow."

Cassidy could scarcely believe her ears. *We are going outside tomorrow, and we will get to dig?* She nearly cried in anticipation. She could hardly wait to tell Colby she was getting to dig.

Colby, in the meantime, was engrossed in the equipment laid out on the tables surrounding the perimeter of his classroom. Like in Cassidy's class, there were shovels, knives, and trowels, but there was also other equipment that he had never seen before. One table contained tools such as an anthropometer, which was used to measure a person's stature using the existing bones, spreading calipers which measured the length and breadth of the skull, and boley gauges which measured teeth. Another table held several pieces of electrical equipment, including a gas chromatograph that separated chemical substances found in remains, a mass spectrometer that helped to identify poisons in a corpse's fluids, and a ground-penetrating radar detector that sent radar waves into the earth to detect the presence of bodies.

Professor Chen walked up beside him. "Hello, Mr. Carson. You are my apple bringing student. You like these things? Yes, yes. I can see. I am so pleased. Will you like to use them on some real cadaver bones soon?" she said.

"Professor Chen, I will bring you an apple every single day if you make that happen," he said with a hearty laugh.

She patted him on the back and laughed along with him. "I will like that very much. You may bring me an apple tomorrow, and I will give you bones to test. That is a deal?"

"Yes, that is a deal," he agreed.

All throughout the Lower Eastern NFAEE Center in Richmond, the participants found themselves in the kinds of courses of which they had dreamed. Tensions were eased, and even the relations between corridors on the floors improved. Men and women laughed and joked and mingled with one another, exclaiming over the wonderful learning experiences they were enjoying.

Stella Cooke was taught to light a cabin without electricity; she fashioned a plate and bowl from wood using sand to create a smooth finish; she wove a watertight basket from grasses; and she could make and keep a fire burning without matches.

Ken Schaffer perfected his knife skills with onions, carrots, celery, and meat; he sampled spices and determined which ones complemented each other; and he roasted cracked beef bones and used them to make a delicious bone broth for a classic French onion soup.

Chester Osceola surveyed the grounds and the walking trail and was able to render a ⅛-inch scale map of the area with surprising accuracy.

Carmine Wells wrote a beautiful evocative poem in rhyming couplets about her friendship with Paulette Jameson and shared it with the class.

Paulette Jameson conducted an interview with Chester Osceola and wrote a compelling human-interest story about life as a Florida Seminole Indian.

*   *   *

At the other NFAEE Centers in the other cities across the nation, the participants were also having "happy week."

In the Upper Eastern NFAEE Center, Clark Banning learned to salsa dance and got to try out his moves at a Latin club in downtown Annapolis. Inez Cohen attended the opera and was given a backstage pass so she could talk with the singers.

Andrew Thibodeau began work on his

sculpture of the Creole Woman in the Lower Central NFAEE Center. Mariana Gonzales visited a newsroom in Frankfort and was able to meet and interview the news editor for over an hour.

In the St. Paul, Minnesota Center, Lou Anne Stevens attended a concert by the Chinese ensemble from the University of Minnesota that wore traditional clothing and played early Chinese instruments. Della Strongbow created a ¼-inch scale map of the grounds of the Upper Central NFAEE Center.

Alma Downey from the Mountain NFAEE got to perform a scene from *Cat on a Hot Tin Roof* in a downtown Santa Fe theater. Gary Campbell painted a gallery-worthy picture of the skyline in varying shades of red, ochre, yellow, and orange acrylics.

Annemarie Cummings of the Pacific NFAEE cooked on the line in a Michelin five-star restaurant. Arlene Yazzi ran the spotlight for a rehearsal of the Salem Community theater. They were all, indeed, sublimely happy.

*   *   *

The band of nine continued their nightly walks, but their conversations were more animated and frequently punctuated with excitement instead of disgruntlement and fear. During the week, nobody left the Center, the course numbers remained unchanged, and there was a general feeling of euphoria in the air.

Colby Carson, however, remained skeptical. Though he was enjoying his sojourn into forensic anthropology, and he was delighted with Cassidy's fervor over her field outings, he could not get over his insistent "inklings." He was afraid they were all getting complacent, and he encouraged them to remain wary, watchful, and careful. The change in the instructors from their generally miserable behavior during the first few days, when they should have been at their most charming, to ideal teachers was too drastic, too abrupt.

Not wanting to put a damper on the women's moods, he talked his feelings over with Glenn during the Friday night walk when Mitzie and Cassidy were strolling up ahead and chattering about their day.

"I can't help feeling this is a honeymoon period, Glenn," he said.

"Mmm hmm. I know what you mean. I've lived with that wife of mine too long to not know that when things go along too smoothly, the other shoe is gonna drop. I'm waiting for the thump, you know?" Glenn responded. "It's too radical. Leopard don't change his spots, and all that."

"Exactly. I don't want to alarm the ladies, but I hate to see them when—and I do think it's when and not if—things change back. I feel like this is a tactic to throw us off balance. Otherwise, why be so crappy in the beginning?" Colby said.

"Oh, you're speaking truth there. I don't care how much Melnyk smiles at me and chats me up, I remember how he put poor Mitzie down. Pissed me off bigtime! Told you she reminds me of my daughter, Colby, and I would never let somebody get away with disrespecting my daughter like that," Glenn said.

"I appreciate that. Mitzie's a real sweetie. It tore me up to see her crying last Sunday night. Tore me up even more when Cassi broke down. But I already told you about that."

"Yeah, you did. Got a real soft spot for her, haven't you?" Glenn said, looking over at Colby.

"Is it obvious, Glenn?" Colby asked.

"To her, maybe not. To me? Damn straight. What are you thinking of doing?" Glenn said.

"I don't know. I'm 45 years old. I live with a cat that my wife had from a kitten. I've been widowed for four years, and I don't know if I can do it again. But I love her. I know that much, even if she doesn't feel the same," Colby admitted.

"... and did you know that Hohokams—that means 'vanished ones'—had mirrors made of iron-pyrite, and copper bells, and even ball-courts. They kept macaws as pets. We each got a macaw feather today. Mighty cool," Glenn said.

"That's amazing. Tomorrow we get to crack open some finger bones to extract blood cells from the marrow," Colby said.

"Sorry, but that is not so awesome to me," Glenn said, and he and Colby shared a hearty laugh as they left the light.

"Was I right about the watches, Glenn?" Colby asked, his eyebrows raised knowingly.

"Yes, you were, and just in time. I saw Melnyk scrutinizing mine and Mitzie's on Monday when we were looking at the spear points. He asked if I was wearing a smartwatch. I told him it was a '*stupid* watch' that I got from a student, and he actually took my arm so he could examine it. You should've seen his face when he realized it was *Batman*. Priceless! Best five bucks you ever spent. I owe you." he said with a chuckle.

"Where *is* your iWatch? Not in the room, I hope. I'm sure they search our rooms, you know."

"I agree. It's around my ankle under my sock. I used a spare shoestring to connect the buckle to the holes in the strap. It's not going anywhere as long as I'm wearing socks during the day. At night it goes under my pillow, shoestring and all."

"Good deal. Hey, ladies. Getting cold out here. Want to head back?" he called.

Mitzie and Cassidy turned around and walked to them. Cassidy slipped her arm through Colby's and snugged up to his side.

"Here, Colby. I'll warm you up," she teased.

"Watch it, watch it. You're getting a bit too familiar Ms. Phelps. I might take a liking to you or something," he mocked.

"Or something," she said with a wink.

Colby clasped her hand and pushed it into his pocket. "Keep my hand warm, girl," he said with a wink and a grin.

"My pleasure, Mr. Carson," she said, "but what about our other hands?"

"Haven't you got a pocket on the other side of

your coat? Put your hand in that pocket, and I'll put my other hand in my pocket."

"Oh, my Lord. Who said chivalry is dead?" she remarked with a rueful shake of her head.

* * *

In the surveillance room behind the grand ballroom, Elizabeth Ford watched the monitor and listened to the audio feed. Mr. Colby Carson had been flagged as person of interest because of his high intellect and powers of observation. Ms. Cassidy Phelps was immediately flagged because of the glowing letters of recommendation she received from her district. Mrs. Mitzie Galloway's flag was due to her extremely creative teaching methods. Mr. Glenn Harding's high aptitude scores and "give a damn" attitude had flagged him.

Elizabeth allowed herself a brief smile. *We've made excellent progress with these flags. A budding interracial romance should just about take care of the first two, and the pair behind them have a father-daughter thing going. This is working out very well.*

She made a few notes on a clipboard beside the monitor, and then she opened her laptop and began tapping the keys. The long email report completed, she sent it to Ronald A. Bowry, with a copy to Ashley Lawrence. She also forwarded blind copies to unnamed recipients in Washington D.C., in Quantico, Virginia, in New York City, in Los Angeles, California, in Portland, Oregon, and in the People's Republic of China.

CHAPTER SEVENTEEN
<u>Week 3</u>

"If your enemy is secure at all points, be prepared for him. If he is in superior strength, evade him. If your opponent is temperamental, seek to irritate him. Pretend to be weak, that he may grow arrogant. If he is taking it easy, give him no rest. If his forces are united, separate them. If sovereign and subject are in accord, put division between them. Attack him where he is unprepared, appear where you are not expected."
~Sun Tzu,
The Art of War

HAPPY WEEK ENDED with the ringing of Koji's bell outside in the corridor. Colby, Cassidy, and Mitzie eagerly exited their rooms, along with the other occupants from their corridor, anxious for another outing into Richmond. Colby was especially glad that he would not have to take a side-trip of his own and miss lunch again. The groups filed out of the NFAEE building and were routed to their respective vans. When they had loaded, Koji again stood at the front waving her itinerary and ringing for quiet.

"Hello red group, it is your guide Koji. I have your excursion information. Today, we visit the Virginia Holocaust Museum. This is a very serious place, and you must be sure to behave respectfully while you are there. Breakfast will be the All-American Café on the way. We meet at the van at 11:45 on the dot to go for lunch at Suzi's Noodle Room. Good Japanese food. Please be at museum entrance at 11:45. Mr. Carson, please be careful what you eat for breakfast. Koji does not want you to miss lunch again. OK? Driver, we go now," she said.

Cassidy gave Colby a stern look. "No field trips today, right?" she asked.

"Nope, just going to be your shadow all day long," he replied.

Because the Holocaust Museum could only accommodate 120 guests at a time, the NFAEE participants were separated into two units. Those on floors seven through 11 were the first ones to tour the museum, while those on floors two through six would take a driving tour around the streets of Richmond with a stop at the site of Libby Prison, a Confederate detention Center during the Civil War considered second only to Andersonville Prison in Georgia in terms of cruelty to is prisoners. After lunch, they would swap out, so everyone could visit both sites.

They arrived at the museum after a light breakfast, and the five vans unloaded. Glenn joined the trio, along with Ken, Stella, and Carmine, who was clearly upset at having been split up from Paulette and Chester. Unlike the Virginia Museum of Art, they toured the Holocaust Museum in parties of 30, facilitated by a docent for each group. The guided tours took about two hours. After that, guests were free to explore the museum and grounds at their leisure for the remaining half hour.

One step inside the doors, and they felt the previous jovial mood begin to plummet. The museum itself was divided into several main exhibit areas. The synagogue auditorium was a place of beauty, a recreation of the famous Choral Synagogue in Kovno, Lithuania; however, the Bucherwald exhibit focused on a Nazi concentration camp on Ettersberg hill near Weimar, Germany in which over 50,000 prisoners died, and it was depressing. The Kristallnacht exhibit, or "Night of Broken Glass," referred to the broken glass shards which littered the streets after German Nazi forces demolished the windows of Jewish-owned stores, homes, hospitals, and synagogues with sledgehammers, and then burned and looted them. It was also a mood breaker. The multipurpose room, conference room, and office areas were not visited.

The first-floor exhibits, for which the docents provided excellent narratives, detailed the brutal and sobering chronological history of the Holocaust and the systematic massacre of European Jews, with over

300 testimonies of Holocaust survivors and artifacts from the time period. In addition, the docent told them the museum possessed collections of authentic historical documents, photographs, and oral histories from World War II, and over 230 digitized personal testimonies from people in the Commonwealth of Virginia who lived through the genocide perpetuated upon the Jewish population. The groups moved about in silence, viewing photographs of atrocities and treatment of which human beings should never be subject.

Cassidy held Colby's hand and wiped tears from her face with her sleeve. Glenn had already given up his handkerchief to Mitzie. Behind them, Ken, Stella, and Carmine walked, each woman clinging to one of Ken's jutting elbows.

One of the most poignant collections they viewed was called "The Violins of Hope," which featured over 60 expertly restored musical instruments belonging to survivors of Dachau and Auschwitz. Though the museum was a loving tribute, its overall feeling was one of despair and shame. Many in the group were crying, and some of them were sobbing, and by the time they finished the tour, they were utterly exhausted.

Most of the guests did not venture through the exhibits a second time, nor did they stroll the grounds or visit whatever might be contained in the gift shop. They were simply too depressed. When the van arrived to take them to lunch at 11:45, they were all waiting out front and boarded without conversation.

"Maybe the next part of our outing will be more uplifting," Cassidy commented, to which she only received downturned mouths from her friends.

After picking at their lunches at the noodle shop, which provided tasty but not satisfying fare, they returned to the vans and listened as Koji pointed out what she considered important landmarks, including shopping spots and her favorite restaurants. They had been cooped up inside the vans for nearly two hours before they headed for Libby Prison, a place known for its harsh overcrowded conditions under which the Civil War prisoners were kept.

There they saw what was left of the three-building brick complex that had originally been a tobacco factory until it was converted into an officer-only prison. The rooms the men were forced to live in were sparsely furnished and open to the elements, which contributed to the deaths of many of them, along with malnutrition, insufficient clothing, and rampant disease.

Over one thousand men had been crammed into the eight low-ceilinged 42 feet by 103 feet rooms on two of the prison's three floors. The very thought made Mitzie hyperventilate, so she stopped listening to the narrative and focused on the sky.

When they finally left the site, they felt drained and were happy to return to their rooms. As it was a few hours before dinner time, they all agreed they would be best served by taking naps or long, hot baths. The mood over the entire **NFAEE Center** was one of sadness and dejection—just as Elizabeth Ford and Ronald Bowry had planned.

Even the excellent food on the buffet line could not lighten their spirits. They ate mostly in silence, avoiding eye contact and sighing often. When Mitzie said she wanted to go back to her room and watch television, Glenn objected.

"No ma'am. That's not happening. If you pull the plug in the bathtub, the rubber duck will sink into the drain," he said.

Mitzie gave him a curious look. "I don't have a clue what you're talking about, Glenn," she said.

"Oh, your mama never told you that saying? Think about your kids. When the tub water ran out, what happened to their little floatie toys?"

"They piled up at the drain. Oh, I get it. Not really a bad analogy. If I give in to depression, it'll just get worse. Is that what you mean?"

"Exactly. Weather report says cold and rainy is coming, so I figure tonight we better have our walk. Might be caught inside for a spell," Glenn announced, "so let's go."

Colby and Cassidy concurred, and they all donned their coats and scarves and hats. They headed for the elevators and then out the doors. It was indeed beginning to get colder outside, so they walked a little more briskly than usual, foregoing the seating areas and keeping their body temperatures up with the increased exercise.

The quartet walked the entire path, but they never ran into Carmine, Paulette, and Chester. They did spot Ken and Stella in a seating area, pressed up against each other, their heads close in conversation. Ken waved but went back to talking with Stella, so the foursome kept on walking until they eventually reached their starting point. Tired at last, but in better moods, they entered the building and departed to their rooms, hoping against hope that the next day would lift their spirits even more. Sadly, it did not.

Glenn and Mitzie were disappointed to see that the fascinating artifacts they had examined the prior week were gone. Instead, Melnyk was standing at the podium waiting on everyone to arrive in the classroom.

"Today we move on to Indian religion, pre- and post-contact. Mrs. Jenkins, would you begin reading at paragraph one on page 98 while the class listens," he said with a visible sneer.

Glenn gave an audible groan, but he covered it by coughing when Melnyk turned his gaze on him. When he looked away, Glenn touched Mitzie's leg gently with his foot.

"Keep your head down, Mitzie dear. It's going to be a pretty bad week, and we're under scrutiny again," he whispered.

Cassidy found herself in the very same disappointing situation when she saw Constance Wright was wearing another hideous frock, her bedazzled glasses already perched on her nose. In no time, the droning monotone of her voice filled the room. Cassidy took out her highlighter and commenced to marking up her book, all the while thinking of how she could apply the written word whenever she did get into the field.

In Colby's class, there were no longer tables filled with equipment; however, Professor Chen was as pleasant as ever and accepted his apple with delight. They delved into the text material, and though he was quite fond of her as a teacher, he found the course content to be extremely challenging. Nonetheless, he did his best to keep up, asking questions for clarification which Professor Chen happily answered.

Ken was chagrined to be back to reading Mario Batali's cookbook. He wanted to chop and dice and puree and perfect the techniques he had literally gotten a taste of the previous week. He figured, since he was stuck in his seat for the time being, he would use his sense memory to put his own creative spin on Mario's recipes.

He took a bit of one recipe and combined it with another, substituting proteins and vegetables until he came up with flavor combinations he thought would pair well together. He painstakingly copied down the prep methods and cooking times. He even tweaked some recipes he had discussed with Stella from her Girl Scout camping days, like "wilderness stew," "sock-it-to-me cobbler," "all-in-one," and "tinfoil meat'n'taters." While it looked to the casual observer as though he was taking copious notes while the instructors Lucy Prince and Javier Rojas took turns reading the recipes, Ken Schaffer was creating his own cookbook.

Stella's class time was taken up with watching an episode of *Little House on the Prairie*, followed by a teacher-led discussion before break, and one more episode and discussion after the break. The instructor announced they would finish all 24 episodes of season one by the end of the week.

Stella was astute enough to know the difference between Hollywood's version of the facts and the real facts, having read all the Laura Ingalls Wilder series of books. So, while the show played, she tuned out the plot and the characters' interactions and instead focused on the set and the props. She watched with interest how Charles Ingalls constructed the log cabin in Kansas, with its sod roof and hand felled timbers. Using the technical drawing techniques Ken had taught her from his years helping boys achieve their drafting merit badges, she sketched out the Ingalls' lofted house in Walnut Grove, speculating on the dimensions with respect to the furnishings. And, in doing so, she figured out how to build her own off-grid tiny cabin.

Chester initially complained about creating the relief map of the grounds in clay; however, he decided to take the old adage of "walking in another man's moccasins" to heart. *If I were a blind man,* he thought, *how could I find my way around?*

He took out his meticulously rendered scale map and laid it on his table. Then he stared at it from all angles, recalling his journey. In his mind's eye, he could see the slight rise as the path moved uphill; he felt the depressions in the earth beside the fence line at the edge of the property and the mounds on which shrubbery had been planted not so long ago; he knew where the peaks and valleys were, where vegetation gave way to rocks and gravel and concrete, and where the lawn sloped and held water. All these things Chester transferred to his modeling clay relief map over the week, and by the time he was finished, he had created a perfect scale recreation of the NFAEE Center grounds.

Carmine's course went back to writing Japanese haiku, and she was distressed at first. She longed to rhyme, for she was gifted with words, but the haiku was not a rhymed poem. It was esoteric and abstract, using the fewest possible combinations of words in ordered syllables to convey imagery. Being a determined young woman, she changed her way of thinking and began to apply the rules for the three-sentence format of five syllables, seven syllables, and five syllables to her understanding of quatrains. Carmine discovered that she could link haiku poems together and, using her superior language skills, she could make them into rhyming stanzas. Suddenly, the class held more meaning for her, and she was able to endure. Her first effort produced a poem that epitomized the band of nine.

Once a frightened bird
Beating its wings to soar high
Its feet upon ground

It lived for a word
Stories it read in the sky
Promise became sound

Friendship's loins were gird
Battling what ere was nigh
Strength and cunning found

Paulette's course time was spent less creatively, but no less importantly. Using her innate investigative journalism skills, she pored over the outdated newspapers and periodicals she had been given and found some interesting articles about Richmond, as well as about some of its local citizens, including several stories about past NFAEE Center participants and their achievements. She was alarmed to note that an overwhelming number of winners went on to work in universities or high-profile jobs and neglected to return to their teaching assignments.

But perhaps the most fascinating thing Paulette discovered was when the course members interviewed each other. By reading the accounts written by her classmates, she was able to confirm that Glenn's population theory was correct. The county populations were categorized on each corridor of each floor, and she made a chart to show her friends.

Floor – color - population	Floor – color - population
2 – violet 80K-100K	2 – purple 50K-60K
3 – turquoise 1K-20K	3 – indigo 60K-70K
4 – yellow 80K-100K	4 – green 40K-50K
5 – red 1K-20K	5 – orange 30K-40K
6 – white 20K-30K	6 – black 70K-80K
7 – violet 80K-100K	7 – purple 40K-50K
8 – turquoise 1K-20K	8 – indigo 50K-60K
9 – yellow 1K-20K	9 – green 60K-70K
10 – red 20K-30K	10 – orange 70K-80K
11 – white 30K-40K	11 – black 80K-100K

The participants were divided into 20 colored groups comprising forty total corridors of rooms. Each floor had four corridors—two for one color group, and two for a different color group.

The color groups began on the 2nd floor with violet and purple; 3rd floor was turquoise and indigo; 4th floor was yellow and green; 5th floor was red and orange; and 6th floor was white and black. The pattern repeated at the 7th floor with violet and purple; the 8th floor with turquoise and indigo; the 9th floor with yellow and green; the 10th floor with red and orange; and the 11th floor with white and black.

Spread throughout the Center were color groups of each population density. Each floor was comprised of sabbatical participants with two vastly differing population groups who were placed in direct proximity to one another.

On Chester's violet corridor on the 2nd floor, the population was 80,000 to over 100,000; the purple corridor was 50,000 to 60,000.

On Paulette's turquoise corridor on the 3rd floor were participant counties with populations less than 20,000; the indigo group had 60,000 to 70,000.

The 4th floor yellow corridor was 80,000 in population to over 100,000; green was 40,000 to 50,000 in population.

On the 5th floor was red, with populations less than 20,000; the orange populations ranged from 30,000 to 40,000.

The white group on the 6th floor had populations of 20,000 to 30,000; the black hall was 70,000 to 80,000 in population.

When the pattern repeated on the 7th floor, Carmine's violet corridor was 80,000 to over 100,000 in population; purple was 40,000 to 50,000.

On Stella's 8th floor, the less than 20,000 turquoise population was bordered by the indigo's 50,000 to 60,000.

On the 9th floor, the yellow population was less than 20,000; Ken's green hall was 60,000 to 70,000.

Mitzie, Colby, and Cassidy, on the 10th floor, were all on the red hall with populations of 20,000 to 30,000; the orange hall had people from counties with populations of 70,000 to 80,000.

On Glenn's 11th floor white hall, the population was 30,000 to 40,000; the black hall was 80,000 to in excess of 100,000 in population.

It was indeed the "haves and have nots," as those from counties with greater population densities invariably had higher incomes and more elevated socioeconomic status than the participants who hailed from counties with smaller populations.

*   *   *

The weather did turn bad and, having no place to escape the confines of the building, the band of nine met on a different floor each night. Sometimes the women and men would split up and gather in the rooms, and sometimes they met all together in the corridors outside the rooms. That was for Mitzie's benefit as they discovered on the first night in her room that nine people caused her undue stress. She had to prop open her door with the chair in order to breathe. Thereafter, they chose a room and pulled as many chairs and pillows into the hallway as they could for comfort. It kept them sane, and though they could not speak as freely as they desired, they found ways to relay their thoughts without saying more than necessary, and they could use the time to enjoy one another's company.

Paulette shared the population table with them, proclaiming it to be one of the stories she had written in her journalism course. They all smiled and gave loud glowing compliments for her "article" for the benefit of the surveillance devices as they digested the implications of the chart. They particularly understood the significance of the class warfare evidenced by the numbers: promote discontent by pairing haves and have nots—exactly as Colby and Glenn theorized.

When they dismissed and went back to their individual rooms, the original Four Musketeers spent time in their bathrooms texting. Colby began the digital conversation.

"GH…U R RIGHT RE: POPS"

"YEP. BIG DOG V LITTLE DOG"

Mitzie joined the conversation.

"4 REAL?"

"FRAID SO, DEAR"

Cassidy picked up the thread.

"Y OFFER US $$ 2 TAKE IT AWAY, COLBY?"

"MORE 2 IT"

Glenn agreed.

"I THINK SO 2. UR THOUGHT CC?"

"BREAK SPIRIT"

Cassidy and Mitzie responded in turn.

"Y? CONTROL?"

"CONTROL WHO AND Y?"

There was no activity for a while as they each thought about what the underlying reason could be. Finally, Colby came back with a terrifying response.

"TEACHERS!"

Mitzie's head jerked as though slapped.

"?????"

Colby paused a moment before writing.

"I HAVE A THEORY. BUT VERY BAD. 2 BAD 2 B TRUE"

"Y?"

"GOES BEYOND NFAEE. NATIONWIDE?"

Cassidy, Glenn, and Mitzie alternated rapid responses.

"(surprised emoji)"

"(thumbs up emoji)"

"???????"

"I M SCARED, CC"

"U SHOULD B, CP"

"OMG. Y?????"

Colby texted his answer reluctantly, realizing it would scare the women.

"CONTROL THE TEACHERS, CONTROL THE WORLD"

Cassidy answered quickly.

"LIKE NAZIS? WWII?"

Glenn began writing, the messages appearing one after the other in rapid succession.

"YES!! THINK VIETNAM. CAMBODIA. KHMER ROUGE. "SOCIALISM=COMMUNISM"

"HIGH INTELLECT=REBELLION SO EDUCATED ARE KILLED"

"KILLED DRS…MUSICIANS…TCHRS!"

"CLASS SYSTEM. NO RELIGION. NO HOPE 4 GOOD LIFE. NO ESCAPE"

"DUMB DOWN EDUCATION. CHILDREN KILL PARENTS" "BRAINWASHING. MASS GENOCIDE."

Mitzie issued a strangled grunt and texted.

"STOP!!!"

"DEAR GOD IN HEAVEN. THIS CAN'T B! CC?"

"IDK SIGNS POINT 2 IT, CP"

Mitzie cried silently as she texted.

"R THEY GOING 2 KILL US, CC?"

"NOT THAT BAD. WANT 2 BREAK US"
"I M BROKEN!!!"

Glenn responded immediately.

"NO, DEAR. U R NOT. U R STRONG"

"I M AFRAID"

"WE ALL R. BUT 2GETHER WE R STRONG. WE R
SMARTER THAN THEY THINK WE R"

Cassidy asked the question they were all
wondering.

"WHO R THEY?"

There was a short period of inactivity as they
thought the question over. Then Colby gave his
opinion.

"WHOEVER CONTROLS THE NFAEE & THE $$. I
THINK SHADOW GOVT. ANTI-USA. GH?"

"AGREE, CC. WE R PAWNS N BIGR CHESS GAME.
MAKE US DUMB...COMPLACENT...COMPLIANT.

IF EDUCATION FALLS, USA FALLS. BRILLIANT PLAN.
WE R 1ST LINE DEFENSE. MUST B UNITED. MUST B
STRONG. STICK 2GETHER. FIGHT W/INTELLECT 4 USA.
ENDURE & WIN"

Colby, Cassidy, and Mitzie echoed his final thought, and it became a mantra for them.

"ENDURE & WIN"

"ENDURE & WIN"

"ENDURE & WIN"

The next texts were comprised of thumbs up emojis and heart icons, and then the four of them signed off and went to bed, each tossing and turning with dreams of their own versions of warfare.

* * *

From the command center on the first floor, Elizabeth Ford saw the four people emerge from their bathrooms with slow steps and hanging heads. *They're broken,* she confirmed. *No need to worry about that group anymore.* She made a notation on a clipboard, and then she moved on to watch others in the building. In her report, she noted the names and statuses of those who remained in the sabbatical.

"Broken: Colby Carson. Cassidy Phelps. Glenn Harding. Mitzie Galloway. No further threat detected from them. Flags removed.

"Distracted: Ken Schaffer and Stella Cooke. Romance, plan to retire. No longer flagged.

"Retiring: Chester Osceola. Flag removed.

"Expelled: Melvin Ward. Lee Wong. Justin Simonds. Carolyn Watson. Sheryl Anderson.

"Exited: Janice Attaway. Spencer Green. Joe Hurst. Fred Rhodes.

"Adapted: Paulette Jameson. Carmine Wells. Originally thought Distracted, merely friends. Further scrutiny required.

"Flagged: Charles Jones. Herman Lloyd. Geraldine Thurston. James Kent. Martin Reed. Amy Luther. Consuela Martinez. Minh Cho. Tan Pham.

"Aware: none confirmed at this time."

CHAPTER EIGHTEEN
Weeks 4 Through 8

"There are few things more pathetic than those who have lost their curiosity and sense of adventure, and who no longer care to learn."

~ Gordon B. Hinckley,
Way to Be! 9 Rules for Living the Good Life

THE REST OF JANUARY PASSED with predictable results: a happy week was followed by a reversion back to the boring and interminable, with Sunday excursions to the Virginia State Capitol, John Marshall House, American Civil War Center, and Tredegar Iron Works, punctuated by meaningless sojourns via van around the city to view numerous points of uninterest. The weather remained dismal, and there were few opportunities to take their nightly walks, so the groups continued to congregate in the hallways. All along the corridor, they noticed people looking downtrodden and dismayed. Entire chunks of participants had disappeared, and the number of vans required for transporting them on the outings decreased as the floor occupants were combined.

Glenn continued to wear his iWatch around his ankle, and the others had taken to doing so, as well. They had already set the call and message volumes to the silent settings, so they were in no danger of someone else hearing a tone, and once the initial video surveillance and instructor observations determined that the watches they currently wore were far from smart, they seemed safe and their flags were subsequently removed.

Colby spent an inordinate amount of time in the bathroom, which failed to arouse suspicion due to his bout of "intestinal distress" that had been reported on the first excursion. Playing to the strength of his inherent geekiness, he developed a way of messaging one another while in areas other than the restrooms. He unveiled his system to the four Musketeers in late January.

By wearing their watch faces on the inside of their ankles, they could tap lightly on the face with their other foot and send short vibration bursts to group message the other three. They could signal a general check-in vibration with one tap, a "meet at Mitzie's room" signal with two taps, a signal to "meet at Cassidy's room" with three taps, a "meet at the dining room" vibration with four taps, a signal for all of them to "meet at the front door" with five taps, and an "S.O.S." signal with six taps. While they used the one through five tap messages frequently, they fortunately never had reason to use the six taps. To be cautious, they never congregated in either Colby's room or Glenn's room because of their proximity to the wide-angle cameras over the elevators and the dining room doors. If they wanted the whole band of nine to meet, they simply called the others on their room phones and issued an innocuous invitation to the 10th floor. Again, it was Occam's razor at its finest: the simplest solution is usually the best.

As January passed into February, more and more people Exited the Center. Some left as broken shells of their once vibrant selves. These teachers would never return to their counties the same persons they left. Generally feeling betrayed and burned by the system that promised them renewal, they would finish the school year depressed and ineffective in their teaching, failing to excite their young students and contributing to the overall dissatisfaction with school and education in general.

Seven teachers who lived in Virginia (from 2nd floor violet, 4th floor yellow, and 11th floor black) got together and hired an Uber to come pick them up and drive them all the way home. Being in the most populated counties, their spouses had significant incomes, so they didn't care about the loss of the monthly stipends.

Several teachers were Expelled for legitimate

infractions—alcohol consumption being the greatest result of their discontent. Countless arguments broke out, along with three fistfights, and five incidents of women screaming, scratching, and pulling each other's hair. These teachers were, of course, Expelled immediately.

Others were Expelled for contrived reasons or after being baited. In one Center, a woman in her Theater class was singled out by the instructor to demonstrate the correct way to perform an onstage kiss. He forced his tongue into her mouth and grabbed her buttocks. She reared back and slapped him across the face. Though she protested she had every right to strike him, she was Expelled.

These Expelled individuals would return to their jobs bitter and resentful, feeling they had been misled or manipulated and mourning the loss of the extra money. They would take it out on their students. A few of them would be transferred to other schools where they would continue the abuse on their pupils, not realizing that the pattern had been imprinted on them while they were at the NFAEE Center.

Of the teachers who stayed, the vast majority were only marking out their time, hoping to collect their full stipends, even if they didn't like the courses they were now forced to attend. Their overall zeal for education was gone and might possibly never return. They had been forced to color within the lines, and for a creative, forward thinking person, there was nothing worse than having to conform to mediocrity.

Within the band of nine, however, because of their comradery, they held fast to their gifts and talents, though they attempted to keep them from showing outwardly. They became as chameleons, seeming to emulate the others in their broken dejected appearances during the sad weeks and allowing themselves to show traces of excitement during the happy weeks. In private, away from the video and audio surveillance, they diligently strived to gather information that would be of use to them if or when the time came to make a stand or escape, if necessary.

In February, they went on an excursion to the Virginia Museum of History and Culture. It was a particularly good outing, and afterwards, they returned to the NFAEE Center with all sorts of do-dahs which cheered them immensely. Ken found an assortment of gourmet items that struck his fancy, including bottles of Virginia Gentleman maple glaze and sauce, as well as the signature steak sauce and barbecue sauce. He wisely asked his guide if he was permitted to buy and keep the sauces, which were prepared with bourbon, in his room. He was granted permission to have them, so long as he didn't consume them at the NFAEE Center.

Cassidy bought herself a tote that read: *"I cannot live without books." Thomas Jefferson to John Adams 1815.* It was a statement Jefferson had written to his friend John Adams in one of the many correspondences they shared.

Glenn bought Iris an apron that read: *"In my*

dreams, I still shop at Miller and Rhoads." Being Virginians, they knew all about the former department store. The friends shared their finds and generally had a great time, knowing that though the following week would again be happy week, the sad week would be right on its tail.

To combat the depressing effects of sad week, they all decided to meet in the corridor between Mitzie's and Cassidy's rooms on the 14th for a Valentine party of sorts. Gifts were not required, but they could certainly be exchanged if they so desired. Most of them so desired.

Ken presented Stella with a large blue ceramic mug he had purchased in the history museum. It read *"Well-behaved Women Seldom Make History".* She broke into a fit of giggles when she read it, and Colby had to explain to Cassidy and Mitzie later that the two of them had been spending long hours in each other's rooms and had even had some "sleepovers."

Stella gave Ken a *"Meet Me Under the Clock"* mug, which referred to the practice of friends meeting for coffee and snacks in the Tea Room of the Miller and Rhoads department store in the 1800s, but it also gave another hint at their relationship.

Paulette gave Carmine a magnetic poetry kit she got in the history museum gift store. It contained over 200 themed magnetic tiles which could be moved around on a steel surface to create poems. A metal serving tray, contributed by a friendly member of the kitchen waitstaff (who was crushing on Carmine) was the perfect surface on which to arrange the tiles.

In return, Carmine gifted Paulette with a touching poem she had composed about friendship that rose above hardship. It was created entirely from individual words which had been clipped from the textbooks she received in her course and glued on a background of lace doilies that came from the dining room, donated by the same waiter. It brought all the women to tears with its beauty, originality, and sentiment.

For Chester, Carmine and Paulette had gone in together to buy four reproductions of Gilmer maps on acid-free paper suitable for framing. When Richmond was burned in 1865, Jeremy Gilmer, the Confederate Chief of Engineers who oversaw the production of maps for use by the Confederacy, salvaged 67 of them from the flames. Chester was overcome. He couldn't keep his eyes off the maps, and they couldn't keep their eyes off his joyful face.

Mitzie gave Glenn a hardcover book entitled *War Against War: The American Fight for Peace 1914-1918* by Michael Kazin. His eyes misted, and he patted the book reverently, thanking her over and over. She gave Cassidy a children's book entitled *The Undefeated* by Newbery award-winning author Kwame Alexander and illustrated by Caldecott Honoree Kadir Nelson. The book was in the form of a poem highlighting black life in the United States, with quotes from Martin Luther King Jr., Langston, Hughes, Gwendolyn Brooks, and other notable black leaders. Cassidy didn't try to hold back tears as she hugged her friend in appreciation.

Mitzie's gift from Cassidy was a collection of six ecru linen tea towels from the history museum, each imprinted with a different design: Richmond landmarks in an archway, a red cardinal in a nest on a bare branch, an outline of Virginia, a sign advertising *"Votes for Women,"* the iconic *"Meet Me Under the Clock,"* and her favorite which read: *Books...because reality is overrated.* Mitzie unfolded them and laid them on the floor in two groups of three.

"I'm going to make them into a quilt," she exclaimed. "This is the best Valentine's day ever!"

There was one gift left to present, and it was saved for last. Colby pulled Cassidy to her feet and stood behind her as she closed her eyes. He carefully draped the Fabergé egg necklace over her head and fastened the clasp. She opened her eyes and put her hand to her chest, feeling the coldness of the enamel and the bumps of the tiny crystals embedded into the egg. She let out a little squeal and ran into Mitzie's bathroom. The rest of them in the hallway heard her shout and laughed when she rushed back out.

"Colby Carson! Oh, my Lord! You have had this egg from our excursion on the first week, haven't you?" she exclaimed, throwing her arms around his neck in a tight embrace.

"Yep. Because I've loved you ever since you first shed tears on the shoulder of my blue checkered shirt," he said, pulling her chin up for a tender kiss.

The seven friends not involved in the kiss were nonetheless part of the moment, and they all hugged and agreed that it was, indeed, the very best Valentine's day ever. Thus, armed with close friendships and two budding romances, they made it through the rest of sad week, although they didn't make it through unobserved.

*   *   *

Elizabeth Ford watched the party on the corridor monitor with unease. Though she approved highly of the romantic dalliances for the distractions they served to promote, she was wary of the group's closeness. Friendship was discouraged. Friendships meant bonds; bonds meant strength; and strength could bloom into unity and resistance.

Ronald Bowry didn't want that; his superiors certainly didn't want that. Despite her earlier decision that these friends were not a threat, Elizabeth reluctantly believed that she now would have to watch them a little more closely, and if they couldn't be discouraged, a more stringent means of deterrent would be necessary. After all, Elizabeth's own life was on the line.

She finished her nightly report and forwarded it to all the required recipients, and then she sat back with her legs crossed staring at the ceiling. Her foot bobbed jerkily. She was irritable and nervous. She had not mentioned the growing closeness of the people she had observed a few minutes earlier. *Maybe it's just a temporary change of mood, a party to make themselves feel better. I'm sure they're still broken,* she told herself.

At least, that's what she hoped. To reverse her decision after she had already removed their flags would make her look weak and unreliable. The superiors didn't like weakness or unreliability. Especially the Chinese man. He was ruthless. Elizabeth was not the first one to fill this position, but she hoped to be the last. She knew what had happened to her predecessor. She began to shiver violently, and then she abruptly ran from the command center to the restroom, suddenly sick to her stomach. She barely made it in time.

CHAPTER NINETEEN
Weeks 9 Through 12

"By failing to prepare, you are preparing to fail."
~ Benjamin Franklin

"I will prepare and some day my chance will come."
~Abraham Lincoln

THERE WAS A BREAK IN THE WEATHER during the last few days of February, and being a happy week, the participants were afforded more opportunities to take outings related to their courses. Because so many had left the NFAEE Center by this time, other classes had been combined, including Archaeology and Forensic Anthropology. Cassidy and Colby were delighted they could spend their days in the same room together.

The archaeologists were given permission to dig in a supervised section of the grounds which they cordoned off in a grid as they had been taught. There was very little chance of them unearthing anything earthshattering, but they enjoyed it immensely.

Cassidy found the skeletal remains of a bird, and one would have thought she had struck gold. She dutifully noted its position in the grid, drawing it in her field notebook, and then she carefully dusted the soil from around the tiny, fragile bones. She showed her excavated find to Constance Wright, who praised her skills enthusiastically and took a picture of it with a small digital camera.

"Well done, Ms. Phelps. I will give you a copy of the picture for your scrapbook. You are quite good at this. If you would like, I will submit your name to a colleague of mine who guides digs across the county," she said cheerily.

"Thank you. I'd like that," Cassidy lied.

"Lovely. Well, perhaps you should take that to Professor Chen and let her people have a look at it," she suggested. Cassidy gave the fragile skeleton to the professor, who thanked her and presented it to her favorite student for testing. He rose to the challenge like a champion.

"I think you may change professions. What do you think about that, Johnny Appleseed?" she said to Colby in a teasing way.

"You could be right, professor. I really do like this," he said.

She clapped her hands and stood over his shoulder watching his use of the equipment. Professor Chen felt it was not necessary to break the spirit of every person in order to control them. Sometimes one need only to change their focus. She believed she had done so with Colby Carson.

"That is very good, Mr. Carson. In a few weeks, I will bring some interesting things for you to examine. You will like to see them very much. Yes, yes. They are deformities! Some very terrible, but you will like them. I am sure," she said.

"Can't wait, professor. Hey, I'm noticing that the bones from this skeleton are pneumatized. They're hollow," he remarked.

"Yes, yes! You are such a good student. That is exactly correct. Look, look, everyone. Mr. Carson has something to show you," she called, gathering the remaining students from the class over and leading a rousing discussion on the composition of bones from humans, animals, and birds.

Cassidy sidled up to Colby. "Colby, that was a good observation," she said quietly. "Did you learn that from your course professor?"

"Oh hell, no, Cassi. Didn't you ever see the 'Jurassic Park' movies?" he confided with a grin. "Sam Neill—playing Dr. Alan Grant—pointed out after the Gallimimus flocking scene that dinosaurs were related to birds. We've learned that some dinosaurs had pneumatized bones with hollow spaces. Mammalian bones are generally solid throughout. Hey, where are you going?"

"I'm going to dig for more dinosaurs, Dr. Colby Geek," she said.

Mitzie and Glenn were able to be with Stella as Indigenous Natives and Early American Pioneers were combined into one course. They all went on an outing together in a van to visit a local tribe of Native Americans, as well as to a former pioneer settlement. Largely unsupervised, they talked freely and learned that Stella and Ken had discussed living together in the off-grid cabin once they finished out their final year of teaching. Since they each had plenty of years in the system and were ready for retirement, it seemed the perfect end of a career for the both of them.

The band of nine prepared themselves for whatever the NFAEE could throw at them. They read their books and applied the knowledge gleaned from every available resource to things they might need to survive whatever was in the future. None of them knew what that entailed, and though they didn't want to be harbingers of doom and gloom, they went about their days and nights with their eyes and ears open.

Weeks nine through 11 passed uneventfully. Thus far, they had spent their Sundays on five enjoyable excursions and had painfully endured five others. And then week 12 rolled around—what they figured to be their last happy week of the sabbatical. They had endured two full months and earned $5,000 of stipend payments which had been sent by registered mail to their homes and was deposited into checking accounts by their families. Cassidy's payments had been sent to Edna Mae and, as she had instructed the NFAEE, were cashier's checks. Edna

Mae dutifully cashed them and put the money in a locked safe in her own house.

The weather had improved dramatically, and their excursion for that Sunday was the Lewis Ginter Botanical Gardens. The remaining NFAEE Center participants were treated to a seasonal garden walk with a special guide who pointed out all the varieties of plants that were blooming in March.

Cassidy was disappointed that they would not be able to see the "Butterflies LIVE" exhibit. Because of the fragile nature of the cold-blooded butterflies, they wintered in Arizona and would not be back at the Lew Ginter Gardens until mid-April. She confided to Colby that she had a recurring dream about butterflies. She had dreamed it since she was a little girl, and she still occasionally woke up amid it.

"I find myself standing in a field, and nobody else is around," she said. "I'm lost and searching for something, but I don't know what it is, and I start to cry. Suddenly, I'm enveloped in a swirling cloud of butterflies. They are all sizes and colors, and they flit around me gracefully, touching my face, my nose. Landing on my hands and my head. And in that moment, I am happier than I have ever been in my entire life, and then I wake up. I think, that must be what Heaven is like. At least I hope so."

"Cassi, that's a wonderful thought. I hope one day you find that field of butterflies," Colby said.

"I do, too, because I know, when that happens, I will be the happiest person in the world," she said.

The friends strolled through the gardens leisurely, enjoying their freedom amid the serenity of nature. Spring was attempting to overthrow winter, and the smell of wild onions was redolent in the air. Crocuses had poked their way through the last of the snows, and the tree branches were beginning to green with tiny buds. Within the 15,000 acres of the gardens, whole beds of flowers had yet to bloom, but the greenhouses were awash in variegated shades of green and other colors. They knew, when they returned to the NFAEE building, they would be wishing it had been the final week instead of next to last.

The romances that had begun in January were in full bloom, and Colby was finally ready to make use of the hinged Fabergé egg which had held Cassidy's necklace. One of the most spectacular exhibits in the garden was the Conservatory, called the "Jewel of the Garden." It was an 11,000 square-foot complex that housed plants from around the world, most of them exotic and unusual. In the center of the 63-foot tall central dome stood a collection of palms and cycads. The North Wing featured plants of seasonal colors and themes. In the East Wing, hundreds of cacti and succulents were on display, and in the West Wing, there were tropical plants and orchids, the likes of which the visitors had never seen.

All throughout the Conservatory were seating nooks, and the band of nine took advantage of a grouping set within an area of ornamental and native grasses. Colby had disappeared to the restroom—thankfully not ill—and when he returned, he didn't sit down by Cassidy. Instead, he handed her a small wrapped package. She giggled like a schoolgirl and took the gift from his hands.

"Now what have you gone and done?" she asked as she tore off the paper. Inside a small box, she found a pair of exquisite dangle earrings made from the wings of a Tailed Jay butterfly, a species native to India, Sri Lanka, Southeast Asia, and Australia. The delicate wings were black with brilliant green spots and were encased in clear resin. A printed note in the box ensured the purchaser that no butterflies were harmed in making the jewelry, that the wings were harvested from the naturally deceased insects. Cassidy was stuck speechless once again.

"I'm sorry we're too early for the live exhibit, but maybe these will make you feel like you're always surrounded by butterflies," Colby said, "and they match your egg necklace, too."

"Well, that's a plus, Colby. Cudos to you for matching them up. I couldn't do that. I'm colorblind," Glenn remarked with admiration.

Cassidy fixed the wings on her ears and shook her head slightly, wishing she had a mirror to see if they looked like she imagined—like butterflies fluttering around her ears.

"Oh, you need something reflective to see them with, don't you?" Colby said, pulling an object from his backpack. "Try looking in this." He held out the larger Fabergé egg he had saved for her.

"Oh, Colby," she managed, gingerly taking the beautiful egg in her hands. "Oh wait. Look. It opens up!"

She pushed the top of the egg back on its hinge. Inside, she discovered a circular bone from the rib cage of the little bird skeleton she had found while she was digging.

"What is this?" she asked, her voice shaking.

Colby took the bone out of the egg and held it up, and then he got down on his knee. "This is a proposal. Cassidy Phelps, will you marry me?" he asked, holding out the polished ring of bone. "I promise I'll get you a proper ring when I can."

"I don't want a proper ring, you damn fool. I will wear this bird bone 'til the day I die," she cried.

"Does that mean yes?" he asked.

"Yes! Now, shut up and kiss me," she replied to the cheers and hoots of their beloved circle of friends. There had been plenty of kissing since that impromptu Valentine's Day celebration, and the group knew there would be much more to come.

Colby slipped the circular skeleton ring on her finger and grinned as she held her hand out in admiration, just as if it were made of gold and diamond instead of bone.

"How did you make it?" she asked.

"I fashioned it from the scapulocoracoid, which is what the bird uses for flight. First, I dissected the coracoid from the sternum, and then I soaked it in vinegar to dissolve the calcium. When it was pliant, I joined the scapula together with thread until the bone dried in the ring shape," Colby said.

"Oh, good Lord, man. Just shut up and kiss me again," Cassi insisted with a huff.

After the high of Colby's surprise proposal, they couldn't imagine anything could bring them down. They went to their classes and, because it was happy week, they got to be hands-on with their course work. To date, the sabbatical participants had withstood 12 weeks of disappointments, threats, fear, monotony, and class warfare and were almost near the end of the sabbatical. They were confident they could withstand through the final week of the sabbatical. They were well prepared, and they were determined to endure to the end.

In Colby's class the following Saturday, true to her word, Professor Chen brought an assortment of deformed bones for them to analyze. Cassidy's group was outside digging, so Colby threw himself into studying a fibula with a large golf-ball shaped growth. He x-rayed it, extracted blood cells from the marrow, scratched the surface and examined the scrapings, and determined it was a malignant cancerous growth that had attached to the bone.

Professor Chen Mei exuberantly praised him for his observations and gave him another item to examine—a femur bent into a Z-shape. At a table across the room, he heard a thud as one of his classmates dropped a bone into a metal pan.

"Holy crap! What is this?" the man barked.

Colby looked over and saw him staring into the pan. Curious, he walked over to see what was so unusual. As he looked at the bone, he felt his hair stand up on the back of his neck, and his mouth became dry. He was lightheaded, and he realized he had stopped breathing. He had never expected to see anything like it.

"Hey, Carson," the man said, "want to trade? This is too gross for me."

Colby shook his head. "No. You work on what you're given. I have my own project," he said and walked stiffly back to his station.

When it was time for the class to end and break for dinner, the students covered their pans with cloths. The next day would be their last Sunday excursion, and then they would only have one week left of the sabbatical. Colby helped Professor Chen by collecting the trays and placing them in a neat row on the table against the wall.

He had kept an eye on the man who wanted to trade, and he knew where his pan was located. As he straightened the tools and aligned the pans, he positioned his back to the door camera and carefully slipped his hand beneath the cloth. He deposited a fragment of a bone he had palmed from another pan and moved his hand to the right. His fingers closed around the other object within. Certain that he was unobserved by both the camera and Professor Chen, he pulled the deformed bone out and stuck it under his shirt.

"All right, Professor. I think that's it. I'll see you on Monday. Thanks for a great week," he said as he walked toward the door.

"Thank you, Mr. Carson, for helping. You are my best student, and you give me apples every day. I see you Monday," she said with a toothy smile.

When he was directly under the door frame, in the one and only blind spot of the fisheye lens, he shifted the bone, pushing it farther down into his pants and wedging it beneath his belt. Then, he turned back into the classroom.

"Oops, forgot my lab coat. Here you go," he said as he removed the white coat and hung it on the portable coatrack. "Goodbye."

Cassidy was waiting for Colby near the elevators. When he approached, he told her he needed to make a stop at his room first and use the restroom. She shook her head and rolled her eyes comically.

"You have a thing about the bathroom, don't you?" she said.

He dashed into the bathroom and was back out in a matter of minutes, smiling, his backpack slung over one shoulder as they headed off to the 11th floor to meet Mitzie and Glenn for dinner.

"Colby, you didn't want to leave your backpack in your room?" Cassi asked.

"Oh! Yeah, I should have. Forgot. No big deal. I'll just carry it on our walk after dinner," he said, hitching it up higher on his shoulder.

The dinner was delicious, as usual, and afterwards, they had a delightful stroll on the path and talked about how much they enjoyed the week's activities. Colby congratulated himself on how well he was able to contribute to the conversations, knowing what lay in the hidden zippered compartment of his backpack: a bone with a skeletal anomaly ... from the hand of a small person ... a person with ectrodactyly.

CHAPTER TWENTY

Attrition

"The condition of alienation, of being asleep, of being unconscious, of being out of one's mind, is the condition of the normal man. Society highly values its normal man. It educates children to lose themselves and to become absurd, and thus to be normal."

~R.D. Laing,
Psychiatrist

THE LAST WEEK OF THE SABBATICAL approached, and there was an unusual mood coursing through the remaining award winners. Most of them were laissez-faire, having made it through on just the promise of the final stipend. Beyond the money, there was no joy in the experience, no jubilation at having completed the sabbatical at all. A few here and there still strove to rise above the mental and emotional warfare, but by and large, they were a forlorn, melancholy lot.

By way of courses, besides the ones that had already been combined, the others were virtually disbanded. Those courses that remained included Archaeology and Forensic Anthropology with eight members, Early Pioneers and Indigenous Natives with seven members, Literary Arts with nine members altogether, Culinary Arts with 11 members (owing to the fact that there was food involved), Performing Arts with six members, Visual Arts and Cartography with five, and the Immigrants—the combination of Africans, Asians, and Europeans—with 10 members in total. Out of the original 500 participants, only 56 remained. Nearly 90% of them had either left or been sent home since the first day of January.

Elizabeth Ford checked the numbers at the other Centers and noted with satisfaction that they were also near the goal of 10% remaining attendees. Among that 10% at each NFAEE hub, almost half had made commitments to accept jobs within the private sector or in universities.

As for the 5% remaining, the projection was that half of those would leave the teaching profession within three years. That left a meager 2.5% of the 3,000 person teaching force that had been recruited and abused with the mind control approaches used by the highly-acclaimed, yet fraudulent National Federation of Academic Excellent in Education Award—the devious front for a subversive organization whose goal was to destroy the best and brightest teachers in the United States in order to gain control of the impressionable minds of America's youth.

As Glenn and Colby had suspected, it was funded by a group, and not an individual. The group had no name, not wishing to identify themselves or take credit for their actions. They operated as a shadow conspiracy, remaining on the fringes to avoid detection. But they were terrorists, just the same.

The members had prominent standing among the highest levels of government, though not in the country's ultimate positions within the White House. They functioned well under the radar of prying eyes in the House and the Senate, although their leaders frequently rubbed elbows with the upper echelon of elected politicians who served the President and the American people.

They were doctors, lawyers, business owners, public servants, politicians, humanitarians, clergy, and even international figures. Behind the scenes, they enjoyed ties to unsavory organizations—drug cartels, organized crime, human sex traffickers, foreign espionage, digital hackers, and the like from which they received payoffs and kickbacks which funded the ersatz awards and stipends given out by the NFAEE, as well as for bribes used to entice the companies and institutions who offered the awardees well-paying jobs and scholarships. They were many, and they were powerful.

The group had operated unchecked for five years, siphoning away the choicest minds from their chosen educational fields. As the bogus award was given biannually—in January and in April—the result was nearly 6,000 teachers a year who either left the profession or became ineffectual. That America had a teaching shortage was largely due to the NFAEE's efforts and incredible success at breaking the spirits of these highly intelligent and extraordinarily creative men and women. It was terrorism from within, and it was working.

The plan was virtually foolproof in its simplicity: create discontent. Discontent turned into despondency; despondency led to decay. And decay was the ultimate goal: the decay of the American education system. However, a select few individuals surfaced among each year's awardees. These astute teachers rose above the mind control methods and figured out the plan. When that happened, other means had been devised to keep the group and its plan from being exposed.

Every participant fell into one or more of eight categories: *Exited* (which constituted those who left voluntarily), *Expelled* (those sent home because of real or contrived infractions), *Retiring* (teachers who had accrued enough years to leave education permanently), *Distracted* (those who either entered into romantic relationships or were offered lucrative employment), *Broken* (the ones who were no longer able to put up resistance and stayed for the stipends), *Adapted* (individuals who seemed to thrive even under the hardships), *Flagged* (participants who needed to be watched carefully), and *Aware* (the adroit ones who understood what was happening).

The *Adapted* and *Flagged* were pivotal. With the right pressure, they could move into the *Broken* category, but the *Aware* threatened the success of the plan, and a more permanent means had been devised to eliminate them. At the private ceremony in Washington D.C., in which the awardees who had finished the sabbatical were honored, presented with a plaque and a final $2,500 cash award, and subsequently appeared in newspaper photographs and televised clips, a public announcement was released which revealed that certain individuals (the Aware) were not in attendance because they had accepted prestigious positions with an American or overseas university, a company, or an organization and had already begun work.

To the rest of the country, those awardees had been given the American Dream, but the ugly truth was the *Aware* mysteriously went missing, along with their entire families, and were never heard from again.

Elizabeth Ford was responsible for identifying the category into which each participant fell. And the two uppermost on her radar as *Aware* at the Richmond Center were Carmine Wells and Paulette Jameson. Had she known better, she would have been alarmed to discover there were nine *Aware* in her own Richmond Center.

CHAPTER TWENTY-ONE
Aware

"There's a time for exposure; until then keep laboring in obscurity."
~Bernard Kelvin Clive.
Ghanaian author

COLBY CARSON WAS FULLY *AWARE*. With the discovery of the skeletal hand with ectrodactyly, he knew he was at risk, and though he didn't want to put her in danger, he had to confide in Cassidy.

He stopped frequently on their walk to kiss his fiancé, letting the others move along at their normal pace until they were a little distance away. It was not unusual, now that they had announced their engagement, for Colby and Cassidy to drift apart from them, so nobody gave it a second thought because Stella and Ken did the same thing.

The band of nine meandered along the path,

shifting positions and changing conversation partners like the ebb and flow of the tide, their pairings fluid as Mitzie and Glenn became Chester and Glenn, and Paulette and Carmine became a trio with Mitzie.

Colby pulled Cassidy into a dark spot and wrapped his arms around her, his mouth close to her ear. He kissed her ear, then whispered to her.

"Cassi, honey, I love you, and I don't want to scare you, so be cool, OK?" he murmured, feeling her body tense.

"What's up, Colby," she asked.

"I found something in my class last week, that day it was so warm outside, and you were outside doing a dig."

"OK. And why will it scare me?"

He pulled back and gazed into her shadowed face solemnly before he answered. "It was a hand, Cassi. A human hand."

"All right. I don't find that so frightening. Haven't you been working on human bones?"

"Not this kind. This hand was deformed."

She gave a self-conscious laugh. "Now, you know I'm not scary. I watch horror movies and read Stephen King. And I teach children, too."

"Baby, this is beyond Stephen King," he said.

She saw the grave expression on his face. "You better tell me a little more. I don't understand."

Colby took her face in his hands and gently kissed her cheek. "This hand had ectrodactyly," he whispered, "a thumb and two fingers."

Cassidy pulled back out of his grasp and stood stock still, shaking her head from side to side.

Colby nodded. "I'm serious, Cassi."

"Well, that doesn't mean anything. You said the professor was bringing in deformities." Her eyes were enormous as she sought to convince herself.

"Cassi, the condition occurs in one in 90,000. How many skeletal ectrodactyly hands do you think can be found in Richmond, Virginia that a group of teachers can have to chip away at?" he said with a gentle tone of voice.

"But Colby, are you saying that … Could it be … What are you saying exactly?" she stammered.

"I'm saying the lady from Georgia who studied archaeology here did not get a position to work in a New York university," he said.

Cassi's eyes overflowed, the tears spilling freely down her cheeks, and Colby folded her into his arms as she wept on his shoulder. Suddenly, she pulled away. Her face held a look of sheer terror.

"Her family!" she said in a hushed voice, "What about her family? They moved to New York to be with her! Don't they know?"

"I'm not so sure about that," Colby said, chewing the inside of his cheek before continuing. "You told me she never went back to Georgia, and her husband and two kids moved to be with her, and none of them ever came back or responded to texts or calls."

"Yes, we all decided they got involved with other affluent folks and didn't want to have anything to do with the rest of us. What are you getting at?"

"Cassi, honey. I'm thinking maybe they *aren't* living the dream in New York. I'm thinking they aren't living at all." He gazed at her sympathetically, trying to be sensitive about the implications.

"What in the hell does that mean, Colby?" she demanded. Her voice and demeanor had become hostile as she denied what she already suspected was the truth.

"Cassi, put it together. *I* have her hand, which I got from bones *my professor* gave *us* to experiment on. I don't believe it's a coincidence it ended up in my class. And if she went missing, her family would have to know, and they would have gone to the police and reported it. If she were d... um, no longer living, they would report it. There'd be an investigation. It would be in the news."

Cassidy shifted her eyes from his face, looking anywhere but at him. "There was no news. The family up and left. Never returned. No word from them for all these years," she muttered.

Colby stood silently; his heart broken for her.

As the pieces clicked into place, Cassidy shook violently. She reached for him, her hands grasping onto his shoulders to steady herself as her knees buckled.

"They have killed her whole family," she whispered, and then she wailed as she collapsed into his strong arms. "Oh Lord ... oh God ... oh sweet Baby Jesus!"

Colby pulled her face into his shoulder to muffle her cries, but Mitzie heard them and came running, followed by Glenn.

"Cass, Colby! What's wrong," she called, barely out of the light.

Colby put his arm around Cassidy's waist, carefully, but deliberately, moving her into the circle of light cast by the path lamp.

"Remember when she found that bird skeleton during her dig? Just now, she happened to step on a dead baby bird on the path. She got a little unhinged. She loves animals so," he explained in a loud voice.

Mitzie immediately put her arms around her friend and rocked her. "Shhh. Shhh. It's all right, Cass. It was already dead, so you didn't hurt it. It's OK. Come on. How about walk with me for a while," she said, and the two of them ventured down the path arm in arm.

Glenn fell in beside Colby and walked quietly through the light. When they got to the dark, he stopped and turned to his friend.

"What the hell, Colby? That was not from stepping on a dead bird. Fill me in, please," he said.

"I took a skeletal bone from my class last week," he said.

"OK. So, you're a thief, among other things. What's so bad about that?"

"It wasn't just any bone. It was a deformed hand like the one Cassidy said the woman that was offered the archaeology job in New York had. Two fingers, one thumb. Exactly how Cassi described the lady's hand, Glenn."

"Holy crap! Are you sure?"

"Positive."

"So that means ..."

"That means she's dead, and I believe she was murdered. I truly believe she and her whole family were killed because of something she knew, and *we* have been playing with their bones in my class," Colby said, his jaw tight. His mouth filled with saliva and he spit it out onto the path, hoping he wouldn't vomit.

"Son of a bitch! They were all murdered because, like us, that lady figured out what was going on. Is that what you're *not* saying?" Glenn asked.

"Yes. And that puts all nine of us in danger."

Glenn reflected on that knowledge a bit as he and Colby continued walking.

"... these womenfolk. They are all just so tenderhearted. My Iris is just like that. See a dead dog on the street, she's crying like it was her granny," he said in the light.

"I love that about her, though," Colby said.

"Sure. Don't we all? Just have lots of tissues everywhere when you two get married. And be prepared for her to go through a lot of crying jags before the wedding. Are you prepared?" Glenn asked as they moved into the dark.

"Very. I gave the hand to Chester to hide. He knows these grounds better than anyone. And I told him it needed to be in a dry place with lots of rocks in case they look for it with ground penetrating radar. He said he knew the very spot, and when the time comes to turn it over to the authorities—whoever that may be at this point—he knows exactly where to find it," Colby said.

"Good. Good. Think we can last the week?"

"I'm damn sure going to do my best. Six days. That's all we have to make is six days. I can do that in my sleep, I think," Colby laughed. "Iris really said that to you on your wedding day? That beats all I've ever heard, Glenn. I'm sure you'll be glad to get back home to her."

"Yes, I will. I'm not sure I'll finish out the rest of this year, though. Iris wants to visit kin folks in Georgia, somewhere near your neck of the woods, and I figure I'll take her around to do it. May not even come back next fall. I don't really know. Have to see," Glenn said as they made their way through the puddle of light.

Way up ahead of them on the path, Chester followed along behind Carmine and Paulette, who had their heads together whispering. He knew what they were discussing, and every now and then, Carmine would shake her head vigorously. Paulette clasped her hand and soothed her. He could hear it in her tone of voice although he could not make out her words. That was good. Chester had an incredible sense of hearing. And if he couldn't understand what they were saying, the NFAEE Center listeners couldn't either.

Chester was not a person who hated, but he came close with whoever was running this shameful place. They were evil people, worse than any he had ever known, and he had known some horrible ones. But the things these did he could hardly believe.

*   *   *

Chester did not go on the Sunday outing. He had other work to do. He told the girls he wanted to finish up some measurements for his maps, but he encouraged them to go on without him. They were disappointed, but the trip that day promised to be short, so they would see him shortly after lunch.

During the Saturday night walk, Colby had given him the woman's deformed claw hand and told him what he believed it meant—a whole family murdered. The next morning, Chester hid the gruesome item in the inside pocket of his jacket as he traversed the grounds, making sketches in his book. There were others who decided to forego the day's outing, and they casually walked the path or sat chatting on the benches, soaking up the sun. He smiled and greeted them as he scoured the land for a place to lay the bone to rest. Passing the low place where the water ran into a little gully, he saw what he had been searching for.

Chester made some more sketches as he ran his survey wheel along the ground, marking off the distances. Then, he appeared to stumble and fall on his hands and knees. Pushing his hands out in front of him, he awkwardly got to his feet and brushed off his knees. A guide came running over to check on him, but he smiled and told the young man he was fine, just a little dirty.

Chester picked up his fallen notepad and pencil and put them in his pocket. Taking his land measuring wheel by the handle, he rolled it in the opposite direction and continued taking measurements. When he looked back, it was impossible to distinguish the white skeletal hand that had been pushed in among the bleached rocks of roughly the same size, shape, and color.

When the vans returned, and after the Sunday night dinner, the band of nine made their customary journey around the path.

Before they left for their walk, Paulette had stopped at Chester's room and had given him a plastic bag with handwritten notes, newspaper clippings, and a composition book inside and asked him to find a place to bury it. Chester knew the contents would potentially get all of them hurt or even killed if Colby's suspicions were correct, so he was very careful to hide the bag in a dark area well off the path beneath the recently disturbed earth where a shrub had been planted. He was also careful to stay out of the view of the solar light surveillance devices which dotted the areas alongside the path. He emerged into the light and rested his hands on his knees, for all intents and purposes an old man with joint pain. Up ahead, the girls waited on him, showing concern for his apparent arthritis.

Chester Osceola, like the rest of the band of nine, was being careful to stay undetected for the last few days of the sabbatical. *Endure and win. Endure and win.*

CHAPTER TWENTY-TWO
Week 13

"I know enough of the world now to have almost lost the capacity of being much surprised by anything."
~Charles Dickens,
David Copperfield

WHEN COLBY ENTERED HIS CLASSROOM that Monday, he expected to see Professor Chen standing at the podium. Instead, she was seated at a table, her mouth stretched into a cheerful grin. The metal trays he had carefully lined up were exactly as he left them on the tables, and the equipment was ready for the students to pick up where they left off.

"Welcome back! I hope you all had a very good Sunday. Please, find your sample and continue where you left off," she said, indicating the covered pans with a wave of her hand.

Likewise, and perhaps even more surprising,

Constance Wright was dressed in her field clothes. She greeted her four remaining sabbatical students with a perfunctory nod.

"I do hope you have remembered to wear your field clothing and bring your gear. If you have not, please return to your rooms quickly and meet me outside. We shall be going back into the grid to dig, and I have surprises for you, so don't waste any time," she said with a broad grin. "And bring your telephones and cameras if you'd care to, so you may take photographs of the work you have done on the dig site."

Having thought it would be sad week, Cassidy was not prepared, nor were the other three students, so they all rushed from the classroom to redress and get their gear. She gave Colby a toothy, albeit forced, smile and a wave as she left.

Colby was delighted. There were only four students left in his class, and that meant he would likely not have to share the specialized equipment with the others, who were simply marking out their time. He grabbed his lab coat from the coatrack, and then he walked to the table and selected the tray with the specimen he had been working on that past Saturday—the Z-shaped femur bone.

He was just removing the cloth and arranging his tools when Bart, the one who had been given the ectrodactyly hand, slammed his fist down on his specimen tray.

"All right, Carson, give it back," he shouted.

"Give what back?" Colby asked.

"Give me back my creepy claw hand. I know you took it," Bart accused.

"Hey, I don't have your claw hand. I told you before, work on what you're given. I've got a femur that I started on last week," Colby said.

Bart angrily stomped to Colby's station. "I want my damn claw, now give it up," he demanded.

"I told you, I don't have it," Colby exclaimed. "Here, look in my tray. See? Not there."

Bart lumbered over to the other two students and checked their pans. "Who the hell got my hand? You, Nakamura?" he accused.

Tom Nakamura, a slightly built Japanese man, regarded Bart fearfully. "I do not have yours. I have only mine. Please, look for yourself," he said.

"That leaves you, Audrey," Bart said to a chubby blond woman in blue jeans and a sweatshirt. "Gimme my hand back, bitch."

Audrey backed away from her table in alarm as Bart upended her pan and looked under the cloth. Then, he circled back around to Colby. "Give. It. Back," he threatened, holding his right fist poised in the air.

Colby knew better than to engage; fighting would get him thrown out along with Bart. He steeled himself for the punch, but it never came. With uncanny swiftness, Professor Chen came up and swiped Bart's feet out from under him. When he landed on the floor, she raised her arm and brought her elbow down in the middle of his abdomen. Bart made a sickening sound like a balloon with air escaping and rolled over to his side in a fetal position. Professor Chen got to her feet just as two of the burlier guides entered the room.

"You had a fight, Professor? We will take them away now," the dark-skinned guide said.

"You take this man," she said, pointing to Bart on the floor. Then she pointed at Colby. "This man you will leave. He did not fight."

"Um, but we're supposed to take out anyone who was involved in a fight. That includes both of them," the guide said as he tentatively approached Colby and Bart.

"I have said you take the one and leave the other," Professor Chen said, putting herself between the guides and Colby.

"But we have to ..." he began.

Professor Chen gave him an icy look, her already tiny eyes completely disappearing into slits.

"Stop talking," she warned. "I have said you will *not*. I am in control of this class. You may make a phone call to Dr. Ford. You tell her I say, 'ask Chen Xio.' That should be sufficient."

The guide retreated to the doorway and pulled out his cell phone, leaving the other guide in the room. He spoke in low tones and then abruptly ended the phone call.

"We will take that one," he said, indicating Bart, still grunting on the floor.

The guides got Bart to his feet and took him out the door. Professor Chen looked at her three remaining students and grinned. "We get back to work now. Yes, yes. Much to do and only five more days to do it," she said, suppressing a big smile as her three students clapped in appreciation.

"Though she be little, she be fierce," Colby said with a smirk.

The professor walked over to Colby and stood beside him. "Yes, Appleseed. I am little, and I am fierce. I like that very much," she agreed. "But somewhere is a sample missing. What do you think has happened to it?"

Colby shook his head, shrugging his shoulders. "I don't know, professor. Do you think maybe Bart took it as a souvenir, thinking we wouldn't be working on the bones this week?"

Professor Chen considered for a moment, and then she nodded. "I think that is a possibility, Mr. Carson. His room will be searched, and the grounds will be searched. The hand will be found. Now, what can you tell me about the bone you are working on?"

Colby swallowed and steeled himself, hoping his voice didn't quiver and betray his disquiet. He was fairly certain of the bone's origin, but he forced himself to compartmentalize his suspicions and appear detached.

"So far, I can tell you, because of its length, it is the femur of a pre-pubescent male, perhaps 10 or 11 years of age. It was surgically disarticulated at the hip and the tibia because neither the ball-and-socket nor the kneecap are intact, but there is no cracking at the joints. The leg bone did not grow this way, and there is no remodeling on it, so it was not broken and then healed in this position."

"Oh, those are very good observations. So, what makes it in this Z shape?" she asked, eyes wide, eyebrows raised.

"My opinion?"

"Yes, yes. Give your *professional* opinion," she insisted.

"All right. My professional opinion is that once the bone was removed from the rest of the torso, it was submerged for a long period of time in an acid-based solution, which dissolved the calcium, leaving the soft bone tissue. Then, by means of a great deal of strength and clamps—because I noticed there are some minute scratches on the bends—it was left to dry until the solution evaporated and the bone dried out, leaving it hardened into the shape of a Z."

Professor Chen clapped her hands and slapped Colby on the back several times. "You *are* Dr. Bones! You are my best student I ever had. I am so proud and honored to have been your instructor." She gave Colby a slight bow, reached into her pocket, and removed a business card which she pressed into his palm. "This is a man who is a friend of mine. Please call him. He will have a job for you to train as a forensic anthropologist. You will be a *real* Dr. Bones. Dr. Bones Carson."

Mitzie, Glenn, and Stella were just as surprised when they entered their class. Standing in front of the room were their instructors, Mikhail Melnyk and Berta Strauss, and another man and woman. The man—obviously Native American—stepped forward.

"Good day. My name is Henry Smith, and I am a member of the Pamunkey Indian tribe. I live on the Pamunkey Indian Reservation here in Virginia. I will be speaking to you today, and I have brought you some examples of the 'blackware' pottery that is made by my people. I have been told that I am descended from Captain John Smith. Perhaps you know him from the story about Pocahontas and the treaty they brought about. If I am not, it is no matter, as I am still Pamunkey," he said, issuing forth a joyful laugh.

The woman who spoke to them was dressed in a long-sleeved high-necked blouse, a simple homespun floor length shirt, and a long white apron that was devoid of frills or ruffles. She had short worn leather boots on her feet and a gingham bonnet tied beneath her chin. She pushed the bonnet back off her face and let it fall onto her back.

"My name is Samantha Caroline Mason, and I am descended from Colonel George Mason, who settled Norfolk, Virginia," she said with a curtsey.

Mitzie looked at Stella's face and saw her eyes welling up. She reached over and squeezed her hand as the woman spoke again.

"Now, before you ask about where to get the

patterns for my clothing, let me tell you that I did not make these clothes; they have been passed down through many generations of women in my family. My grandmother many times removed wore this very outfit when she traveled with her family on a covered wagon. I am not a pioneer, but I am certainly descended from them. Who is in the Pioneer class? You three women? Wonderful! Today, we will be going outside to cook from a tripod over an open fire in cast iron pots. I hope you brought your muscles with you," she said, walking toward the door with the three women like little ducklings in a line behind her.

Mitzie hoped that all the classes would be as enjoyable this week. Though she relished talking with Henry Smith, she was anxious to meet the others at lunch and find out about their day.

At noon, because there were only 54 participants left, everyone ate together on the 5th floor. Mitzie, Glenn, and Stella hurried to the elevators. Mitzie failed to notice that she rushed into a full elevator until it reached their floor. Glenn noticed, but he thought it wise not to mention until she got into the corridor and it was too late to get claustrophobic. They entered the room and were met by Colby, who wore a very serious face.

"What's wrong, Colby?" Mitzie asked.

"Paulette didn't come to her class. Carmine is frantic. She and Chester have gone to Paulette's room to check on her."

"What should we do?" Mitzie was wide-eyed.

"We go ahead and eat lunch as usual, dear," Glenn said, leading her by the elbow to the buffet line. "Act naturally, Mitzie. We don't know what's happened. It's possible she is not feeling well. Get some food and let's sit down. No sense in you getting all upset."

"You're right. I'm just on edge. But I am hungry. I think I'll have something cooked for me. A panini! That's what I'll have. Meet you at the table," she said, heading off to speak to one of the chefs in tall paper hats.

The band of nine, which was now just six, sat at the table together and discussed the fact that they had been granted two happy weeks in a row. Not only that, the speakers and activities were even better than those they had experienced during any of the other happy weeks. Colby told them about the near fight with Bart and the guides who came to take them away.

"Yeah, he accused me of taking his bone and tried to punch me out. Professor Chen knocked him off his feet and elbowed him in the belly. The guides arrived at the door only seconds later. She wouldn't let them take me," he said.

"My Lord, Colby," Cassidy exclaimed, "You were almost sent home." She clung to his arm.

"Not in the professor's game plan. She wants me to stay. She gave me a guy's name to call for a job," he said, showing the business card.

"Are you considering it?" Glenn asked.

"Aw, hell no," he said with a snort. "Why

would I do that? Nope, I'm just trying to survive. Strange thing, though. She dropped a name. Somebody Chinese. When the guide called to find out what to do, he backed off me like I was contagious. Whoever she mentioned must've been somebody important."

They continued eating lunch, chatting happily. The only blot on the meal was the absence of Paulette. They ate and talked and waited for word. Soon, Chester came back, his arm around a distraught Carmine. He sat her down and went through the line to get them both a plate of food.

"Carmine," Cassidy said, "tell us what's going on with Paulette."

"I don't know," Carmine said. "She didn't come to class, and I don't have a key, and she wouldn't answer the door. I don't know if she's inside or gone or what!"

"Has anything happened to make you suspect she was going to leave?" Colby asked.

Carmine looked uncomfortable. She checked around the table to see if there were any people within earshot. Seeing that they were reasonably isolated, she leaned forward and pretended to take a bite of the sandwich Chester brought her.

"Last night we were arguing. Paulette wrote an article for the newspaper. She was determined to type it up and email it. It had information about the floors, and the populations, and the stipends, and the rotating happy-sad schedule, and some things she had found in the old newspaper articles about missing people. She had so much damning information in that article. If the newspapers got hold of it, they would investigate the NFAEE, which was OK with me, but if the NFAEE got it, I was scared they'd send her home," She struggled to swallow the bit of sandwich.

Colby slowly blew out his breath. "Whew, that's chancy. She's a toughie. I didn't realize she had that kind of strength and resolve," he admitted.

"That's not all," Chester said. "She had me bury a plastic bag on the grounds. Inside she had a notebook with all the whole story and the newspaper clippings. She said that was her insurance policy if she got caught."

"Well, that's a little comforting," Cassidy said.

"Not really," Carmine interjected. "She was going to email her story to the paper today. I told her not to, and she said she would wait. But I think she did send it after all."

"What makes you think she did, Carmine?" Stella asked gently. "Is there more?"

Huge tears fell from Carmine's eyes and landed on the table. She hastily brushed them away with her napkin while making it look as though she was wiping her mouth.

"Everybody, please continue eating," Cassidy said, scooping up a forkful of macaroni and cheese. "Keep up appearances. Remember, we are watched even if they can't hear us. Tell us what else you know, Carmine."

"Well, you know she gave me that magnet set with all the words. Every night before she left my room, she'd leave me a message on the metal tray propped against my bathroom mirror, so I'd see it first thing in the morning. It was usually something like *'have a good day,'* or *'see you in class'* or something similar. This morning, the message was different. It felt like a good-bye," she said.

"What was the message, Carmine? Do you mind telling us?" Mitzie took a sip of orange soda.

"Yes," Carmine said with a trembling voice, "She wrote, *'You are my winter suddenness—a glass of red wine spilt across a white tablecloth.'* It's a line from a poem by John J. Geddes that I read to her."

The group at the table was silent, not knowing how to address the next question. Mitzie, being closer to the girls than the others, broke the silence.

"Carmine, is Paulette your lover?" she asked.

Carmine smiled beautifully and shook her head slowly from side to side.

"No, but that doesn't mean we don't love one another. I know she wanted us to be more, but she never forced the issue. Paulette understands I'm straight, but I truly love her as my dearest friend." Carmine's voice dropped to barely a whisper.

Cassidy got up from her seat and approached a female guide who was standing across the room. The guide followed her back to the table.

"Hello, Miss. I am Antoinette. I see that you are upset. How can I help you?" the guide said.

"Her friend did not come to class, and she's terribly worried she may be ill. Can you please find out if something is wrong with her? Carmine can go with you to the room," Cassidy said.

"And so will I." Stella rose from her seat. "I have a stew cooking in my pot outside and it won't be ready to check for another hour. I'll go with Carmine. Don't worry, love," she said, noting the panic on Ken's face. "We'll be back in our classes as soon as we check on Paulette." And with that, the three women left the dining room.

Having no reason to hang around and be late for their classes, the others disbanded and went their separate ways.

When Stella returned from Paulette's room and after checking on her pot of stew, she walked directly over to Mitzie and Glenn's table and sat down. Her face was pale, and it was obvious she had been crying. Mitzie held her hand until they were dismissed from class.

"Let's go up to my room before dinner, Stella, and get freshened up. Glenn, will you let Colby and Cass know, please?" Mitzie said.

Glenn nodded and tapped the watch strapped to his ankle two times. When they got to Mitzie's room, Colby and Cassidy were waiting for them.

"Stella?" Cassidy said.

"Paulette's gone. Her room's cleaned out. That's all we know. We took Carmine back to her room. She laid down on her bed and cried herself to sleep. Chester stayed in the room with her." She searched the corridor beyond them with wild eyes. "Has anybody seen Ken?" she cried, her voice shrill.

"Right behind you, doll," Ken said.

Stella whirled and threw her arms around him.

"Ha," he barked. "I should sneak up on you more often. Let's have dinner folks, and then we need a nice walk outside. I think that will make everybody feel better. Come on Stella, let's get some food in you."

Dinner conversation was sparse. Chester and Carmine did not come down to eat, and Mitzie worried they would be hungry. Glenn got two plates from the buffet and filled them with sandwiches, fruit, and chocolate cake. "Women always say chocolate cake makes them feel better," he stated with a shrug.

On their way to the lobby, they took a detour to Carmine's room and tapped on the door. Chester answered and gratefully accepted the plates. Carmine was still asleep, and he intended to stay with her all evening. Overnight sleepovers were not against the guidelines, so he figured it was safer for them to be together, just in case. Before they left, Colby noticed Chester's modeling clay relief map on the desk.

"She likes it," Chester said simply.

There was not much talk on the night stroll. The two couples clung to each other, and Glenn and Mitzie walked behind them talking to Iris and Phillip on their cell phones the entire time. After a few minutes, they returned to the building and went to their separate rooms until morning.

CHAPTER TWENTY-THREE
Final Eliminations

"Intellectual growth should commence at birth and cease only at death."
~ Albert Einstein,
German Theoretical Physicist

PAULETTE'S BODY WAS REMOVED late that night as the remaining participants slept. Chester Osceola, sitting at the picture window in Carmine's 7th floor room overlooking the side entrance to the building, saw the headlights as the long dark vehicle pulled up. His vision was as acute as his hearing, and he recognized the familiar shape of a hearse. The driver opened the back, and two male guides appeared from the building, carrying a small person between them. As they unceremoniously deposited the body into the hearse, the overhead light caught the reflective chevrons on her white tennis shoes. Chester bowed his head and allowed the tears to fall.

* * *

In the command center, Elizabeth Ford and Ronald Bowry stood together talking to Ashley Lawrence. They were all tense, their lips pressed tightly together in between conversation.

"I thought we might get through this session without having any *Eliminated*," Bowry said.

"No matter," Elizabeth replied with a dismissive flip of her hand. "Besides, Dr. Chen needs more samples for the next session."

Bowry pressed his lips together and nodded in agreement. "That woman does like her bones."

Elizabeth consulted her chart and checked off Paulette's final status. In addition to the other eight categories of participants, there was a ninth category—the title which came after *Aware*. *Eliminated*. It meant exactly what it suggested. Failing to turn an *Aware* person by means of fear, compliance, or promise of a new job, the *Aware* person became a serious risk. Those who didn't succumb to intimidation or payoffs were subject to crossing the line and were flagged to be *Eliminated*. Paulette Jameson crossed that line, and for that reason, she was *Eliminated*.

On day one, while they were in their first class, all participant cell phones and computers had been hacked, so every keystroke, every conversation, every text was available for monitoring. When Paulette sent the email, the command center registered a warning, and Ashley viewed the correspondence. She notified Elizabeth, who promptly called the editor (a longtime supporter of the NFAEE) and informed him of the breech. He deleted it from his home computer, which was linked to his newspaper network, and the emailed exposé vanished.

Paulette was awakened early and brought to the command center before breakfast. There, she was sternly questioned by Ronald Bowry, punctuated by frequent vicious slaps to the face by Elizabeth Ford. Bravely refusing to implicate anyone else in her band of friends, she swore that she had acted alone, not even informing her closest friend Carmine.

While the interrogation was being conducted and the morning session of classes had begun, guides were dispatched to Paulette's room to clean it out and bring everything to command. They sorted through her possessions and found no other items of interest, other than her computer and cell phone which reflected that she had neither called nor texted her story to Carmine, Chester, or the other friends, and the exposé email had not been forwarded to additional news media.

After offering one last chance at redemption if she gave up any co-conspirators, Elizabeth smiled and spoke quietly to the young woman.

"All right, Miss Jameson. I can see that you were overly zealous in reporting the things you imagined were taking place here. We have decided you are no longer a threat, so we are going to lift that flag," she purred with a convincing expression. "Ashley, sweetheart?"

At that signal, the wholesome Ashley Lawrence stepped forward and stood behind Paulette. With surprising quickness and clinical detachment, she pushed the girl's head forward, stabbed a needle into the back of her neck, and injected a bolus of air into the basilar artery. The arterial air embolism traveled to the brain relatively quickly, and Paulette Jameson suffered a fatal stroke.

She was kept in the refrigerated cooler in the kitchen until that evening when the coroner (another longtime friend of the NFAEE) arrived and removed her, as Chester Osceola watched from Carmine's window.

* * *

The next morning, while their friends were enjoying the first part of their classes, Carmine Wells accompanied Chester Osceola to his 2nd floor room where he packed up his meager belongings. Then, they returned to her room on the 7th floor, packed up her things, and waited for the lunch hour to arrive to say farewell to their friends of the last three months.

* * *

In the command center, Elizabeth changed their status to *Exited*, pending their departure from the NFAEE Center.

* * *

Mitzie Galloway was approached by the new guest speaker of the class, a Bureau of Indian

Education representative, who offered her a position in the administration at the Miccosukee Indian School in Miami, Florida for a good deal more than she made in Jefferson County.

"But I'm not Indian," she explained, flustered and honored at the same time.

"Yes, but your husband and children are Creek, so you are affiliated. We do not seek just Indians for our positions," he said, "we seek upward thinking and creative people who can provide a better education for our people," he said.

She told him she would consider it, and she kept his card, but she knew she would decline.

Glenn Harding was also approached and offered a position on the district level in Cherokee, North Carolina. He would be overseeing education in the elementary, middle, and high schools. He took the man's card, having no intention of accepting, but he told him he would talk it over with his wife Iris.

On the command center computer, their flags were removed, and their statuses were officially changed to *Distracted.*

Colby Carson's designation had already been upgraded to *Distracted* after Professor Chen arranged for his job offer to obtain his doctorate degree and train as a forensic anthropologist, though they had no way of knowing he would never accept the position.

Cassidy Phelps was offered a full university scholarship, conveniently located in the same city as Colby's job offer. She was free to pursue archaeology at the PhD level and promised a position in the school as a professor. She said she'd consider it, but she lied. Her status was upgraded to *Distracted*, too.

Of the 53 remaining awardees, the ones whose statuses were *Flagged* or *Adapted* were offered positions in their areas of interest which were too good to pass up. Most of them accepted and were upgraded to *Distracted*. Those who did not accept were reevaluated. If their being *Adapted* was deemed to be benign and it was determined they were simply waiting to receive the last stipend, their flags were removed. If they seemed to be moving toward becoming *Aware*, they were bated into breaking a guideline so they could be *Expelled*. The *Broken*, *Distracted, Retiring,* and *Exited* were considered no threat. Paulette Jameson remained the only participant *Eliminated* from the current sabbatical at the Lower Eastern NFAEE Center.

*   *   *

In the other NFAEE Centers across the nation, the same process was followed. Though Ronald Bowry and Elizabeth Ford oversaw all the Centers, each place had its own "Ashley Lawrence"— an "Enforcer" who performed the procedure to render participants *Eliminated*. For this sabbatical session, a total of nine persons had been *Eliminated* across the country, including Paulette Jameson. It was a good year, and the NFAEE was proud to have the fewest *Eliminated* thus far in its five years of operation.

*   *   *

When their lunchtime arrived, Chester and Carmine came in to sit and eat with their comrades for the last time. They had both decided not to finish out the sabbatical and planned to go home before the ceremony, but for different reasons. Carmine was heartbroken that her dearest friend had decided to leave without even telling her "goodbye." Feeling she did not object strongly enough when Paulette insisted on exposing the NFAEE, she assumed it was her fault the girl ran away.

Chester, on the other hand, knew the truth but had yet to inform Carmine. He intended to tell her much later.

"Carmine has asked me to come live with her family in St. Augustine. I will do this. It is still close enough to Holopaw to visit my loved ones, but this young one needs me now. I am happy in my decision to go with her," he said.

"We'll miss you, Chester, but I'm glad you and Carmine will be together," Mitzie told him.

"If you don't mind hurrying up, we have some things in my room we want to give each of you before we go," Carmine said, putting on a cheerful smile in spite of her sorrow.

The band of eight finished their meals quickly and made their way up to Carmine's 7th floor room. Dutifully aware of the proximity of her room to the elevator surveillance, they stood in a half circle outside the door, their backs shielding their faces to keep the watchers from lip reading.

"This is for you, Ken and Stella," Chester said, giving Ken the surveyor's measuring wheel. "I think you two can use this tool to help you build your small cabin in the woods."

"And for you, Glenn, I am giving you my notes and sketches. You are very good at puzzles and with numbers. I think you will find this helpful when you go to solve the puzzle of this place." Chester handed Glenn several small notebooks and deliberately tapped them.

"Colby, I want you to have this clay map. It is exactly accurate on a ⅛-inch scale. By looking at it and imagining yourself a tiny pin within it, you can see everything that is around this building. Use it well to find what you seek." He handed Colby the modeling clay relief map.

"For you, Cassidy, as you will be Colby's mate, I will give you the paper map I used to create the clay one. It is arranged in grids just like you have learned to do in your archaeology course, and everything is marked. Apply that knowledge, and you can pinpoint locations, too. Combine the two together, just as you and Colby will be together," Chester said, giving her a rolled-up blueprint of the NFAEE grounds.

"To you, Mitzie, I give my personal addresses and telephone numbers," he said, handing her a worn black book the size of an index card. "Seminole and Creek were once one, so some of the names in here may be your husband's people. You and your family will always have an invitation to call or visit them."

Mitzie gratefully accepted the small book, clasping it to her chest reverently.

"I have nothing else to give to you all except my great affection and thanks for having met you and been called your friend." He hugged the ladies tightly and kissed their cheeks. "May the Master of Breath keep you safe in all you do."

Chester's words and gifts left more than a few tears. And then Carmine spoke to them.

"I don't have anything for you men, but I want you to know that you're the best guys a girl could ever know, and I'll miss you. I want you to text me and come visit if you can, so I'm giving you my cell phone number and my home address. Please don't forget us," she said.

"Now ladies, I do have something for each of you, Stella, I want you to take lots of pictures of your cabin and everything you build out there, and your dog, and Ken, too," she laughed. "I want to give you this. It's poems that I read to you guys when we visited each night. When you're out there in the woods, read them to Ken by the fireside. Sometimes the most cherished memories come from hearing the written word read aloud." She gave Stella a thick book of poetry and several notebooks filled with her original poems. Stella broke down into tears as she cradled them in her arms.

"Ms. Cassidy Phelps," Carmine said, taking a deep breath. "When I think of books, I think of you, so here's a little something I picked up from the museum on our first outing. I think it'll be better for you than for me." She held out a small box. Inside was a gold filigree brooch in the shape of an open book, with colored Austrian crystals dotting the pages. "It's not a Fabergé egg, but I think it'll match your necklace well enough."

Cassidy sucked in her breath, and then she threw her arms around Carmine. "You keep on writing poetry, Carmine. You have a God-given gift, and I love you," she said.

Carmine then turned to Mitzie, her eyes overflowing. "Mitzie, you've been a good friend to both Paulette and me. You knew she was special, but you never judged her or me either. Whenever she feels like she can return my phone calls, I know she'll want to talk to you and say so herself. Until then, I want you to remember us both. I got this at that first outing, too. I was going to give it to Paulette for her birthday, but I'm sure she won't mind if I give it to you instead." She held out the tiny box and placed it in Mitzie's hand. "I know you cussed someone out that night, and I sure didn't want you to cuss me out, but anyway, this is for you."

Mitzie hesitantly opened the box, and then she threw her hand up to her mouth, her eyes wide.

"What is it, Mitzie?" Cassidy asked.

"Oh, Carmine, No. I can't accept this. It's too much," Mitzie objected.

"Oh, yes you will, but keep it in your pocket until you leave this hateful place," Carmine said.

Cassidy's curiosity was killing her, so she moved Colby aside and stole a look inside the box. Stifling a squeal, she looked back and forth between the box and Mitzie's face, her mouth hanging open.

"For God's sake, what is it, dear?" Glenn asked, trying to get a look at the gift.

Mitzie and Cassidy spoke in a hushed tone at the same time. "It's a Persian turquoise ring!"

The women gathered around and exchanged embraces and kisses. In the meantime, the men collected all the luggage and started walking toward the elevators. They all rode down together and went out the door into the gardens, down the path toward a waiting cab. When they were almost to the gate, Chester stopped in a spot between the overhead path lights that would be dark at nighttime. He put his arms around Colby in a final hug and whispered in his ear. Colby flinched, and then he stood up ramrod straight and waved as the two friends entered a waiting taxi.

The alliance of six slowly walked the path back toward the building. Colby stopped in a safe place and held Cassidy tightly, kissed her, and continued to keep her in his strong embrace as he put his lips to her ear.

"Paulette is dead. Chester saw them take her body away last night. Make no noise. This is serious. Go hug Mitzie and tell her to show no emotion, and then hug Stella. We can't keep this a secret, Cassi. We are all in great danger."

Cassidy wiped the tears from her cheeks and graced him with a brave, beautiful smile. Then she went to Mitzie and Stella in turn. Each woman accepted the news with strength and understanding of the situation.

Colby strolled up to Glenn and Ken and shared the sad news with them. They knew the rules of the game had changed. The stakes were higher, but they were armed with knowledge, fierce resolve, and Chester's gifts.

That night, when the sun went down and they were cloaked in darkness, they made their plans to stay alive, to find what Chester had hidden for them, to endure and win the evil sabbatical directive.

CHAPTER TWENTY-FOUR
The Last Day and Night

"Our rapidly moving, information-based society badly needs people who know how to find facts rather than memorize them, and who know how to cope with change in creative ways. You don't learn those things in school."
~ Wendy Priesnitz,
Canadian Alternative Education Advocate

COLBY ENTERED HIS CLASS on the last Saturday and saw Professor Chen talking with two guides who were wearing jeans, gloves, and sturdy boots in place of their usual navy suits. She waved at Colby and beckoned him over.

"Mr. Carson, today we will work outdoors with the GPR equipment," she said.

"That's cool. What are we looking for?" he asked. His voice was calm, but his stomach was not.

"We are seeking the NFAEE Center property

that was stolen. You know what I mean ... the deformed hand that Bart took from our classroom."

"Oh, you didn't find it, then?" His face was bland, his tone expressionless.

"We searched his room and his belongings before he left. No hand. What do you think he might have done with it?"

"I ... have no idea, Professor, unless he tossed it in the trash," he said.

"No, no. I think he hid it somewhere on the grounds. So, today, you will lead the hunt for the hand," she said with a grin. "That sounds like a good title for a movie. Yes, yes. 'Dr. Bones hunts for the hand.' Yes?" She giggled.

"Sure thing. It's my pleasure," he replied.

Colby followed the two guides out the door and into the elevator. "So, where's the equipment?" he asked a guide as they descended to the first floor.

"It's outside already"

"You guys ever used one before?"

They shook their heads.

"Super. This should be fun," he said as he went through the revolving doors.

Just off the path outside the door stood the bright yellow Utility Location GPR. It was a state-of-the-art ground penetrating radar. It looked like a souped-up self-propelled lawnmower with four heavy-duty wheels and a computer tablet attached to the handle. The monitor displayed a vertical slice of the ground that was made visible by means of radio waves. The high frequency radio waves were emitted in pulses and imaged objects in the subsurface by transmitting echoes of the reflections of materials hit with the waves to the monitor in picture form.

Colby had not operated the machine before, but he had read all about it in his texts. Extrapolating written information to practical application came easily for him. It was one of the reasons he was originally flagged by Elizabeth Ford.

"All righty, let's get this thing going," he said, powering up the machine.

Colby began walking in a linear path, sending the radio waves deep into the ground. The two guides flanked him on either side, their eyes darting back and forth from the path ahead to the computer screen, though they didn't know what they were seeing.

He stopped every few feet, checked his monitor, and entered surface flags and subsurface interpretations into the computer. As he walked, he could see Professor Chen sitting on a bench in one of the seating areas, monitoring the data with the WiFi connection on her cellphone, actively interpreting the data as he displayed it. To his left, he saw Cassidy with her instructor and remaining three classmates digging in the gridded section of the grounds. She waved tersely and continued digging.

He scanned the surrounding area for the greater part of the morning, stopping for a short break, during which Professor Chen brought him a soda and a bag of corn chips and patted him on the back. He had surveyed the outer perimeter and most of the interior of the gardens. He was nearing the center rock pile in which Chester had hidden the hand. Wiping his face with his shirt sleeve, he advanced toward the pile.

The Professor walked up alongside him as he carefully rolled the GPR over the rocks. She was holding three round stones slightly smaller than grapefruits, which she laid to the side of the rock pit. She put her hand on Colby's arm and made him wait as she stared into the monitor. She made a few adjustments to the data and interpreted the results.

"Go back over this section, Mr. Carson," she directed, pointing to the pile of rounded stones.

Colby obediently turned the machine and slowly pushed it over the spot she indicated.

"Stop. Let me look closer," she said, prodding the stones with a small trowel.

Colby's heart thumped heavily in his chest as he watched her. She picked up the uppermost stones and carefully cleared them away.

"Here. What is here?" she said.

He moved the GPR over the area, and she stared at the screen. Then, she bent down, dug into the dirt, and carefully removed a small, fist-sized round white object.

"Ah ha!" she exclaimed, holding the object aloft. "It is what I thought." She tossed it to Colby, who caught it awkwardly.

"Here you are, Mr. Bones. You can keep this baseball to take home. I think some little boy is very sorry to throw this over our fence. Yes? Come, it is time for lunch. I think we will not find the hand on our grounds. You did well with the GPR. I think you will be a great forensic anthropologist." She patted him on the back and walked back to the building.

*   *   *

Colby Carson entered the 5th floor dining room and sat at the table. Cassidy had fixed him a tray of his favorite lunch items, and it was waiting for him. He looked around at the anxious faces.

"Well?" Ken said.

"Well … it was a ball … literally." He reached into his pants pocket and withdrew the baseball, chuckling.

"My Lord, you scare me to death sometimes," Cassidy said. "Eat your lunch, you crazy man."

He kissed her cheek and took a bite of his double cheeseburger. "Oh heavenly. Got something for me, Glenn?" he asked as he chewed.

Glenn leaned back. Between his legs on the floor was Colby's backpack. "Think maybe I should hang on to it for the rest of the day in case she does a search in the classroom?"

"Not a bad idea. Thanks," Colby said.

"I sure do hate that the band's breaking up tomorrow. We've had a helluva time," Glenn said.

"Yeah, you men had a helluva time last night," Stella said. "I worried about Ken for two hours."

"Oh, I wasn't in any great danger, doll. You're just gonna have to learn to let me be one of the guys every now and then or you and I are gonna have problems all alone out there in the Georgia mountains," Ken joked.

They had all worked as a team the previous evening. Chester's gifts had particular significance, and it took all six of them to sort out the clues and distract the watchers as they retrieved the evidence.

It was imperative that they find both the skeletal hand and the bag of evidence Paulette had compiled before Sunday, the end of the sabbatical. As soon as dinner was finished, Colby complained of an upset stomach and went to his room. Cassidy and Mitzie both agreed they were tired and went back to their own rooms. Glenn announced that if Colby wasn't going on a walk, he wasn't either, so he headed to his room.

Ken and Stella turned off the lights and climbed atop Stella's bed to watch an old movie on television. It was a spaghetti Western, and there was lots of shooting and whooping.

Colby entered his bathroom and loudly dropped the toilet seat before pulling the door shut. He sat there fully dressed for a long time.

Mitzie sat in her barrel chair and called Phillip. She carried on a loud conversation with him and with each of the children.

Cassidy yawned and turned on the television to the music channel. Then, she entered the bathroom with her bedclothes and ran the shower.

Glenn sat at his desk and, with the television

broadcasting Pat and Vanna on *Wheel of Fortune,* he methodically studied the notes and sketches Chester had made of his survey of the grounds. He deciphered the clues that pinpointed the location of the hand in the stone pile and the plastic bag beneath the shrubbery. Then, he tapped his ankle and went into the bathroom. From there, he texted Cassidy, who was waiting in her bathroom, and she signaled Colby to be ready for messages.

"CP…GOT UR CHART?"

"(THUMBS UP EMOJI)"

"4 HAND: LOCATE ROCK PIT"

"GOT IT"

"COORDINATES?"

"E-14"

Glenn directed his texts to Colby.

"CC…GOT UR MAP?"

"ON THE SINK"

"E-14?"

"YES. ROUND DEPRESSION IN CLAY. HAND?"

"(THUMBS UP EMOJI)"

"THX 2 CHESTER (SMILEY FACE EMOJI)"

Cssidy texted.

"CC...CAN U FIND?"

"WILL NEED KEN"

"K WILL GET HIM. FROM DOOR, 32 FT FWD, RT 40 FT"

"GH...HOW ABOUT BAG?"

"NEAR CP'S DIG GRID"

"DIRECTION?"

"TOWARD GATE."

"HOW CLOSE?"

"DEAD BABY BIRD"

Colby texted to prompt Cassidy.

"REMEMBER, CP?"

"(THUMBS UP EMOJI)(SAD FACE EMOJI)"

"WHERE?"

"GRID J-2"

"SURE?"

"(THUMBS UP EMOJI) YES"

Glenn rejoined the thread.

"CC?"

"FOUND IT. CHESTER MADE X"

"JUST OFF PATH"

"YES. GOT IT. L R R SIDE, CP?"

"STEP L. GO 10 FT. LOOK R. 3RD BUSH, GH"

"THX, CP. CC...R U READY?"

"FLUSHING NOW"

"TMI (WIDE EYES EMOJI)"

Coly laughed at Glenn's response.

"CP...TEXT MG. WE NEED KEN. HAVE HER BRING SC TO UR ROOM"

"K. BE CAREFUL. ILY (HEART ICON)"

"(HEART ICON) ILY 2"

Glenn joined in.

"ME 2 (WINKING EMOJI)"

Cassidy turned off the shower and sent Mitzie one tap, which signaled her to get to the bathroom. Then she waited for the response.

"HERE, CP"

"CC & GH COMING 4 KEN. U GET SC. BRING 2
MY ROOM. B HERE IN 5 MIN"

"(THUMBS UP EMOJI) (HEART ICON)"

Less than five minutes later, Mitzie and Stella approached Cassidy's room and knocked loudly on her door.

She answered and stood before them in her pajamas. "Hi Mitzie. Hi Stella. What's going on?"

"Hey, there! We wanted to have one last girl-gab before we all go home. The men went for a walk, but they'll be back after a while. Are you packed? I'm not. I think I'm just going to throw it all in and be done with it," Stella said.

"I was thinking the same thing," Mitzie said.

"That won't happen," Cassidy laughed. "Your OCD will kick in. You have to make it just so."

"Yeah, I guess you're right, dammit," Mitzie conceded with a chuckle.

While the ladies chatted in the room, the three men meandered down the path, talking about this and that and the other. After they had gone about 30 feet from the door, Ken stopped to describe the cabin he and Stella planned to build.

"Yeah, I stepped it off the other day. She wants to build it just like the Ingalls' farmhouse on 'Little House on the Prairie.' Damn those videos. I told her we're too old to be going up and down a ladder to a loft," Ken said.

"How big .... or tiny ... are you planning to make it, Ken?" Glenn asked.

"Well, let's see," he said, turning to the right. "If I remember my piece of land, there's a little flat place about 15 feet in from the property line."

Leaving the path and moving toward the center of the garden area, he took measured steps which, he knew from experience having been a scoutmaster, were almost exactly three feet in length. Five steps were equivalent to 15 feet. Colby and Glenn followed him.

"Now, this is the place I'll build the house." He spread his arms wide, indicating a broad, flat area, making sure his voice was loud and clear and he was in full view of the surveillance devices.

"The house itself is going to be 24 feet wide." He took eight measured steps. "That puts the corner right here about where this pile of rocks is. Hey, Glenn. You stand here and be the corner."

Glenn moved to the center of the rock pile and sat down cross-legged.

"Whatsamatter old man? Are you tired?" Colby joked.

"Yeah, yeah. You give yourself another ten years and you'll be wanting to sit every chance you can, too," Glenn remarked, idly running his hands in and around the rocks.

"OK. You stay there, Glenn. Wait, how 'bout grab me a few of those bigger rocks so I can mark the other corners."

Glenn obliged by picking up four large round rocks the size of oranges and handing them to Ken.

"Now, this wall will be another 24 feet." Ken took eight more strides toward a darkened area and dropped one of the stones onto the ground. "This is the other corner," he called.

"Can't see ya. Too dark over there," Glenn called. "Colby, you go stand at that corner."

Colby sprinted over and stood by Ken, waving to Glenn.

"Can just barely make you out. It's pretty dark," Glenn said.

Ken and Colby paced off the next 24 feet through the darkness and dropped a rock at the corner, then they walked the 24 feet back to the point of origin and dropped the third rock. Ken came back to Glenn and helped him stand.

"Come on, I'll show you how the interior will be laid out now that we have our corners," he said. Ken and the other two men walked all around the inside of the square as he pointed out where the front and back doors would be, where he planned to build Stella's attached kitchen, how he would arrange the bedroom, and the area for the bathroom.

"And right where you were sitting ... where this pile of rocks is ... that's going to be a corner fireplace that we will use to heat the cabin. So, whatcha think?" he said with a smile.

"I think it's awesome, Ken," Colby said.

"I think I'm cold and need to walk some more, guys," Glenn complained, heading back to the path.

The three friends strolled along the path until they reached a specific dark area between two lamps. Colby left Ken and Glenn talking loudly on the path while he took a detour to the left. He counted three large bushes on his right. Squatting so as not to get dirt on the knees of his pants, he held onto the bush with his left hand while reaching beneath it with his right. The trowel he held encountered no resistance when he scraped, and he knew he was digging in the right place.

Five minutes later, he emerged and joined the conversation, the zippered section of his backpack holding the plastic bag of Paulette's evidence he unearthed, along with the ectrodactyly hand he had gotten from Ken after Glenn pulled it from the rock pile during their contrived cabin measurements.

As the men returned to the Center, they discussed Colby's engagement and his future together with Cassidy. Glenn shared details about the trip to Georgia he was planning with Iris. They were still talking of their plans when they entered the building, rode the elevator to the 10th floor, and knocked on Cassidy's door.

CHAPTER TWENTY-FIVE

End of Sabbatical

"Education is the passport to the future, for tomorrow belongs to those who prepare for it today."

~ Malcolm X,
American Human Rights Activist

IN THE GRAND BALLROOM on the last Saturday night in March, the remaining sabbatical participants were treated to a formal dinner much like the one they enjoyed when they first arrived, except for one noticeable fact: there were fewer than 10% of the awardees in attendance. The guides performed their duties admirably, ushering in their dwindled number of charges to their tables with the ringing of their silly bells. Mitzie, Colby, and Cassidy sat together at one table, while their friends Glenn, Stella, and Ken were separated and sat at tables reserved for their floors. The mood was considerably less jovial than it was at that first dinner, and the applause for Ronald Bowry was much less enthusiastic when he took the podium.

"Good evening NFAEE Award Winners! We are delighted that you have been with us for the past three months at the 2020 Winter Sabbatical. We hope your stay was enjoyable, exciting, and memorable. You are among the finest teachers in America, and we celebrate you. Before we start our dinner, I would like to recognize the award winners from each of the counties in the Lower Eastern time zone who have completed their courses and stayed throughout the entire three-month sabbatical. When I call your state, would you please stand and receive applause from your fellow teachers.

"From Florida, we recognize six teachers from the 67 counties." Mitzie stood and graciously smiled, and then she sat down with the rest of the Florida awardees.

"From Georgia, we recognize ten teachers from the 159 counties." Colby, Cassidy, and Glenn rose. When their state awardees sat, Bowry recognized the rest of the award winners in turn.

"From the state of North Carolina, we recognize nine teachers from 100 counties. From South Carolina, we recognize six teachers from 46 counties. From Virginia, we recognize eight teachers from the 95 counties. And from West Virginia, we recognize five ... er ... four teachers from the 55 counties. I thank all of you teachers for fulfilling all the obligations of your award. I will speak to you again...*after* dinner. Enjoy!"

Though the meal was exquisite, the appetites of the six friends were lacking, and they had trouble finishing all that was on their plates. They each felt personally stung by Bowry's stumble on the number of participants from West Virginia. As soon as dessert was finished, though most of them just picked at it, Bowry again took the podium, giving virtually the same speech he gave that first night, but with minor changes.

"Ladies and gentlemen. I hope you enjoyed your dinner. I don't know about you, but I am stuffed!" There was little more than half-hearted polite laughter on this occasion.

"You were not here to merely eat, although you did plenty of that. You were here to experience renewal and arm your minds for battle against the institution of education that has sadly been failing you as teachers. Many of you will be going back into the same battlefields from which you came. We wanted to make you ready to be exemplary movers and shakers in the field of education. We wanted you to lead. We wanted you to mold our young ones' minds so they could go on to be movers and shakers in their own generations. You thought it could not be done, but I am here to tell you that in finishing this sabbatical, you are the ones who will do it.

"You were each given a course of study that we hope expanded your minds to include possibilities you had never before dreamed, and some of you will be moving on in those fields of study. Dr. Elizabeth Ford is with us again tonight to relay some exciting news. Dr. Ford, please come up and share your thoughts," he said before returning to his seat. There was no air kiss between the two of them before she took the microphone.

"Ladies and gentlemen, teachers all. We have been honored to host you at the NFAEE Center for this sabbatical. You recall I told you that some participants enjoy their course of study so much they go on to make careers of them? Well, guess what? For some of you there will no longer be bus duty, no more cafeteria duty, no students to supervise in your future. Isn't that great?"

She giggled and rotated her shoulders, but there were no rousing hoots and applause throughout the room. "I truly hope you enjoyed what we provided for you. We wanted you to enjoy yourselves and be renewed. Teaching is hard work. You deserved to be pampered." Her simpering smile brought no reaction other than a few hand claps. She faltered slightly; then, she recovered and set a paper on the podium in front of her.

"When I call your name, please stand. Please hold your applause until I have finished naming these individuals. Thank you.

"William Woolery. William has accepted a job offer from University of Richmond to teach a class on drawing and painting. Sharon Lawson. Sharon has accepted a job offer from Randolph Macon College to teach a graduate class on Immigration in America. Hammadah Hadad. Hammadah has accepted a job as a journalist for the Richmond Times-Dispatch. Oliver Sessions. Oliver has accepted a scholarship to complete his PhD in theater and dance at Virginia State University. Lacy DeGrasio. Lacy has accepted a scholarship to complete her master's degree in music education at Virginia State University. Charles Franklin. Charles has accepted a scholarship to complete his master's degree in creative and technical writing from Virginia Union University."

These people sat down to polite applause, and Elizabeth turned the page on her list.

"Mitzie Galloway, please stand. Mitzie has accepted a position in the administration at the Miccosukee Indian School in Miami, Florida. Glenn Harding. Glenn has accepted an offer to head the district offices in Cherokee, North Carolina and oversee all their schools. Cassidy Phelps. Cassidy has accepted a scholarship to complete her PhD in archaeology at Virginia State University, after which she will be employed on staff as a professor. Colby Carson. Colby has accepted a scholarship offer to complete his PhD in forensic anthropology at Virginia State University, after which he has been guaranteed employment in a private firm as a professional forensic anthropologist."

When Colby's name was mentioned, Professor Chen stood up at the instructors' table and loudly applauded her star pupil. Afterward, Elizabeth named off the retiring individuals, which included Stella and Ken, and participants who would be returning to take administration jobs in their own school districts. Of the 49 remaining teachers, only 19 were going back into the classroom from which they came.

"Tomorrow morning at 10:00 a.m., we will all board a chartered bus. That's right, Mr. Bowry, Miss Lawrence, and I will be joining you on the bus trip in place of your guides. We will arrive in Washington D.C. a little after noon. We will enjoy a fabulous luncheon at the St. Gregory Hotel Dupont Circle, and then we will join the graduating awardees from the rest of the NFAEE Centers, along with the members of your immediate families who have been flown in for the day for your congratulatory ceremony. Be sure to wear your best suits, gentlemen, and ladies, apply that makeup carefully. There will be newspapers taking pictures and coverage by the television stations. Afterward, you will accompany your families back home as we have secured your airfare, as well. It should be a most enjoyable and enlightening day, so go now, get packed, and get plenty of rest. We will meet at the bus in the morning after breakfast. Good night, all!"

And with that, the 2020 Winter sabbatical was officially ended.

The alliance of six took their last walk on the grounds, passing in and out of the dark and light circles, speaking of things which should be heard and things which should not. Several small groupings convened in the darkened areas of the path to make everyone aware of the next day's plans, with plenty of activity in the light to distract attention away from the ones who were in the darkness. When at last they retired to their rooms, they all agreed on one thing: tomorrow would, indeed, be a most enjoyable and enlightening day.

CHAPTER TWENTY-SIX
The Sabbatical Directive

"To fill the young of the species with knowledge and awaken their intelligence ... Nothing could be further from the truth. The aim ... is simply to reduce as many individuals as possible to the same level, to breed and train a standardized citizenry, to put down dissent and originality. That is its aim in the United States ... and that is its aim everywhere else."

~ Henry Louis Mencken,
American Journalist,
Public Education,
The American Mercury, April 1924

ELIZABETH WATCHED WITH DISINTEREST as the six people took their last nightly stroll. Their flags had been lifted; they were no longer a threat to the NFAEE. She was relieved that they had been contained so quickly after the *Eliminated* disappeared from within their midst. It served to confirm her suspicions that Paulette Jameson was the instigator. Elizabeth had almost made a fatal error by failing to recognize the danger the small-town girl from West Virginia posed. The misclassification could have ended her own life. She shivered.

Elizabeth was confident she had performed her duties admirably, and all the Sabbatical Directive leaders were pleased. Though the Chinese man would be at the ceremony the next day, she had no reason to fear him, even after the threat from his cousin, Professor Chen. She was comforted in the knowledge that she, Ronald Bowry, and Ashley Lawrence had successfully completed another phase of the Sabbatical Directive. Another group would arrive on Monday, and the Sabbatical Directive would begin anew for the spring session.

The shadow conspiracy had been operating for five years, effectively ridding America of over 6,000 teachers annually. Throughout history, when a regime attempted to overthrow an existing government and control its population, they targeted education. Young minds were like sponges, soaking up whatever was presented to them in a palatable way.

The overall field of education was rife with imperfections. An insatiable love of the almighty dollar spurred companies to develop teaching materials that put money in the pockets of those who created the content, not put knowledge into the minds that were fed its version of the facts. School districts, unable to fully fund the programs they were required to present, found themselves cutting corners on the most necessary of their resources—their educators. As a failure to make their own ends meet combined with the overwhelming responsibilities required of these teachers, discontent was bred. By placing activists in the teacher unions, further damage was done. Riled up teachers, expecting to receive their fair share, left their classrooms and went on strike, leaving the impressionable students in the charge of those less qualified and not as well suited to work with children. The students themselves were faced with moral dilemmas as well as educational deficiencies as their role models, who were so crucial in the early stages of development, left them.

The attack on education was documented and evidenced across the world, yet Americans failed to recognize it. In Cairo, the Arab educational system became inexorably linked with the current political leaders. An entire curriculum, including the teachers, books, and the classrooms themselves were subject to the parties in control.

Extremist policies in many countries had been enacted that prohibited any form of education that wasn't sanctioned by the regime in power. Teachers, parents, administrators, and even students were arrested and brutalized if they disobeyed, and teachers were made to solicit statements from security forces that deemed them acceptable only if they adhered to appropriate behavior.

World cultures had been controlled and restructured due to the indoctrination of their youth and the adults who were denied good educations that encouraged forward thinking. The Moscow Young Pioneer Guards of Honor operated by the communist party, the Hitler Youth organization of the Nazi Party in Germany, the Communist Party of Kampuchea (also known as the Khmer Rouge of Cambodia), the People's Republic of China, the Republic of Cuba, the Democratic People's Republic of Korea, the Socialist Republic of Vietnam, and radical Islam were just a few examples of the molding of young impressionable minds to shun what was right and embrace what was wrong. It was no surprise that one of the founders of the NCAEE Sabbatical Directive, Chen Xio, was a member of the Communist Party of China, and there were other affiliates who existed on the fringes of mind control.

Elizabeth Ford heaved a great sigh and left the observation room of the command center. One more day, and she would be done with the current batch of "movers and shakers." She laughed to herself, *if they only knew.*

*   *   *

If they only knew, Colby thought as he stared at his reflection in the mirror. He was in the restroom outside the dining room of the St. Gregory Hotel Dupont Circle waiting to make "the exchange."

*   *   *

The night before, in his own bathroom at the NFAEE

Center, he had sent a message from his iWatch to a trusted friend from school—the Sheriff, of Peach County, Georgia. The two old classmates texted back and forth, and Sheriff Lang helped him work out a plan for contacting the Federal Bureau of Investigation through law enforcement channels that would keep Colby and his friends safe. He had explained they didn't know who to trust, that they were in extreme danger, and that they were in possession of highly sensitive evidence that needed to be conveyed to the authorities.

A career lawman, Leonard Lang had a long arm and was able to contact people with whom he had a trusted relationship in Washington, D.C. It was well after midnight when he got back to Colby, but he assured him the FBI and D.C. Metro Police would be ready for the operation the following day. In fact, Sheriff Lenny Lang said he would make the trip to D.C. and be there to ease Colby's mind and be sure things went as planned.

During the bus ride, Colby and the others kept up a valiant pretense at conversation, acutely aware that Bowry, Ford, and Lawrence were on the bus and within earshot. Cassidy, Mitzie, Glenn, Ken, and Stella were all aware of the operation and the high stakes, but they managed to hide their trepidation beautifully.

Because it was the last day of the sabbatical, all the remaining participants freely used their cell phones. Colby kept his smartwatch handy, beneath his phone, constantly exchanging messages with

Sheriff Lang. When they disembarked the bus, his friend was waiting for him at the entrance to the Hotel, wearing civilian clothes and looking like any other good ole boy.

"Colby Carson, you old so and so. It's great to see you again," Lang said, pumping Colby's hand up and down.

"You, too, Lenny," Colby responded. "Here, I want you to meet Cassidy, my fiancé, and these are my friends Mitzie Galloway, Glenn Harding, Ken Schaffer, and Stella Cooke."

Lenny Lang greeted everyone with a smile and down-home southern charm, but his eyes also took in Ronald Bowry, Elizabeth Ford, and Ashley Lawrence.

"Will you be joining us for lunch, Lenny?" Cassidy asked.

"No, no, but thank you for asking. I've got another appointment, but I'll be real close by. Don't you worry," he said with a wink. "Colby, I'll be talking to you soon. You just go on about your business. It's all good."

Lenny sauntered over to the bathroom, stuck his head inside to make sure it was empty, and then leaned up against the wall.

"Yes, I know. Bathroom time again," Cassidy remarked with a trembling smile. "I'll be at the table. I love you." She kissed him quickly and followed Mitzie into the dining room.

* * *

Inside the restroom, Colby continued to stare

at himself in the mirror. His eyes were bright and dilated, and a sheen of sweat kept creeping out beneath his nose. He wiped his face once again with the damp paper towel and took a deep breath.

Turning, he viewed the empty stalls along the back wall. Counting from the left, he selected the 4th door and opened it, as he had been instructed. He stepped inside, closed and locked the door, and sat down on the commode. Pulling his backpack onto his lap, he unzipped the hidden compartment and withdrew the dirt-flecked plastic bag containing Paulette Jameson's evidence. He balanced it on his knees as he carefully removed the napkin wrapped skeletal hand from his pack and placed it in the bag with the other items. He slung the backpack over his shoulder and sat, waiting for the handoff.

After a couple of minutes, someone entered the bathroom. Colby remained quiet. He heard the stall door to his right open and close, and then he heard splashing water as the occupant urinated. There was a flush and a zip, and then the door opened again, and the person left the room without washing up.

Ew. Wish I had seen his shoes. Sure don't want to shake his hand, he thought. He shifted uncomfortably on the toilet seat as he continued to wait. He didn't wait long. Another person entered. The room was silent for a moment, and then the person whistled the tune to the first line of a song: *"Take me out to the ballgame."* That was the cue.

Colby stood and opened the stall door. He

found himself face to face with an unremarkable looking man wearing a dark suit. His eyes were steely grey, and he regarded Colby without blinking. He whistled the tune again, waiting for a corresponding response from Colby.

Colby licked his lips and forced his dry mouth to whistle the tune to the next part of the song: *"Take me out with the crowd."*

The man nodded. He extended his hand, and Colby held out the plastic bag. The man took the bag and gave a small smile.

"Enjoy your meal, Mr. Carson," he said before leaving the room.

Colby did an about-face and hurried back into the stall where he immediately emptied his stomach. After washing up and making sure he was presentable, he exited the washroom and rejoined Cassidy and the rest of the group at the table.

*   *   *

Once they had finished a delicious luncheon, the awardees assembled into six groups and entered the Grand Banquet room reserved for the ceremony. The venue was filled with family members who beamed as the 49 participants from the Lower Eastern Center walked in and arranged themselves in four rows, waving to their families as the media snapped pictures and filmed the proceedings, and then the awardees sat in chairs reserved for them in front of a raised platform with a podium positioned at the end of the room. After they were seated, they were followed in order by the participants from the Upper Eastern Center, the Lower Central Center, the Upper Central Center, the Mountain Center, and the Pacific Center.

The crowd cheered the 288 awardees, and then their attention was focused on the platform behind them. There was an audible exclamation in the room as Dr. Elizabeth Ford stepped up to the podium.

The six friends sat together and watched as she worked her spell on the assembled guests. The crowd loved her, probably because she looked like a composite of their favorite actresses, and she milked it for all it was worth. Ronald Bowry, likewise, knew how to work an audience to his best advantage. He addressed the guests and gave a short speech.

The 288 awardees who had "graduated" from the NFAEE were posed and paraded, photographed and interviewed, complimented and praised until Colby thought he might throw up. He smiled at his parents who waved from the crowd. He wondered what they would think of his new fiancé, but he was not worried because he was his own man, and they knew it.

Cassidy waved to her Auntie, the only family member she had in attendance as both her parents had passed on. Edna Mae was not officially family, so she was not flown up. Cassidy rotated the bone ring on her finger and smiled, and then she touched the brooch she had received from Carmine. It pained her to know that Paulette had been killed and that Carmine would grieve.

Mitzie's children could be heard shouting as she smiled for the cameras. Phillip gave her a thumbs up sign, and she laughed when Gabe, sitting on Phil's lap, gave her the same gesture. She was wearing her new ring, and though it felt conspicuous on her small hand, it gave her a sense of contentment and peace.

Glenn saw Iris and burst into tears. He really was a softie, despite his gruff exterior. When Mitzie pointed out her family, he waved at them just as hard as she did.

Stella and Ken stood hand in hand. Ken had already told his grown children he would be getting married soon and they would be building their own home on a little piece of land Ken owned in the north Georgia mountains near Dillard.

The ceremony headed to a conclusion, and the families prepared to return to the airport for their flights. The alliance of six clung to each other, loathe to disband after the ordeal they had faced. Though they would be miles apart, they knew their friendships would endure. They hugged and kissed and promised to keep in touch. There was sorrow over the loss of Paulette and for the way in which Carmine and Chester left, but the sabbatical had not yet ended.

Ronald A. Bowry, Dr. Elizabeth Ford, and Ashley Lawrence stood side by side at the podium with the other five "Enforcers" from the other facilities, holding their hands up in a salute to the 288 participants. Suddenly, the double doors in the back of the room opened.

Momentarily flustered, their hands drooped and then fell to their sides completely as uniformed officers entered the room and marched up to the platform, followed by two men in dark suits and Sheriff Lenny Lang, badge now in full view, who gave Colby a wink and a smile. One of the suited men turned and directly faced the television cameras. As he did, a squat Chinese man slipped unnoticed out the double doors.

"Mr. Ronald A. Bowry, Dr. Elizabeth Ford, and Miss Ashley Lawrence. By authority of the Metropolitan Police Department of the District of Columbia and with the cooperation of the Federal Bureau of Investigation, I hereby place you under arrest for crimes committed on and against citizens of the United States including cyber-crimes, espionage, collusion with anti-American foreign entities, operating a fraudulent organization, terrorism, and murder in the first degree of Paulette Jameson and Olivia Roberts, her husband, and their two sons."

Ronald Bowry, Elizabeth Ford, and Ashley Lawrence were handcuffed and led away through the doors, along with the five "Enforcers" from the other facilities. A smiling Sheriff Lenny Lang took up the rear of the procession, his thumb up in victory.

CHAPTER TWENTY-SEVEN
Butterflies

"Believe nothing merely because you have been told it ... or because it is tradition, or because you yourselves have imagined it. Do not believe what your teachers tell you merely out of respect for the teacher. But whatsoever, after due examination and analysis, you find to be conducive to the good, the benefit, the welfare of all beings—that doctrine believe and cling to, and take it as your guide."

~ Gautama Buddha,
Nepali Philosopher

BUTTERFLY WORLD in Coconut Creek, Florida was hailed as the largest butterfly house in the United States of America, encompassing three acres of botanical gardens, butterfly aviaries, and a working butterfly farm and research center. It produced up to 1,000 butterfly pupa per week and provided a home for over 10,000 butterflies of more than 150 different species of the beautiful insects.

In April of 2020, it was the site of a special wedding. The bride and groom recited their vows while their families and six of their most cherished friends stood in attendance.

The 40-year-old bride wore a white lace dress that highlighted her dark skin, close-cropped black hair, and the green lacquer and crystal miniature Fabergé egg necklace that hung around her slender neck. A gold and multicolored crystal brooch in the shape of an open book was pinned to her shoulder. Earrings made of the black and green spotted wings of a Tailed Jay butterfly hung from her tiny earlobes and attracted other butterflies. They swirled around her head like a living halo, giving her an otherworldly appearance.

The 45-year-old groom was handsomely dressed in a blue and white checkered shirt, khaki slacks and matching sport coat, with a bright blue bowtie that matched his striking azure eyes. He was also covered in butterflies from head to foot.

At the conclusion of the ceremony, the bride and groom turned to their guests and with them, recited a single verse by John J. Geddes:

> *"You are my winter suddenness—a glass of red wine spilt across a white tablecloth."*

CHAPTER TWENTY-EIGHT
<u>The Award</u>

"Those who cannot remember the past are condemned to repeat it."

~ George Santayana,
Spanish novelist, poet, philosopher

CYNTHIA CROMWELL, A FIRST-YEAR TEACHER in Coconut Creek, Florida, eagerly tore open the fat envelope and read the enclosed letter.

"Dear Miss Cynthia Cromwell,

We are pleased to announce that you have been specially selected as an award winner by the Educational Consortium of America, based on your entry questionnaire, your teaching philosophy, your written essay, and the letters of recommendation from your principal, your district superintendent, and your fellow teachers at Coconut Creek Elementary School.

You are one of the 67 candidates chosen from the state of Florida to attend an all-expenses-paid three-month educational sabbatical at the Lower Eastern ECA Center in Atlanta, Georgia.

At the end of your sabbatical, you will travel to the ECA headquarters in Los Angeles, California where you will be joined by your family and the winners from each of the 3,142 counties in the United States of America, during which you will be recognized in a private formal ceremony.

Please return your signed, dated, and notarized acceptance packet in the enclosed envelope, along with your preferred course of study and one alternate course of study for the sabbatical. We will make every effort to accommodate your preference.

Congratulations on your award! You should be proud to be one of the premier educators in America.

Sincerely,
Mikhail Melnyk, President
Professor Chen Mei, Director of Instruction
Educational Consortium of America"

ABOUT THE AUTHOR

M.M. BUSBY is a retired educator who won the Florida Center for Teachers Award given by the Florida Humanities Council for her original essay about the Apostle John working as a public-school teacher after living 2000 years on earth. She is certified by the prestigious Renaissance Learning Systems, Inc. as an Accelerated Reader Model and Master Class instructor. As a teacher, M.M. Busby contributed to the creation of computerized reading comprehension and literacy programs and developed a highly acclaimed interactive sing-along system to promote reading fluency. She is a member of *Sisters in Crime (SinC)*, *National Association of Independent Writers and Editors (NAIWE)*, *American Copy Editors Society (ACES)*, and *Society of Children's Book Writers and Illustrators (SCBWI)*. M.M. Busby lives in Florida with her family.

Readers can visit her at patentprintbks.com.

www.ingramcontent.com/pod-product-compliance
Lightning Source LLC
Chambersburg PA
CBHW030415180626
46812CB00005B/2014